*Also by Patricia Sprinkle*
*in Large Print:*


But Why Shoot the Magistrate?

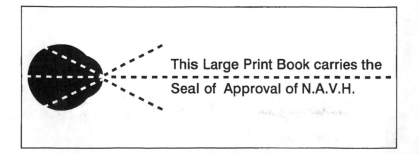

This Large Print Book carries the
Seal of Approval of N.A.V.H.

# WHO INVITED THE DEAD MAN?

A Thoroughly Southern Mystery

Patricia Sprinkle

WHEELER PUBLISHING

Published in 2002 by arrangement with NAL Signet, a member of Penguin Putnam Inc.

Wheeler Large Print Softcover Series.

The text of this Large Print edition is unabridged.
Other aspects of the book may vary from the original edition.

Set in 16 pt. Plantin by Christina S. Huff.

Printed in the United States on permanent paper.

**Library of Congress Cataloging-in-Publication Data**

Sprinkle, Patricia Houck.
    Who invited the dead man? : a thoroughly southern mystery / Patricia Sprinkle.
        p.   cm.
    ISBN 1-58724-349-0 (lg. print : sc : alk. paper)
    1. Women judges — Fiction.   2. Georgia — Fiction.   3. Large type books.   I. Title.
PS3569.P687 W49 2002
    823'.914—dc21                                    2002028243

# THANKS TO:

Robert Bremm, of Parrot Jungle, Miami, Florida, for his invaluable information about parrots, particularly scarlet macaws, and for giving me the chance to meet a parrot face-to-face.

Helen Rhea Stumbo, founder of Camellia and Main gift store and catalogue, who explained the fascinating world of catalogue merchandising.

Donna Van Lier, who frankly shared her own experience dealing with a husband with Traumatic Brain Injury, and steered me toward two excellent books: *Where Is the Mango Princess?* by Cathy Crimmins (New York: Alfred A. Knopf, 2000) and *Over My Head: A Doctor's Own Story of Brain Injury from the Inside Looking Out* by Claudia L. Osborn (Kansas City: Andrews McMeel Publishing, 1998).

Dorothy Cowling, who proofread and suggested good changes in the book. Judge Curt St. Germaine, chief magistrate of Burke County, Georgia, and Judge Mildred Anne Palmer, Mac's inspiration and consultant on being a Georgia magistrate.

The expertise in these fields is theirs; any errors in their fields are my own.

# Cast of Characters

**MacLaren Yarbrough:** amateur sleuth, Georgia magistrate, co-owner of Yarbrough's Feed, Seed and Nursery

**Joe Riddley Yarbrough:** MacLaren's husband, a former magistrate, co-owner of YFS&N

**Clarinda Williams:** cook for MacLaren and Joe Riddley

**Ridd:** the Yarbroughs' older son, a high school math teacher and small farmer

**Martha:** Ridd's wife, an emergency room supervisor

Cricket (3) and Bethany (16): their children

**Walker:** the Yarbroughs' younger son, an insurance salesman

**Cindy:** his ornamental wife

Tad (9) and Jessica (11): their children

**Augusta Wainwright:** autocratic leader of Hopemore society

**Meriwether Wainwright:** her granddaughter

**Alice Fulton:** Augusta's personal secretary and companion

**Florine Jackson:** Augusta's housekeeper and cook

**Winifred "Pooh" DuBose:** Augusta Wainwright's oldest friend, a widow

**Lottie and Otis Raeburn:** Pooh's cook-housekeeper and driver-yard man, respectively

**Slade Rutherford:** new editor of the *Hopemore Statesman*, a weekly paper

**Kelly Keane:** newspaper reporter

**Darren Hernandez:** Joe Riddley's physical therapist

**Hiram Blaine:** local character who carries a parrot and believes in aliens

**Hector:** Hiram's brother, convinced the Confederate treasury is buried on his land

**Jed:** their nephew, an Atlanta lawyer

**Hubert Spence:** MacLaren and Joe Riddley's nearest neighbor and old friend

**Maynard:** Hubert's son, the Hope County Museum curator

**Selena Jones:** Maynard's girlfriend and a nurse

**Police Chief Charlie Muggins**
**Sheriff Bailey "Buster" Gibbons**

*It is unfortunate when you are a newly appointed judge, and the chief of police finds a dead man at your party.*

*It is downright mortifying when the last words out of your mouth were, "Don't look behind that screen. You know good and well I put it there to hide things I don't want seen."*

*File that under Life Moments I Would Rather Forget.*

# 1

## SEPTEMBER

Knowing where to begin this story is like finding the end of a ball of yarn after it spends an hour with my beagle Lulu. Maybe the best place to begin is with the first death, which was as unexpected as the second, but not half as mystifying.

Garlon Wainwright dropped dead on the seventeenth hole at the Hopemore Country Club during the Labor Day Tournament. Poor Garlon was in the lead for the first time in his life, and some said his heart just couldn't stand the excitement.

According to his obituary in the *Hopemore Statesman*, Garlon was "fifty-five, only child of Augusta and the late Lamar Wainwright of Wainwright Mills, survived by his mother, one daughter, Meriwether, and his second wife, Candi (35)." I suspected Gusta had a hand in writing it. Nobody was surprised after the funeral to see Gusta and Meriwether riding to the cemetery in the first Cadillac and Candi, alone, in the second.

I kept meaning to get over to see Gusta after the funeral, but couldn't find a minute. That was the autumn after my husband, Joe Riddley Yarbrough, got shot in the head. He'd survived, but recovery from a head wound is slow, uphill work. I was busier than a bird dog in hunting season between driving him to various kinds of therapies and running Yarbrough's Feed, Seed and Nursery without him. As if that weren't enough, I'd agreed to serve as a Georgia magistrate in his place, and while I was used to watching Joe Riddley fit that in around work at the store, I hadn't realized quite how much time it took.

On Wednesday morning a whole week after Garlon's funeral, I was pushing Joe Riddley's wheelchair up the back porch ramp after physical therapy when I heard the phone.

"You gotta answer," our cook, Clarinda, called through the open screened door. "I'm makin' rolls and my hands're covered with grease and flour." Clarinda came to help me when our older son, Ridd, was born forty years ago, and has worked for — and bossed — me ever since.

The voice on the other end was chillier than a healthy dog's nose on a frosty morning. "MacLaren? I need you here right away." I knew it was Gusta. Anybody else in town would have told me who they were. Even my sons announce "Mama, this is Ridd" or "Hey, it's Walker." Gusta belonged to that highly self-confident elite who believe the rest of us have so few friends we will always recognize their voices.

Augusta Wainwright was the closest thing we had to royalty in Hopemore, Georgia. Her granddaddy was governor back when she was young, and her brother was a U.S. senator for three terms. She never bragged, but their names cropped up in a lot of conversations. She also never bragged that after Lamar's death she sold his daddy's cotton mills for more millions than I have fingers and toes, but she expected us to let newcomers know, so she got due respect. Gusta ascended to the throne of Hopemore within a few days of her birth, and never relinquished it.

"I can't come right now," I informed her. "I've got to get Joe Riddley settled. Then I have a reporter coming by to interview me for the paper." I tried to say that casually, but to tell the truth, I was a bit nervous and even a little excited. In the past it was Joe Riddley who got stories in the paper, for winning almost every award in the county. All I'd done was help him run Yarbrough's Feed, Seed and Nursery, raise two boys, and serve as treasurer to a lot of clubs. Treasurers don't get stories in the paper, unless they abscond with funds. Of course, I wrote a monthly gardening column, and my name was sometimes in the paper for helping our ungrateful police chief, Charlie Muggins, solve a murder. But those weren't stories about *me*.

Gusta didn't say a word about my interview. A bit miffed, I warned, "It will be close to dinnertime before I get there." For Gusta, as for us, dinner was still eaten at noon.

She sighed. "Well get here as soon as you can. I need you to come talk sense into Meriwether."

"What's the matter?"

"I don't want to mention it over the telephone." We've had private phone lines longer than Meriwether has been alive, but Gusta still thinks somebody might be listening in on her.

When I hung up, Joe Riddley spoke in his new, careful way. "Who was on the phone?"

Joe Riddley was the best-looking man in Hope County, as far as I was concerned — with long, rangy bones from his Scots grandfather and dark hair and eyes and a tinge of copper in his skin from his Cherokee grandmother — and it broke my heart to see him sitting in a wheelchair with a half-there look in his eyes and his cap dangling from one hand. All his life Joe Riddley had worn a succession of red caps with YARBROUGH'S in white letters over the brim. Our boys joked they'd bury their daddy in his cap and me with my pocketbook.

I set my pocketbook on the counter. "Gusta, commanding me to come talk sense into Meriwether. Hang up your hat."

Joe Riddley carefully centered his cap on its hook beside the kitchen closet. "Meriwether *has* sense," he said belligerently. Meriwether was one of Joe Riddley's favorite people. "Meriwether's going to be all right. You just wait and see."

He'd been saying that for twelve years, since

Meriwether came home from college silent and pale as an ice princess and let out word that her engagement to Jed Blainc was over. When folks have watched you fall in love in preschool and stay in love with a hometown boy all the way through college, they feel they have a right to know more than that, but Meriwether never offered any explanations. Just moved back into her grandmother's house (where she'd lived since her own mother died in childbirth) and volunteered in charities Gusta thought would fold if Wainwrights didn't personally oversee them, accompanied Gusta on two or three trips abroad every year, wrote Gusta's letters, paid her bills, balanced her checkbook, and helped her host small elegant parties several times a year. Joe Riddley and I got Christmas cards from Jed, so we knew when he finished Mercer Law School and joined a practice in Atlanta, but he never came back to Hopemore and Meriwether never, ever mentioned his name.

Clarinda snorted from where she was rolling out the biscuits. "Best sense you can talk to that girl is, tell her to move out of her grandmother's house and get a *life*. Prince Charming ain't gonna ride his white charger up Miss Gusta's steps, and he may not recognize she's a princess once she gets wrinkles."

"I'll tell her you said so."

Clarinda opened her mouth to say more when we heard tires crunch on our gravel drive and knew the reporter had arrived.

No taller than my five-foot-three and wearing a khaki skirt, yellow cotton sweater, and sandals, she scarcely looked old enough to be out of college. Silky auburn hair swung down her back halfway to her bottom. Only the wire-rimmed glasses perched on her pert nose and the expression in her brown eyes were businesslike. "I'm Kelly Keane" — she held out one slim hand — "from the *Hopemore Statesman*. It's such a pretty day. Could we talk on your porch?"

Hope County is located in that strip of Middle Georgia between I-20 and I-16, right on the edge of the gnat line, and while nobody knows why gnats come to a certain Georgia latitude and stop, Joe Riddley always said it's because they know our climate's the next best thing to heaven. That September day the grass and trees were dark, dark green and an egg yolk sun floated near one startling white cloud in a deep blue sky. As we carried brownies and glasses of tea to our screened side porch, bees buzzed, young birds sassed their parents in the manner of adolescents everywhere, and the air was thick with the scent of our old apple tree.

"This is lovely!" Ms. Keane exclaimed as she took a rocker and looked over our three acres of grass, trees, and flower beds.

"Why, thank you. Our son Ridd does most of the work. He loves to dig in the dirt, and we're too busy selling plants to have time to fool with them."

She poised her pen over a pad. "Now, you and

Judge Yarbrough —" She turned so fiery red I nearly went for water to put her out.

"That's all right. People do that all the time. They still think of him as the *real* judge."

"Are you both lawyers?"

"Oh, no. In Georgia you don't have to be a lawyer to be a magistrate. The chief magistrate in each county is elected, and she or he appoints the rest. Most of us are part-timers, running our businesses while we serve. The state gives us training every year."

She checked a list of questions she'd brought. "How long have you all been married?"

"Married, or together?" From her expression, I knew she thought we'd lived in sin before getting hitched, so I hurried to set her straight. "Joe Riddley and I have been married forty-one years, but we've known each other nearly sixty. We met when I was four and he was six, when my daddy stopped by his daddy's hardware store for cotton seed and fertilizer. That's the same store we now own, Yarbrough's Feed, Seed and Nursery. But everybody already knows that."

"That's romantic." She turned a little pink. "I think your husband has physical therapy with a friend of mine. Darren Hernandez?"

"That's right." While she consulted her notes, I was thinking I'd have to ask Darren if he'd taken Kelly out. His love life could use some sprucing up — he was pining for a two-timing woman down in Dublin. Kelly lifted her head. "You have two sons, right? Ridd teaches at the high school and Walker owns an insurance company?"

"Yes. They grew up in this house, just like their daddy. He was born upstairs." When she looked around at the big blue house in astonishment, I surprised her some more. "Joe Riddley is the fourth-generation Yarbrough to live here. His great-granddaddy owned a sawmill and lumber company back before the War. He could afford to build big after General Sherman lit through town and created an unprecedented demand for lumber. The Civil War," I answered her puzzled look. "Sherman burned the houses."

"Oh. Well, it's a gorgeous house." Then she stepped out of her reporter shoes to ask, "But aren't you nervous, living way down a dirt road so far from the highway?"

"It's a gravel road." I spoke a mite tartly, thinking of the fortune we'd invested in gravel over the years. "And it's just half a mile. Besides, we've got good neighbors."

She wrinkled her forehead. "Just two other houses, and one of them is empty."

Considering that one owner of the place on the corner had been a killer and another a kook, empty was a vast improvement. I didn't want to go into that, however. "We love it down here. It's very quiet except for crickets, owls, and frogs."

"Oh." The way she kept tapping her toe on the floor, quiet wasn't something she valued.

She peered at her questions again. "Did you always want to be a magistrate?"

"Heavens no. I think the main reason they chose me is because I went to magistrate school with Joe Riddley so many times, and have watched him do magistrate business for thirty years in our office. Our son Walker, though, swears the county appointed me so they could save money by recycling the Judge Yarbrough sign on our office door."

"Could you, uh, tell me something about your husband's, uh, accident? What happened, and how you, uh, felt?" She had prepared that question ahead of time and was still embarrassed to ask it. Most people were embarrassed to talk about Joe Riddley right then.

"It happened too fast for me to feel anything. Everything changed in less than a minute. One night in August Joe Riddley went down the road looking for our beagle, who'd escaped her pen. A killer thought Joe Riddley was on his trail, and shot him. Luckily Joe Riddley had bent toward Lulu at the time, so the bullet just grazed his head. The same man also shot Lulu."[1]

"You'd never know it." Across the lawn, Lulu was chasing a butterfly.

I chuckled. "That bullet turned her into the fastest three-legged beagle in Georgia."

"And your husband?"

How could I tell her that the bullet had

[1]*But Why Shoot the Magistrate?*

turned Joe Riddley into a stranger? One evening I had a husband who was wise, gentle, funny, and occasionally grumpy, but who loved me more than life. When he woke up from his coma, I had a husband who could not read, who could not put words together in coherent sentences, who could not send signals to his legs to make them walk, who erupted in unexpected rages at the slightest thing, and who didn't even seem to like me most of the time. Sometimes he got so mad at me I was afraid of him.

That's not what I told Kelly Keane, of course.

"Joe Riddley's injury is mild compared to many," I said, quoting his doctor. "He ought to be back to normal eventually." I didn't add that "eventually" could seem like a very long time.

She wrote a pretty good article, except she never mentioned Yarbrough's Feed, Seed and Nursery and she quoted Walker about that dratted sign.

The next time I'd be in the paper would be in October, when Hiram Blaine was found dead in my dining room.

# 2

As I gathered up my pocketbook to leave, Clarinda asked, "You reckon I ought to hold back your dinner?"

"Gusta didn't ask me to eat, if that's what you're asking."

"Even if she had, you wouldn't get much. That woman hates to lay out money she doesn't have to. Speaking of laying out money, did you ever talk to the florist about centerpieces for the judge's birthday party?"

"No. Ridd says to put a pot of chrysanthemums on each table."

She rested both hands on her stout hips. "We don't want to look like we're advertising the store. Go over to Flowers 'R' Us and talk to them. They did arrangements for our Sisterhood meeting at church, and they're real good. Reasonable, too."

"Maybe I'll talk to them, then." We sounded, I thought, like two Old Testament wives planning a birthday party for our joint husband.

I stopped by Joe Riddley's room, where he was lying in bed staring at the ceiling. "I'm going to see Gusta and Meriwether." He liked to know exactly where I would be.

He gave me an anxious look and carefully pronounced every syllable. "Is 'go see Meriwether' in your log?"

"I don't have a log, honey. You have the log." Joe Riddley's log was a notebook in which we had to write down every blessed thing he needed to do in a day, so he could check on himself. His memory was slowly coming back, but he still couldn't remember things like "get dressed," "go to therapy," "eat dinner."

I deposited a kiss on his head. "You be good, now, you hear me?"

"I'll be good or I'll be careful." His eyes had the ghost of a twinkle.

It was a good thing I'd lived in that house more than thirty years, because my eyes were so blurred with tears I'd never have found my way to my car. It was real confusing, smack in the middle of all the strange things Joe Riddley's brain was doing, for a shutter to go up and suddenly give me a glimpse of the man I'd loved all my life. Those were the times that shattered my self-control.

Gusta lives on Oglethorpe, which has three blocks of fine Victorian houses and even three antebellum houses just down from the courthouse square. Gusta's is one of the antebellums, spared by General Sherman on his comet-trail trip through town — "not by intent," Gusta insists in her gravelly voice, "but because those Yankees had a hard time getting Georgia heart pine to burn."

Normally I didn't mind driving behind gawking tourists, but that morning I was impatient. What could Meriwether be doing to get Gusta in such a tizzy? They'd had some rousing disagreements back when Meriwether was dead set on marrying Jed and Gusta was just as determined no granddaughter of hers would ever marry a Blaine. But once Meriwether had come home with a broken heart, the two of them had never disagreed on anything more serious than which author should speak at the Friends of the Library banquet.

Gusta's son, Garlon, now that was another matter. When her husband died, Gusta inherited everything. Garlon had a good job in the cotton mills and a nice bequest from his first wife, but when Gusta sold the mills, he wanted her to advance him funds out of his daddy's estate to buy himself a business. Gusta refused. She said she already had enough business to keep Garlon busy, since Lamar had owned real estate as well as the mills, and had a good bit of stock. Joe Riddley always said that's when Garlon realized he'd moved back to his mother's house lock, stock, and soul.

The noise of their discussions kept the neighbors up for several weeks. Then Garlon stormed out of the house, arranged his own financing for the business, and bought a nice town house across town. After Meriwether went to college, he went down to a New Orleans business convention and brought back Candi — who, Gusta claimed, jumped out of a cake into his lap. Of course, Gusta had been known to stretch the truth a bit when it served her prejudices.

Candi had wide blue eyes, curly peroxide hair, and a knack for making Garlon laugh. Meriwether seemed to like her well enough at first. She divided her time between their town house and Gusta's house on her college vacations. But when she came home for good and found Garlon and Candi fixing to move into a house he owned over on Liberty Street, she got furious. Some folks speculated she was jealous at seeing her daddy so happy when she was miserable. Others claimed she loathed that particular house. In any case, she refused to set foot in it. She was perfectly cordial to Garlon and Candi at her grandmother's or in public, but she never visited them at home.

It was half past eleven when I parked behind Gusta's old black Cadillac. As I climbed out of my Nissan and worked my way past a big hydrangea planted too close to the drive, I had a sudden memory of Jed Blaine in high school, a shock of blond hair and a friendly freckled face, waiting behind that hydrangea for Meriwether to sneak out to tell him good night. He was never handsome, but he was always an endearing youngster.

Gusta's maid, Florine, ushered me onto Gusta's large, screened side porch. Sun lay in wide warm bands across the red tile floor and brightened the faded floral cushions on Gusta's white wicker. Beyond the screens, bees buzzed the late-summer flowers and mockingbirds sang in the magnolia.

Seeing Gusta in leaf-dappled sunlight, I was shocked at how much Garlon's death had aged her. Up until now, although her hands were knotted with arthritis and her long spare frame stooped a bit, she had never looked old. Today, her face was lined and frail, and although her yellow cotton dress was fresh and every one of her iron-gray hairs knew its place, she looked older than the eighty I knew she was.

Her gray eyes and tongue, however, were sharp as ever. "She's hightailed it out of town," she greeted me with satisfaction.

"Meriwether?" Startled, I backed to a big wicker armchair and more fell into it than sat.

"No, Candy cane. Florine," she interrupted herself, "please tell Meriwether we have a guest and bring Judge Yarbrough a glass of tea." Gusta had no problems adjusting to new titles. Florine, understanding those instructions, headed back to the kitchen to hold dinner until I left.

Gusta would never do anything vulgar, like talk right away about whatever she'd hauled me all the way over there to discuss, so she asked, "How are you coming along with plans for your little party?"

Gusta always considered other people's parties "little," but that morning I edified her. "It's getting pretty big. We are even going to have dancing on the lawn."

25

She waved one bony hand through the air. "Oh, how I remember the parties Granddaddy used to have in the governor's mansion. The people all loved him, of course." They didn't love him enough to vote him in for a second term, but I didn't mention that.

Meriwether herself brought the tea with a gaily flowered paper napkin. Thirty-two that year, tall and slender with blue-green eyes in a heart-shaped face and naturally blond curls that looked great with just a tad of frosting, she was far and away the prettiest unmarried woman in Hopemore, but her smile seemed a bit strained as she set the glass on a table near my chair. "It's good to see you, Mac. We really appreciated the donation you sent the Heart Association in Daddy's name." She blinked a couple of times, because she had genuinely loved her daddy and her eyes had filled with tears, but a Wainwright seldom showed emotion in public.

She took another wicker chair and stretched her long legs before her. They were shapely legs, ending in long aristocratic feet. I sipped my tea and thought that Meriwether had the prettiest skin I'd ever seen. Clarinda would have been hard put to find a wrinkle.

Since I'd known Meriwether since she was a baby, I felt comfortable informing her, "I've come to talk sense into you, but you don't look like you've lost what you already had."

"I haven't. It's just that Nana doesn't think I'm old enough to live alone."

I looked in surprise from one to the other. Gusta's face was as frosty as the tea glass on the table beside her. "This child," she said with emphasis, "has taken the notion to move into her daddy's house over on Liberty Street, since that creature —" She stopped.

"Candi has left," Meriwether finished smoothly. "She went back to New Orleans last evening. Daddy willed the house to me, and I've decided to live there."

"She has a perfectly good home right here. Why should she live in that poky little place —"

"Built in eighteen ninety, charming, with three bedrooms and two baths. I told you, Nana, I've loved that house since I was in grade school. Daddy bought it originally for me and —" She stopped to take a breath, then turned to me. "He told me several years ago it would be mine one day." Her eyes again sparkled with tears. "I didn't think it would be so soon."

Gusta ignored both the tears and the interruption. "A poky little place," she repeated, "way over there —"

"It's not in Macon, like you make it sound, for heaven's sake. It's three blocks away."

"— and leave me to rattle around this house all by myself? Who is going to keep up with my stocks, pay all the bills, and enter checks into the ledger every month?"

That last item could take some time. Gusta's husband had been a fine upstanding gentleman in many ways, but he'd owned more run-down

27

little properties across three counties than I liked to remember. He'd blocked Hope County from building public housing for years, saying loudly and at every opportunity, "We take care of our own. We don't ask gov'ment for hand-outs." The fact that most of his houses had leaky roofs and no insulation never came up.

The first thing Joe Riddley said when he heard Lamar Wainwright was dead was, "Maybe we can finally get some decent public housing around here."

We did, but it never seemed to be enough. Gusta probably still got more than a hundred rent checks a month. Maybe two hundred. Little dribbles that swelled to a river by the time they reached her account.

I came back to the conversation as Meri-wether was saying, "I told you, Nana, you can hire somebody to do all that."

"Let somebody read my private correspon-dence? Keep my books? Write my checks? You know my arthritis is so bad I can scarcely hold a pen."

Meriwether gave an impatient little huff. "Other people deal with this." She turned to me. "We even have a good candidate. A few weeks ago we got a letter from Nana's college friend, Bitsy Herrill, over in Macon —"

"Odd girl, Bitsy," Gusta interrupted. "Smoked like a chimney, but never drank coffee or tea. Claimed it was bad for you." She took a long swallow of her own tea to prove that wasn't so.

"Drank that grass stuff they call herbal tea. Didn't do her a speck of good. She's dying anyway."

Meriwether went on like she hadn't heard. They were used to doing that with one another. "She owns a small chain of gift stores, but now she's dying of lung cancer and wrote Nana that she's got a girl working for her whom she'd really like to find a place for before she dies. Says the girl is real sweet and honest, good with old women" — she gave me a mischievous wink, knowing full well her grandmother could see it — "a little shy, but competent. She was asking Nana if we knew anybody who needed someone. We said we didn't, but now that Daddy's left me his house" — she took a deep breath to steady the wobble in her voice — "I've decided it's time Nana gets somebody to replace me. I want to restore that house. I went through it this morning, and you wouldn't believe what Candi did to it. She lowered the ceilings, replaced the dining room chandelier with track lighting, installed wall-to-wall carpeting over oak floors, painted the kitchen pink, put in dark rose cabinets, even put a mirror on one entire bedroom wall!"

"Deplorable," Gusta agreed, "but what could you expect? Garlon never had any taste after your mother died. At least he didn't expect you to keep up his little hobby."

It took all my fortitude not to kick her in the shins. Garlon's "little hobby" was a perfectly re-

29

spectable lawn and garden tractor business. Garlon loved that business, and worked as hard at it as we work at Yarbrough's Feed, Seed and Nursery. Owning several huge cotton mills instead of one decent store didn't make Gusta better than the rest of us.

The whole town already knew that Garlon's will stipulated that the business be sold on very generous terms to his manager, a nice young man who was likely to make a go of it, and proceeds from that sale were to go to Candi. But that wouldn't matter to Meriwether. The rest of Garlon's money and what was left of her mother's now passed to her. After thirty-two years of depending on other people for every penny she spent on exquisite clothes, little silver Mercedes convertibles, and the kind of grooming most of us have neither the time nor money for, Meriwether could pay her own bills. No wonder Gusta was upset. The two of them glowered at each other across the porch.

"Children have to leave home," I reminded my old friend, "and this young woman from Macon sounds like she could use a job. Why don't you at least talk to her? She could be very grateful."

I could almost hear Gusta's thoughts. A grateful employee might be easier to order around than a thwarted granddaughter.

"Go bring the portable phone out here and call her," she said grudgingly to Meriwether. "And you talk to her, Mac. You're used to hiring people. You'll know what to ask."

I didn't know if that was a compliment or an insult.

Apparently Bitsy had her office phone forwarded to her home, because a soft voice answered. "Alice Fulton. This is Miss Bitsy Herrill's residence." She sounded soggy and sad, like she had a bad head cold.

"This is Judge MacLaren Yarbrough," I told her. "I'm calling for Augusta Wainwright, a friend of Bitsy Herrill's. Is she there?"

"No, ma'am." Her voice grew even sadder. "Miss Bitsy died last night. I was over here trying to pick out something for them to bury her in." She sniffed, then said as if trying to convince us both, "She's finally at peace. And she didn't suffer at the end. Please tell her friends that. I was going to call them later today, after all the" — she paused to sniff again — "arrangements have been made."

"Honey, would you like me to call back another day? We wanted to talk about a possible job down here, but this doesn't sound like a good time."

"Oh, no, ma'am, I can talk now if you like. It would take my mind off things."

When I asked about her business skills, she said, "I just did whatever Miss Bitsy told me to. I went to work for her to put myself through community college. But she was so nice, I quit school and worked for her full time. She taught me what I needed to know." Her voice broke. "I'm sorry," she explained through a series of sniffs, "but losing her is almost as hard as losing Mama two years ago. I've been with her seven years, and she was real easy to work for."

I doubted if she'd find Gusta easy to work for, but didn't like to discourage her right off the bat. And what did it matter what skills she'd needed to work for Miss Herrill? Apparently she was used to following orders, which is the only skill she'd need at Gusta's. Nobody who ever worked with or for Augusta Wainwright had need of initiative.

"How soon do you think you could come?"

She hesitated. "Do you think I could take a couple of weeks off first? I need to help them close up things here, and my sister has invited me to go scuba diving down in Clearwater. It sounds like a lot of fun, but if Mrs. Wainwright needs me right away —"

She'd have time enough to cater to Gusta's whims once she got to Hopemore. "I think you *ought* to take some time off between jobs, honey. It will refresh you."

"Yes, ma'am, I think it might. But I'll come as soon as we get back. I know I'll like it there. I prefer small towns."

Gusta reached for the phone. "This is Augusta Wainwright. The job isn't much. A little typing, helping me with parties, entering checks into my ledger, and keeping me company, since I'll be alone in the house." She frowned at Meriwether.

Meriwether and I shared a grin. "She makes

slavery sound like a long vacation," I said.

Alice must have asked a question, because Gusta said, "No, I don't have a computer. I do everything by hand. Can you do that?" Alice must have said she could, because Gusta said, "Fine, then, come whenever MacLaren — Judge Yarbrough — told you to. Now tell me about Bitsy." She finally expressed proper regrets, ending, "She was a good friend to us all."

"She sounds like she'll do fine, doesn't she?" Meriwether asked a bit anxiously. "Nana can get so out of sorts with people." "Out of sorts" was putting it mildly. Mean as a junkyard dog was more like it. I didn't envy shy little Alice Fulton, but at least she'd have a job.

As I stood to leave that afternoon, I felt real proud of myself. I'd helped the Wainwrights solve their little dilemma, and everything would be rosy in Hopemore.

For a very short time.

# 3

As Meriwether walked me to the car, a navy-blue Cadillac pulled up their drive, making a Cadillac sandwich with my Nissan as filling.

Meriwether wrinkled her forehead. "I wonder what Pooh wants."

Winifred "Pooh" DuBose is Gusta's oldest friend — born two months later — but Pooh is as sweet as Gusta is tart, and has a far greater claim to our local throne: She is a direct descendant of William Few, who signed the Declaration of Independence. Pooh's husband, Lafayette DuBose, started with one truck and built a national trucking line, so she's almost as rich as Gusta, too, but Gusta set Pooh straight about who was number one in their baby carriage days. Pooh doesn't seem to mind. She doesn't mind, either, that everybody, from the old to the very young, calls her Pooh. The only people in town who call her Miss Winifred are Otis Raeburn, her driver and general helper, and his wife, Lottie, Pooh's housekeeper.

Neither Gusta nor Pooh ever bought a car when their husbands were alive, so neither of them knew how to buy one after the men died.

Gusta still drove Lamar's 1980 model. Pooh's was five years old. Otis polished them both and took them to be serviced or repaired.

That morning Otis climbed stiffly out of Pooh's Cadillac and, with immense dignity, hoisted a wheelchair from the trunk and rolled it to the back door.

Otis is thin as a rail, and must be nearer eighty than seventy. He and Lottie were working for Pooh long before I got married. They had seen Pooh and Fayette through the birth of their only son, Zachary, through Zach's death in Vietnam, and, most recently, through Fayette's own death a couple of years ago. Now the wheelchair was almost too heavy for Otis's thin wrists. I wondered how much longer he would be able to haul it in and out of that high trunk.

He opened the door, and Pooh wriggled herself out, a small plump woman moving with arthritic difficulty. She could stand and even walk a few steps on her own, but barely, so she balanced against the car for a mere moment before lowering herself into the chair. Then she threw both hands up in delight. "I'm here!" A frame of silver curls surrounded round pink cheeks and sparkling eyes as light blue as the autumn sky. "I didn't know you were coming, MacLaren. It's so good to see you."

I gave her a hug and Meriwether bent to give her a kiss.

Pooh gave her a worried frown. "I do hope Gusta remembered I don't like canned asparagus. She's had it the last two times I've been here."

Meriwether's dark brows moved together in consternation. "Are you here for dinner?"

Otis gently shook the handles of Pooh's chair in reproach. "I tol' 'er she wadn't invited today. Tol' and tol' her. But she wouldn' listen."

"Of course I'm invited." Pooh's hands fluttered in irritation. "Come Tuesday, Gusta said."

"That was last Tuesday, Miss Winifred," Otis said in equal irritation. He turned to me. "I tol' her twenty times she already *had* dinner here *last* Tuesday. But she won't listen to nobody since Mr. Fayette died." He slapped one bony thigh in frustration.

Pooh turned and spoke over her shoulder with dignity. "Go on home. Gusta invited me herself. Meriwether will help me in. I'll call you when I'm ready for you to come get me."

Meriwether threw me a look of appeal.

"Why don't you go check with Gusta, and let me visit with Pooh?" I suggested.

She turned and hurried up the walk.

Pooh cocked her head. "How is that dear Joe Riddley?"

"He's coming along, but he's not real patient with his therapy."

I was about to invite her over to visit him when Meriwether loped back. "I am dreadfully sorry, Pooh, but Nana forgot all about inviting you, and we're having leftovers. Canned asparagus, too. How about if you come next Tuesday?

36

I'll have something very special for you."

"No canned asparagus?" Pooh quavered.

"No canned asparagus." Meriwether gently turned the chair back toward the car so Pooh could climb in more easily. "Will you remind her, Otis?"

"I'll bring her," Otis promised as he climbed back into the driver's seat. "I surely will. Thank you, Meriwether. Very kind."

"Oh, well," Pooh said almost to herself. "We'll probably get home about the time Zachary gets back from the store."

The blue Cadillac inched down the driveway.

Meriwether watched it creep down Oglethorpe past three houses and turn into the drive of Pooh's large yellow Victorian. "I hate her getting like that. I just hate it!"

"I do, too, honey, but at least she's happy and sweet. And she'll have forgotten lunch at Gusta's by the time she gets up from her afternoon nap."

Instead, Pooh got up angry at crows.

It wasn't shots I heard, it was the siren tearing down Oglethorpe Street.

Sirens are so unusual in Hopemore that I raised my head from the checks I was writing. With only thirteen thousand people in what the chamber of commerce proudly calls Greater Hopemore, any cause for alarm probably involves somebody I know. I feared a car accident on the other side of town, where folks hadn't gotten used to a new four-way stop. When the siren's wail stopped soon after it passed our store, though, I listened harder. It was just a matter of time before somebody came to tell me what was going on.

Sure enough, my granddaughter Bethany — Ridd's daughter — burst through the door. "You didn't knock," I reminded her for the hundredth time. Bethany, a high school junior, had started working afternoons after school to earn money for college. She was having a hard time remembering that my office door now belonged to her employer, not her grandmother.

"Sorry." She backed out breathlessly, knocked, and waited.

"Come in. What's going on out there?"

"It's Pooh. She's in her backyard shooting!"

My first instinct always is to think I have to get up and do something about any situation. Now that I don't have Joe Riddley to remind me I don't, I try to remember to remind myself. But before I sat back down, I asked, "Shooting what?"

"A gun, Me-mama."

"I know that. I mean what is she shooting *at?*"

"I don't know. They just said shooting." "They" being the Hopemore grapevine that gets news around so fast we scarcely need a newspaper at all. "Maybe at the police," she added.

That sent me out of my office in a hurry, toward the front sidewalk. Yarbrough's Feed, Seed and Nursery is on Oglethorpe one block west of the square. Pooh, like Gusta, lives one block east of the square. Hopemore is so old that our earliest first families built their homes in easy walking distance of their banks, businesses, and law offices.

From the sidewalk we heard another shot.

"What you reckon she's shooting at?" one of my clerks asked.

"Don't know. It's not huntin' season," a Yankee tourist replied. You'd have thought Hopemore was Alaska, with game roaming the streets.

Just then, to my relief, the shots stopped.

"Where would Miss Pooh even get a gun?" a young man asked near the front of the crowd.

"Probably one of Mr. Fayette's old ones," said one of his contemporaries.

"Pooh used to have guns of her own," I informed them. "She was one of the best shots in the county. Hunted with Fayette for years, and brought back squirrels, rabbits, even a buck back in nineteen —" I stopped, remembering I was close to giving a clue to my own age. "I don't remember the exact year."

A second siren wailed from another direction and a second cruiser pulled up to the curb down the street. We saw two officers jump out. One carried a bullhorn, the other had his hand on his pistol.

Two more shots rang out. "She just stopped to reload," a woman announced unnecessarily.

The bullhorn bellowed indistinctly.

Bethany turned to me. "Me-mama, go down there. You know how confused Pooh gets now'days. She might shoot somebody." What sent me scurrying to my car instead was the fear that an overexcited officer might shoot Pooh.

I drove a tad more quickly than a judge ought to, and was embarrassed at the screech my tires made on the gravel drive as I stopped. Before I could even get my door open I heard the bullhorn thunder. "Put down the weapon. Put it down."

I was shaking so hard I could hardly get the door open, and I must have set an Olympic record for women over sixty sprinting up a long driveway. I found three young officers at Pooh's back gate. One had the bullhorn and one actually had his weapon drawn.

"Don't shoot!" I yelled, puffing for breath. "Let me talk to her."

As they turned in surprise, Otis stepped from behind a big camellia bush. He was gray and shaking, sweat running from his temples. "I sure am glad to see you! Folks has gone plumb crazy 'round here." He waved both hands in the air.

"What's going on?" I asked.

The officers replied in official jumble-ese, but Otis gave a clearer picture. "Miss Winifred got up from her nap, got in her power chair, and wheeled herself out in the yard with her shotgun before I knew she was awake. When I saw her through the kitchen window, I came right out after her, but she said she's gonna kill those pesky crows that keep her from napping. I tried to talk her out of it — tol' her and tol' her you can't shoot a gun in the city limits. But she was bound and determined."

Another shot was fired in the backyard and the bullhorn roared again. "Put down your weapon or you will be considered armed and dangerous."

Otis's eyes widened in fear. "I called the police thinkin' they'd come talk sense to her. Instead, next thing I know we've got po-lice all over the place drawin' *their* guns. We gotta get that gun away from her" — he gave the officers a rebuking glare — "but we don't hafta shoot her to do it."

"Subject is armed and dangerous, Judge," one of the officers informed me stiffly.

I treated him as formally as he was treating me, although I'd lifted him up to water fountains when he was crawling around my shoelaces. "Let me see if I can talk to her, Officer."

I rounded the big camellia and saw Pooh sitting in her wheelchair in a lavender-and-blue cotton coffee coat with a wide white pique collar. She looked perfectly harmless except for the shotgun on her shoulder. As I watched, she aimed at the sky, pulled the trigger, and brought down a spiraling black form.

"Good shot, Pooh! You haven't lost your skill. But what're you doin'?" I called from the gate. I started walking toward her like I was just curious.

41

She lowered the gun and turned in her chair, swinging the barrels in my direction. I saw that her arms were shaking from the exertion of holding the gun. And while she could still remember how to shoot, she apparently couldn't remember not to aim a loaded gun at friends. That was one of those times I wished I was someplace else, especially since the young officer behind me probably had a protective but trembling finger on his own trigger at my back.

Pooh's face was flushed with heat. "Why, hello, MacLaren!" We could have been at a garden club party except for the gun pointed at my chest. "I'll be with you in just a minute. First I have to shoot the rest of these pesky crows. They've taken up residence in my magnolia and simply won't let me get my nap."

She turned back to aim toward the towering magnolia that stood between her yard and her neighbor's. Just beyond that particular tree was her neighbor's kitchen window.

I considered trying to dissuade her, but knew that wouldn't work. "Can you get a clear shot from your chair? Looks like you've got a branch between you and the crow." I walked closer to her and bent down to sight over her shoulder.

"Get the gun!" one of the officers called.

I ignored him.

Pooh nodded seriously. "That's what I've found." She started to move awkwardly, waving the gun about. "If I get up, will you hold me so I can stand?"

"Maybe I ought to shoot the crows."

I could tell the officers were having fits behind me. I flapped one hand behind my back to keep them from rushing us both.

Pooh's forehead puckered like she was thinking it over. "Are you a good shot, MacLaren? I don't rightly remember."

"Used to shoot rats in Daddy's henhouse, and never hit a chicken."

She thought about that while the courthouse clock chimed four. Then she gave me her sunny smile and held out the shotgun. "That ought to be all right, then."

I took it and sighted along the barrel, wondering how long it would be before those young policemen's patience ran out. "You know, I can't get a clear shot, either. I'm likely to shoot right through your neighbor's downstairs window. I sure don't want to rile anybody, do you?"

"Well, no, I don't want to upset the neighbors. But we've got to get rid of those crows."

I lowered the gun's muzzle to the grass. "You know what? We've got some artificial owls down at the store that will scare them off. How about if I send somebody over with some? He'll even install them for you."

"That would be wonderful!" Pooh clapped her hands in delight. "I should have called you in the first place."

"I wish you had. I'll send one of our men down within the hour. Okay?"

"That will be fine. Otis? Where's Otis? That man is never around when I need him."

"Here I am, Miss Winifred." He came through the gate and took the handle grips of her chair. "Let me get you inside so you can get dressed for the afternoon."

Pooh looked down in surprise. "Why, MacLaren, I am ashamed to have you see me like this. I came out in such a hurry, I forgot to put on my dress." She put her chair in gear and started up the ramp to her back porch.

One of the officers stepped forward. "Just a minute. We're going to have to cite you . . ."

I turned and motioned him back toward the gate. "Would you say this woman is competent to stand trial, officer?" I asked softly.

"Well, no, Judge, but —"

"Would you say she ought to be sent to an institution?"

Pooh used to stand on her front porch steps with warm home-baked cookies when he walked home from elementary school. Maybe he remembered those cookies, or maybe he thought of his own grandmother, who had never been the same since his Uncle Jack was killed in Vietnam. When you live in a small town, you know so many things about each other. "She can't be trusted with firearms in the house, Judge."

"We'll get the guns out of the house this afternoon. All of them. I'll see to that myself."

"Yes, ma'am. May I put that in my report?"

"Sure. Say that Judge Yarbrough personally oversaw the removal of all firearms from the premises."

As soon as the officers left, I followed Otis inside and we collected all the DuBose hunting rifles, shotguns, and ammunition. "I hate to take 'em without her knowin'," Otis worried out loud, "but we have to for her own safety."

"If she asks, say I took them away to clean them. You're sure there aren't any more?"

He furrowed his brow above his grizzled eyebrows. "Used to be a little bitty twenty-two pistol, but I think she gave it to Miss Augusta after we had all those robberies a good many years back. Miss Winifred never had much use for *little* guns."

"I'll ask Gusta. Meanwhile, you search for it. If you find it, bring it to me right away. I gave my word that I'd oversee the removal of *all* firearms from these premises."

That promise would come back to haunt me.

# 4

When I called Gusta to ask about Pooh's gun, she said Meriwether put it somewhere and she'd ask about it. Since it wasn't at Pooh's, I forgot about it. I pretty much forgot about Gusta and Meriwether, too, for two weeks. Then, on Saturday, I went to Phyllis's Beauty Parlor for a long-overdue perm. Phyllis was almost finished rolling me when somebody came in and demanded, "Is it true Meriwether's painting her house red, white, and blue?"

"Sounds real tacky, if you ask me," said a customer at a station I couldn't see.

Phyllis held the last hank of my hair straight up in curling paper and turned to whoever spoke. "Buck says it's gonna be gorgeous. The actual colors are creamy magnolia, slate blue and old burgundy, with just a tad of forest green up at that point near the roof. He's head contractor on the project, you know." Phyllis — who was Buck's wife — picked up the last pink roller while the biddies cackled on.

"Wonder what she has against plain white paint?"

"Same thing she has against those gorgeous

kitchen cabinets. Is she really gonna rip them out and put in plain old wood?"

Phyllis set that one straight. "They aren't plain old wood. They're solid oak, Buck says, with oak and white ceramic handles. She's taking the kitchen floor down to wood, too."

"Doesn't she know you can't mop wood?"

"Probably never mopped a floor in her life."

"You can mop anything if you put enough polyurethane on it."

"When's it gonna be ready for her to move in?"

Phyllis tied a net around my lumpy curlers. "Buck says she's gonna move in as soon as Miss Gusta's new help arrives, even if it's not done. Says she wants to be on hand to supervise. Buck wishes she'd stay where she is and let him get on with his work. Okay, MacLaren. Let's put you under the drier a few minutes."

They kept talking as I slid down from the high chair and headed to the driers.

"She can't cook, can she, until the kitchen floor's done?"

"Can't cook, anyway. She'll be going back for Florine's meals the rest of her life, I shouldn't wonder."

"Must be nice to have that much money plus a cook to go back to."

"When's the new girl coming?"

The last thing I heard before the drier roared in my ears was, "Late Monday, I believe."

I wasn't thinking about Alice Fulton, though,

47

on Monday afternoon when I left the store. I was going to see the florist to discuss centerpieces for Joe Riddley's party so Clarinda would stop nagging me about it. To my surprise, we agreed on what I needed so quickly that I decided I had time for a piece of pie and a cup of coffee.

The place for pie in Hopemore is Myrtle's Cafe, a local restaurant that still advertises "Food as Good as Mama Used to Make." That hasn't been true since her husband had his bypass and Myrtle stopped frying her chicken and fish or putting a slice of fatback in her vegetables. Nowadays she only cooks as good as Mama did if your mama was a Yankee. But Myrtle's is still the best place in town for dessert. Her meringue stands two inches thick with sweet sugar beads on the top. Just like Mama's.

Myrtle and I visited a little and I said what I always said: "You have simply got to replace this floor. You've got so many holes in the tile, somebody's going to trip one day and sue you for all you've got."

Myrtle said what she always said, too: "I don't have much to sue for, what with Jack being so sick and all. I'm saving for a floor, though. I just haven't gotten around to it." Which would have made me a lot sorrier for her if I didn't know she drove a new gold Chrysler, took a long vacation to Branson last year, and paid her kitchen help dirt. You don't have many secrets when you live in a small town.

Finally I asked for chocolate pie.

She jerked her head in the direction of a back booth and said, "Sorry, Mac — I mean Y'r Honor — I didn't know you were coming, so I gave that girl back there the last piece." She leaned down and whispered, "I think she must be Miss Gusta's new help. She had a letter signed by Meriwether on the table when I took her order, and I heard she'd be arriving late this afternoon. Must have got here early, and stopped for pie and coffee to fill up the time."

I saw a cloud of dark hair so lively it looked electric. Its owner was a slender girl with her head bent over a paperback book and both hands cupping a mug. She carried it absently to her mouth while she read.

"Meriwether's moving out tomorrow," Myrtle confided. "The poor thing's got her job cut out for her, wouldn't you say?"

I didn't have time or inclination to gossip. "How fresh is your banana pudding?"

"Made not half an hour ago, and we broiled the meringue, so the bananas aren't one speck cooked. You want a big bowl of pudding and black coffee?"

She wrote down my order without even waiting for my nod. Myrtle knows the vices of her regulars. As she passed the newcomer's table, the young woman raised one hand. "Miss? I need more coffee."

Gusta herself couldn't have done it better, but Myrtle didn't take bossing by newcomers.

49

"I'll be back in a minute." She headed for the kitchen.

I settled back in my booth, opened the new *Statesman*, and was astonished to read that our newspaper editor was fixing to retire to Florida that very week to live near her grandchildren. I knew she had been thinking about retiring, but figured she'd take her time. The article said Slade Rutherford from the Asheville paper was coming to take over as editor.

"You see this?" I asked Myrtle as she came from the kitchen carrying my banana pudding and coffee.

The girl at the back called impatiently, "Miss? I need more coffee."

"Hold your horses," Myrtle told her shortly. "I'll be there soon as I give Mac here her pudding." She bent over my table and said under her breath, "Miss Gusta'll soon take her down a peg or two." She cruised off with the coffeepot and I tucked happily into warm banana pudding.

When I finished, the young woman was still reading in her booth. On impulse I went back to say hello. She slid the book into her lap and looked up curiously. Her big dark eyes were set in a long thin face framed by that soft black mass of hair that sprang from her scalp with a life of its own.

"I'm MacLaren Yarbrough. I spoke with you a couple of weeks ago for Mrs. Wainwright."

I could tell by the flicker in her eyes that she'd

forgotten, but she recovered almost at once and stuck out her hand in a businesslike manner. "Oh — yes. How do you do?"

When we'd finished the little courtesies, I asked, "Did you take that week's vacation with your sister before you came? And was it fun?"

To my amazement, her eyes filled with tears and she regarded me with horror. She pressed her lips together, but they still trembled.

"Oh, honey, is something wrong?"

She nodded and blinked to stop the tears. "My sister drowned," she whispered.

The starch went out of my knees. Without asking permission, I sank into the booth across from her. "Oh, my goodness! What happened?"

She dabbed her eyes with her napkin. "We went down to Clearwater to scuba dive. She hadn't been before, and on our very first dive she caught her fin in a hole in the coral. When she tried to get it out, her foot got wedged. Several of us tried to help her, but we couldn't free it —" Her voice choked and she pressed her hand to her mouth. That didn't stop tears from brimming over her eyelids. "It was horrible! She had plenty of oxygen in her tank, but she was terrified. The dive master had gone up with another novice, so one man went to get him while the rest of us stayed down to try and help her, but she got disoriented and panicky, and jerked off her mask." She closed her eyes and her shoulders shook. "They tried to get it back on her, or to make her breathe with a buddy, but she fought and fought, and gulped water. . . ." She covered her face with her hands and shuddered. She finally added in an anguished whisper, "It was awful!"

I put out a hand to touch her gently. "I am so very sorry."

Breathing heavily, she looked away, her eyes stark. "They made me go up to the boat and wait while they brought her up. Then they worked with her for ages — even radioed the Coast Guard. But she was gone." She pressed both hands to her cheeks and shook her head as if disagreeing with her sister's fate. "It happened so fast." She wiped away the tears and used the tissue I handed her to blow her nose. "We were real close. It's been hard." Her voice was muffled by the tissue.

"It must have been especially hard on you following the death of your employer. You should have taken more time before coming here, Alice." I'd remembered her name, and thought it might make her feel more welcome if I used it.

She took a deep breath, then gave me a shy, watery smile. Her voice was softer, too, as she said, "I really need to work right now. It didn't take long to clear out both our apartments, and there wasn't any reason to stay there. So I came on." She looked at her watch. "I'd better be getting over to Miss Wainwright's. I told her I'd arrive around four." Fumbling in her purse again, she brought out a black cloth scrunchy and, with one smooth motion, pulled all that lovely hair to the nape of her neck and fastened it back like some old-fashioned schoolmarm. She also brought out a pair of horn-rimmed glasses and set them on her nose, and she went from lively and pert to quiet and drab in three seconds. I thought about telling her Gusta appreciates women who look nice, but decided that was their business.

As we slid out of the booth to pay our bills, she left half a cup of the coffee she'd been so insistent about getting.

At the curb she started toward a little white Acura with a Georgia vanity plate: TERRI. When she saw me reading it, she explained, "It was my sister's. Her name was Teresa. I didn't have a car, so —" She stopped and took a deep breath. "I need to transfer it into my name and get a new tag as soon as I can."

Just then a man from our church ambled down the sidewalk. "Afternoon, Judge Yarbrough."

I couldn't help laughing at how upset Alice looked. She'd plumb forgotten what I was. "I won't have them lock you up today. Just get that tag as soon as you can."

"I will. I sure will!" She slid easily into the driver's seat and drove away.

I stared after her, thinking how fragile life is, how it can shatter in one afternoon — or one evening when your husband goes out for a routine walk. I felt like shouting to everybody passing me on the street, "This day is precious.

53

Do you know that? Enjoy it while you can. Your whole life may be different tomorrow."

As I walked back to my office, I winged a short prayer that Alice Fulton would find peace and comfort in Hopemore. Whichever angel was supposed to carry that prayer must have been on its cell phone, though, because in another few weeks Hiram Blaine would come home and Hopemore's peace would be shattered.

# 5

Slade Rutherford came to town first, and caused his own kind of ripples.

I heard he'd come, but before I could get down to the *Statesman* to introduce myself and ask tactfully whether he planned to keep my garden column, I bumped into him as I was coming out of the bank. Literally. I was saying "good morning" over my shoulder to Vern, the security guard, and wasn't looking where I was going. I didn't know a soul was there until my nose hit a dark green tie with gold fleurs-de-lis. Mortified, I turned my head and got my new perm tangled on his tie tack. We stood on most intimate terms until he could disentangle me. After that it seemed odd to introduce ourselves.

My son Walker could have told within a few dollars how much he'd paid for that light camel jacket, matching slacks, soft creamy shirt, and tasseled loafers, but all I knew was they'd cost a lot. He looked to be around Walker's age, too — thirty-five or so — and had a high forehead, dark, fuzzy black eyebrows, and eyes so brown they looked black. They burrowed into my own without giving away any secrets.

I could see myself reflected in his pupils — a short plumpish woman wearing a cotton knit sweater with a coordinated print skirt. Joe Riddley used to say, "Honey, you aren't plump, you're just voluptuous." How I missed having somebody who thought I was the most special person in the world. The man I'd run into seemed to be deciding whether I was worth another second of his time.

"I beg your pardon." I knew I was pinker than a sunburned flamingo. "I don't generally make a habit of running into people. I am MacLaren Yarbrough."

"You all own the big nursery business?" As soon as I nodded, his eyes crinkled in delight. "I'm Slade Rutherford, new editor of the *Hopemore Statesman*, and you're one of our best advertisers."

"I'm also very embarrassed. I should have been looking where I was going."

"Hey, don't worry about it. I stumble over my own feet so often, I make a habit of forgiving folks who stumble over them, too." After that, I couldn't help looking down at his shoes. He must have worn fourteens.

I was wondering whether it was the time to tell him I wrote the paper's monthly gardening column, and delicately inquire whether he would continue to run it, when Vern hobbled out the door shouting, "You can't park there! You know you can't park there!"

Slade raised eyebrows like dark brown caterpillars. "Come see the fun," I suggested.

Immaculate in a blue linen suit, Gusta climbed from her elderly black Cadillac and brandished her silver-headed cane at poor Vern. Vern had a bum leg, but he could still hop in rage. "You can't park there! You know that!" He waved fists in the air. Gusta brandished her cane again.

Sensing that Slade might be about to go to somebody's aid, I held him back. "Don't worry, this goes on all the time. It's a perennial battle over whether Mrs. Augusta Wainwright can park in the handicapped zone in front of the bank without a sticker."

"Marvelous car." His eyes roved admiringly over the polished black paint and shiny chrome.

On the sidewalk, Vern was wringing his hands. "You know that place is for people who's got a sticker, Mrs. Wainwright. All you gotta do is get a sticker from your doctor. Or park 'round the corner and come in the side door. Or park just down the block."

"I am not handicapped, merely old," Gusta informed him, stomping across the sidewalk with the help of her cane, "and I have no intention of walking extra steps or skulking into the bank by a side door. You never had a handicapped zone there when my husband was alive. He'd never have permitted it. Wait in the car," she called over her shoulder, "and by no means move that car. I will be out soon." That's when I noticed Alice at the wheel in Meriwether's place.

Gusta paused in the doorway. "Good afternoon, Judge Yarbrough." She gave my companion a significant look, waiting to be introduced.

His own eyebrows rose. "You should have told me I was in the presence of the law."

"I'm one of three magistrates in the county. Let me present you to Mrs. Augusta Wainwright. Augusta, this is Slade — uh —" I bogged down in the morass of bad memory.

"Rutherford," he supplied helpfully. "New editor for the *Hopemore Statesman.*"

Gusta rested on her cane and peered closely, searching his long frame for flaws. She apparently found none, because she extended her hand. "How do you do? Where did you come from?"

"Asheville, I was with —"

"Ah, one of the North Carolina Rutherfords?" He barely nodded, but she went right on, satisfied that she'd placed him. "We may be distantly related — through my mother's side. Come by one afternoon. I'm just up Oglethorpe Street. Anyone can direct you." She swept past us and into the bank, leaving Vern still wringing his hands and looking for a police car. Alice waited by the curb, avoiding Vern's eye. I and everybody else in town pretended we didn't notice the car. We all knew Gusta didn't need to do any more walking than she had to.

Slade watched Gusta's progression through the bank with an amused smile. "I take it that

Mrs. Wainwright is important in town?"

"Assumed the throne at birth and hasn't shown any sign of stepping down."

"I'll keep that in mind." He touched his left hand to his forehead in a mock salute and followed her toward the counter.

Any woman with eyes in her head could see that Slade's wedding ring finger was bare. It didn't take long for him to be approached by every unattached woman in town between twenty-five and forty except Meriwether Wainwright. And by their respective mamas. Especially after Gusta discreetly spread the word that Slade was "one of the North Carolina Rutherfords — you know, like Rutherfordton?" She pronounced it *Rolfton*, like I'd heard native Carolinians do.

Suddenly we had a spate of little Welcome Autumn cocktail parties, football get-togethers with cute food instead of the usual nacho cheese and chips, a group jaunt down to Dublin to watch car races, a Harvest Barbeque, even a Scarecrow Dance at the country club. We also had a round of what our women like to call "just a casual dinner, nothing formal, mostly family" that involves two days of silver polishing, tablecloth ironing, and cookbook consulting to pick something not too ostentatious but certainly not what the family sits down to as a rule.

Slade Rutherford, of course, was the guest of honor at all those events, tall, slim and handsome. With Slade invited, the parties did double duty. Not only did they parade eligible women in their native habitat, they also gave hostesses a chance for a small paragraph in the paper. A few even got pictures. But while the *Hopemore Statesman* duly reported our social whirl, Slade seemed immune to all Hopemore's blushing belles. The only woman he seemed the least bit interested in was Gusta. I heard he stopped by her place several times a week with flowers and candy.

Gusta called one Tuesday to invite Joe Riddley and me to a musicale the next Sunday afternoon. "Only a few people," she assured me. "I've got a chamber orchestra from Augusta and am tuning the Steinway." She made it sound like she turned those little screws herself.

"You know Joe Riddley doesn't go out right now," I reminded her.

"It would do him good to get out. He can sit in a corner and listen to the music, and you can go home whenever you feel like it. Don't let me down. I'm counting on your being here."

Thinking it might do Joe Riddley good, I wrestled him into a suit that hung on him, thin as he'd gotten. I gussied myself up in my favorite long green dress that everybody says flatters me. I put blusher on my cheeks and mascara on my lashes, for I like to look nice. I struggled to get both Joe Riddley and that dratted wheelchair into the car. And then, when we got there, I discovered it wasn't Mac and Joe Riddley she'd wanted, it was

60

Judge and Judge Yarbrough. She also had the chief surgeon from our local hospital and his wife, the president of our community college with her husband, and Maynard Spence, my nearest neighbor and the new curator of the Hope County Historical Museum. He brought Selena Jones, whom he'd been squiring for over a month. Maynard had lived in New York for ten years before coming home to Hopemore, and outshone our dark-suited men in a natural linen suit and a dark green shirt. Selena beside him was a whirl of orange, green, and yellow silk that set off her deep red hair.

After Gusta presented Slade to all the other guests, she added as if it were an afterthought, "And I don't think you've met my grand-daughter, Meriwether."

Meriwether was wearing a soft green-and-blue dress that made her eyes look like emeralds. With her hair fluffed around her face and her mother's large pearls in her ears, she could have flown in from Paris, but her grandmother gave her a prod like she was a backwards sixteen-year-old. "Meriwether, why don't you get Mr. Rutherford a drink?"

While the instruments tuned up, I wheeled Joe Riddley to a corner, got him a drink and a plate of finger food, and sat fanning myself. Joe Riddley took one sip of his drink and took one look at his plate and said loudly, "Gusta's watering her sherry again, and this sandwich isn't big enough for a flea."

I motioned for him to be quiet, which irritated him more. "Don't shush me, Little Bit. I know what I am saying. As much money as that woman's got, she could afford to feed us."

I pointed to Kelly Keane, moving purposefully from group to group with her notebook and ballpoint pen. "There's that reporter who interviewed me. You don't want her quoting you in the paper, do you?"

As Kelly moved to talk to somebody hidden from me by a potted palm, Joe Riddley exclaimed, "There's Darren!" He waved a cracker spread with cheese and one slice of olive. "Hey, Darren! Come eat a flea sandwich."

I was surprised and delighted when Darren Hernandez, Joe Riddley's therapist, stepped out from the palm and headed our way. He must have taken seriously my suggestion that he look up Kelly. Well-dressed women and men in starched shirts and suits looked askance at his black jeans and T-shirt — or was it his bright green hair and silver earring? His handsome swarthy face lit with a smile. "Hey, J.R. You need more to eat? I'll get it for you."

"We need to go," Kelly said softly at his shoulder. She gave us an apologetic smile. "I have another event to cover this afternoon, too. Slade's going to write up the music part here."

I was sorry they had left when I saw Alice Fulton come from the back part of the house and stand looking around uncertainly. They'd been the only people her age in the room. I smiled, and when she smiled back and headed our way, I remembered with surprise how pretty she could be. Since she'd started work, I'd only seen her in flat shoes, neat dark skirts, and cotton sweaters. Today she wore a simple sleeveless black dress that showed off a lovely figure and brought out her dark hair and eyes. Gold hoops in her ears and a gold chain around her neck glittered in the light. High heels called attention to her tiny feet. But she still had her hair dragged back instead of letting it spring loose around her face.

With his current lack of tact, Joe Riddley put my next thought into words. "Let your hair down and put on a little makeup, you could be downright beautiful." He waved a scrap of pimento cheese sandwich at her. "Won't get fat eating at Gusta's. That's for sure."

Alice gave him an anxious smile. "Can I get you something else?"

"Get me about fifty of these. Takes that many to make a good meal." As she scurried off, he looked around the room and called to nobody in particular, "Did Gusta sell her furniture?"

Gusta herself heard him. "I put it in the back room to make space for the concert." The way she said it, you'd have thought she'd personally moved the couch, chairs, and tables.

"Don't need to clean up for a party if you do what Little Bit does. Puts everything in corners and hides it with screens. Isn't that right, honey?"

"That's right," I agreed ruefully.

I have seven tall screens scattered around our house. Joe Riddley made them years ago, papering them to match various rooms, so whenever we have a party I can shove things behind them and have the house looking halfway decent. It is an old joke in Hopemore that "the size of a Yarbrough party depends on how much space MacLaren has left after she sets up her screens." As I later told Police Chief Muggins, though, when I say I "shove things behind them," I mean paperwork I've brought home, or projects for church, the A.A.U.W., and the Garden Club. I don't mean dead people.

Alice hurried back from the dining room with a plate piled high with food.

"Heavens!" Gusta exclaimed. "How many are you planning to feed?"

"It'll do me for starters." For an instant the old Joe Riddley twinkled up at us. Alice was so startled she nearly dropped the plate. I knew what she was feeling. It was something like having somebody peer at you from what you'd thought was an empty house.

"You'll never be able to eat all those. Take what you need, and I'll pass the rest." Gusta passed the plate to him long enough for him to take three sandwiches, then snatched it away.

"Old skinflint," Joe Riddley growled as she moved to other guests.

"Honey, try to be nice," I begged.

"Spent my life being nice, and where did it

ever get me? Time I spoke my mind." Joe Riddley waved a piece of stuffed celery like a baton. I bent to wipe pimento cheese from Gusta's thick Chinese rug and hoped she hadn't seen him spill it.

I could tell it wasn't any use sticking around for the music. If he didn't take a mind to sing along, he'd talk and spoil the afternoon for everybody. As soon as he'd eaten his "flea sandwiches," as he kept calling them, I went looking for Gusta to lie about how much we'd enjoyed being there and say he was getting tired and had to go.

I didn't see Gusta, so settled for Meriwether, who was with Slade Rutherford in the dining room. They seemed to be enjoying one another's company a good deal. I heard her laugh aloud as I approached them — a sound as seldom heard in Hopemore as a discouraging word back home on the range.

"I need to take Joe Riddley home." I gestured toward his chair. "He's having a bad day, and he's going to bother everybody. Will you tell Gusta for me?"

"Let me help you get him to the car," Slade offered at once. "I'll be back in a minute," he promised Meriwether. "Don't go away."

He pushed Joe Riddley out to the back porch and down the ramp installed after Lamar Wainwright had his first heart attack. Slade helped Joe Riddley into the car as gently as if he were his own daddy, and stowed the chair in the trunk for me. "Can you get that out when you get home, Judge? Want me to follow you home and help?"

"I'll be all right," I assured him. "You go back in and enjoy the music."

White teeth flashed in his dark face. "I was sure enjoying the company, as I'm certain you noticed. May I ask you a question?" He leaned close to me and spoke softly. "Is Meriwether seeing somebody?"

I patted his arm. "Only Gusta. You'd be a vast improvement."

He threw back his head and laughed, then shut my car door after me.

As I backed down the drive, Joe Riddley growled, "Man brays like a donkey."

The next Wednesday evening about eleven, a deputy called to say he needed me down at the detention center for a hearing, and he was coming to get me. Joe Riddley used to drive, of course, but they were still treating me like Hopemore was a hotbed of crime and I wouldn't be safe driving myself the two miles each way. On our way back we came down Liberty Street and I saw a big green Lexus in front of Meriwether's house. "Looks like that newspaper fellow is making time with Meriwether," the deputy said with a grin.

The next Saturday at the beauty parlor I heard that Slade had been over at Meriwether's house several times that week "bugging Buck to death with suggestions for how things could be done better. He's more finicky than Meriwether, even."

That same evening Walker and his wife, Cindy, saw them at By Candlelight, our most exclusive restaurant, for dinner.

Sunday evening, Ridd and his wife, Martha, reported they were out at Dad's Outdoor BarBeQue, a large barn with long tables and benches and the best barbeque in our part of Georgia.

"She was laughing," Martha reported. "I can't remember the last man I saw Meriwether laugh with."

I could. Jed Blaine. But she hadn't done much laughing with anybody since she'd moved back in with Gusta. She smiled, but happiness never reached her eyes.

"Were her eyes laughing?" I asked.

Ridd looked at me like I was crazy, but Martha looked thoughtful. "No, they weren't."

I sighed. "Oh, well. Give him time."

But time was something they were not destined to have — not right away. When I saw Gusta at the Garden Club luncheon the following Tuesday, she announced, "We won't be here for the A.A.U.W. meeting. I've decided to go to China. I haven't been there for several years, and there's a wonderful tour some Agnes Scott alumnae have put together. Hong Kong, Beijing, Shanghai, and several other places."

"You won't miss Joe Riddley's party, will you?" If she did, I'd never forgive her.

"Of course not. We'll be back more than a week before that."

"We? Who's going with you?"

"Meriwether will accompany me, as usual."

"Not this time," Meriwether corrected her, joining us. "I've got my house to work on. They're about to finish the kitchen. Besides, Slade and I have been invited —"

Gusta lifted her chin. "There will be other invitations, my dear. Besides, you know what they say: Absence makes the heart grow fonder."

Meriwether lifted her own chin while I looked down at my piled-up plate and tried not to feel guilty. Mine was full of fats and starches, Meriwether's full of lettuce, carrots, and other bunny food. "I am not going," she declared, "and that is final. Take Alice."

"I have every intention of taking Alice. But I want you, too. She's not used to my ways."

"What's there to get used to?" Meriwether demanded. "All she has to do is obey you."

Gusta ignored her supremely.

"You could do me a favor," I told Gusta. "While you're there, get a pretty tea set for me to give Maynard and Selena for their wedding, if he ever gets around to asking her. I've been wanting something real special for them, and they both like tea. You can either bring it back or send it back." Maynard Spence had lived next door to us since he was born, and he and I

68

had gotten real close that past summer. I'd even introduced him to Selena.

"I'll see what I can find," Gusta agreed. I wrote her a check on the spot, and our conversation turned to other things.

As it turned out, circumstances worked in Gusta's favor. The hot water heater in Meriwether's new house fell through a soft spot in the floor. As somebody said down at Phyllis's Beauty Salon, "Faced with cold-water baths, Meriwether decided to go to China."

"Wish somebody would give me that choice," said somebody else. Trapped by running water, I couldn't see who was talking.

"Okay, Mac, let's get you rolled." Phyllis turned off the water.

As she wrapped my head in a towel and I moved to her work station, I joked, "I'll bet Buck loosened that water heater on purpose, to get her to go away and leave him in peace."

She leaned real close and muttered, "He didn't, but he said he might of if he'd thought of it. If she'll go, Buck says he can be done by the time she gets back, but she wouldn't even think of it until this happened — and until that new newspaper editor said he'd stop by every afternoon to check things out."

"Does Meriwether like that? She's pretty independent as a rule."

"Buck says Slade always checks with her before he makes a suggestion. He's sweet as pie to her, but gives orders to the men like it was his house."

"Maybe it will be one day. I hear they're seein' a lot of each other."

"What about that girl who's come to help Miss Gusta?" somebody called from the other side of the long mirror. "Looks like she'd be scared to stay in that big house by herself."

Finally I had a bit of news to contribute. "She's going, too. They leave Wednesday." Nobody asked how I knew. Information like that floats on the air in a small town, as untraceable as perfume in a crowded room. I probably heard it at the store, or maybe Martha told me.

"Lah-di-dah," the woman next to me jeered. "That girl sure fell into a good position."

"Honey" — Phyllis leaned over to look her straight in the mirror — "would you work for Miss Gusta, even for a trip to the Orient?"

"Not for a trip around the world five times."

"She's got a sick aunt to look after, too," Phyllis continued. "Came in here to get her hair trimmed yesterday and said she had to run down to Jacksonville today to see her sick aunt before they leave."

"How long're they gonna be gone?" somebody called from the shampoo sink.

"Two weeks, I understand." That was from behind the mirror again.

"Two weeks without Miss Gusta? How will Hopemore manage to survive?"

"Peacefully, probably." Everybody tittered.

We didn't know at the time that Hiram Blaine was giving notice that very day in Atlanta, planning to head back to Hopemore. Poor Hiram, even he had no idea of the trouble he'd bring back with him.

# 6

## OCTOBER

One afternoon in the second week of October, I was working in our back office when Walker came in rubbing his palms together. "I can't believe I fell for that old trick."

Looking at Walker is like looking in a mirror. We have the same brown eyes, the same stocky build, and the same honey-brown hair, except Walker's is beginning to show some gray and mine, thanks to Phyllis, is not. Busy with the payroll, I scarcely looked up. "What trick?"

He slumped into his daddy's desk chair, still rubbing his palms. "Hiram Blaine is back, with that same old electric button he hides in his hand to shock folks with. Must have fresh batteries though." He held out a palm as pink as boiled shrimp. "That thing nearly sent me to Mars." As he settled into the chair, he added, "Speaking of space travel, Hiram said he's come back home because Atlanta's full of aliens and they're as slippery as turkey turd."

"You don't have to quote him. Hiram's got the foulest mouth in Georgia."

"Good pun, Mama." Walker flipped on Joe Riddley's computer, then flexed his right hand again. "He's still got that old Yarbrough's hat Daddy gave him years ago, and the same obstreperous red parrot perched on his shoulder."

"Old Joe?" I grinned even though Walker wasn't looking. "Don't forget that parrot was named for your daddy, son. Watch how you insult him."

"Hiram sent you his love." Walker spoke without turning around. "His exact words were, 'Tell Mizzoner I'll come by to see her soon's I get time.' "

"Lucky me."

The main reason Gusta had objected to Meriwether's dating Jed was that while he himself was a very personable young man, he belonged to one of the most peculiar families in Hopemore. In the South, "peculiar" can mean anything from a tad eccentric to downright dangerous, and generally we tolerate peculiar folks unless they do bodily harm. But the Blaines came close to being intolerable.

They had been the despair of Hope County for nearly a century, a shiftless family always more willing to annoy people than to bathe. In our generation the family had finally dwindled to Hector, Hiram, and their younger sister, Helena. Their mother had been a schoolteacher before she gave it up to marry a charming smile and a shock of black curls. She wasn't the first wife to discover the wrappings were better than the package.

Our family hadn't had much to do with any of

the Blaines until thirty years ago, when Helena came back from being a civilian worker at Warner Robbins Air Force Base during the Vietnam War. She brought a little boy and no explanation. Just showed up at our store one day with the baby, asking, "You all got any work I could do?"

Joe Riddley felt sorry for her and hired her to work at the counter, but she was helpless with a register. We tried her in several positions before he found she had a knack for growing flowers. She cared for all our bedding plants, and under her care they were gorgeous.

Hector was a shiftless skunk who tried to wheedle a loan from anybody he met. He was also convinced the Confederate treasury was buried on their family farm, and for years he'd been arguing with the bank about a loan, using that hypothetical treasury as collateral. He'd been sent to jail several times for minor crimes.

Most of his fifty years, Hiram had been the less disgusting of the two boys, wandering around with a big red parrot on his shoulder, playing practical jokes. Then a few years back, he took up with our neighbor Amos Pickens, who was convinced earth was in danger of imminent attack from outer space with Venus as the launching station. After Amos died, Hiram saw himself as Hopemore's only informed citizen. He petitioned the county commission to order everybody to buy blackout curtains so telescopes on Venus couldn't peer in our windows at night. When they refused, he begged them to magnetize an old steel building down by the railroad tracks to attract any spaceships that attempted to land. The commissioners pointed out that a magnet that size would attract trains, tracks, and every automobile in town, but Hiram didn't give up.

One night he was caught by a police officer on top of the water tank with a five-gallon bucket of vinegar. He had three more buckets on the ground, and claimed that putting vinegar in the water was the only surefire way to stop spies the aliens already had among us. "Alien bodies cannot tolerate vinegar," he explained. "They shrivel."

I vividly remember the morning the indignant officer brought Joe Riddley the warrant. "Son," Joe Riddley said, stroking his jaw with one long forefinger, "carrying a bucket of vinegar is not exactly possession of implements of a crime, and scratching that old water tank a little getting it up there is hardly criminal damage of property. You're reaching a bit, aren't you? Let me try to talk Hiram out of this foolishness."

But Hiram was so determined about the need for that vinegar, and the commission was so irate, Joe Riddley finally concluded that sending Hiram to jail for six months might be the best thing for everybody. When Hiram got out of jail, he went up to Atlanta, where Jed was already practicing law. Joe Riddley always said Jed was the only good thing to come out of the Blaines in three generations. Hiram had been in Atlanta nearly four years.

"Has he come home permanently or just to visit?" I asked Walker.

He spoke over one shoulder, already intent on his computer screen. "Didn't say."

We worked in companionable silence, broken only by a police officer coming in for me to sign a warrant of arrest for a man who'd held up a convenience store in a stocking mask but left his wallet on the counter when he drove away. The office at the back of Yarbrough's was as much home to all of us as our house. Our boys came there every day after school until they were old enough to ride their bicycles home alone. The oak rolltop desks, chairs, and filing cabinets were put in by Joe Riddley's granddaddy when he bought the store. My in-laws set the big comfortable chair by the window. We added computers and other modern equipment, and I occasionally put up a new ruffle at the window or got the big chair re-covered, but the office hadn't changed much over the years. It was both modern to work in and very comfortable.

I had always kept the books and done the billing while Joe Riddley supervised the front and ordered inventory. Since Joe Riddley got shot, he might come in for an hour now and then, but you couldn't call his little bit of thumbing through catalogues "work." He still couldn't read properly. Now Ridd came after school to check on the plants and how things were running out front, and Walker had started coming by for an hour or two each afternoon to check inventory and order what we needed. Ridd had always loved plants and being around the place, but Walker never had taken much interest. It was surprising to find that while he didn't care for plants one way or the other, he was better than his daddy, even, at the business side of things. He was also tactful about not letting Joe Riddley know how much work he was taking on.

Around three he stopped, stretched, and asked, "You want a Coke?" When I nodded, he fished quarters from the Cane Patch syrup can we kept on Joe Riddley's desk and went out to get us both a drink. As he came back, he asked, "Do you have any idea where I might have known Slade Rutherford before?"

I popped the tab from my chilly can as I thought about that. "Maybe he went to Davidson? He's from North Carolina."

"Nope." He took a long swallow of Coke, emitted a belch, and gave me a grin to say it was designed only to irritate his mother. "I checked my annuals. Even hauled down my old high school annuals, in case he attended high school here a year or two." He flung himself into his daddy's chair but didn't turn back to the computer. "I've thought about all the logical places — insurance conventions, Rotary, Jaycees. It's not any of those. I keep connecting him with huge buildings, but if it wasn't at college —" He shook his head like he was trying to clear it.

I turned back to my desk and asked absently, "But you think you have met him?"

"I'm sure of it. The first time I laid eyes on him, I thought he looked familiar, and when I heard his name was Rutherford, I immediately asked, 'Slade?' It's not exactly a name you pull out of the first barrel." He gave an embarrassed little chuckle. "The weirdest part is, as soon as I said his name, I wanted to knock him down." He made a fist and rammed it into his sore palm, then winced.

Now he had my full attention. Walker had always been a pounder, but he pounded furniture and pillows, not people. "For what?"

"I don't know." He swiveled his chair toward the computer. "Oh, well. We've got enough on our plates without worrying about that."

I eyed my own screen thoughtfully. It wasn't like Walker to dislike somebody. Was there something about Slade I ought to know as a magistrate? Walker's back was to me, so instead of continuing to work on payroll like I ought to, I went on-line and checked the Asheville paper archives. Slade was listed as one of their editors up to six weeks ago, but I couldn't find a bio.

As long as I was reading papers on-line, I might as well look up another article I'd been wanting to read. I found the Clearwater paper and the archive article on page one: "Novice Diver Trapped in Coral Rock." As I read, I squirmed that I'd harbored even a suspicion that Alice killed her sister. The story was worse than she'd told. Several other divers had been interviewed, and the writer pulled out all the stops telling about beautiful young Teresa Civilis frantically trying to release her foot, panicking, fighting off her helpers, ripping off her mask, and drowning right before their eyes. "We could have saved her," one man was quoted, "if she'd stayed calm. We could have gotten her free. It was panic that killed her, not danger." Terri had a degree in business administration from Georgia State, but was unemployed at the time of her death. She was survived only by a half sister, Alice Fulton. Half sister sounded distant. It didn't convey Alice's obvious grief. Her eyes were always anxious and sad.

As I went back to my payroll, I sent up a prayer that Gusta wouldn't be too difficult and Alice would have fun on their trip.

Then my mind returned to where Walker might have known Slade.

"Maybe he went to scout camp or church camp with you," I suggested aloud.

"Let it alone, Mama. It'll come to me one day."

I didn't say any more, but it kept niggling at me. Walker's reaction to Slade was utterly out of character. You don't build up a good insurance business if you aren't the kind of man who likes and gets along with almost everybody.

I looked out the window. The weather was so

gorgeous that as soon as Walker left, I'd mosey over to the newspaper office. I needed to take my column, anyway.

Hopemore is a pretty town, with elevated sidewalks and trees lining all the streets. I paused to admire our own sidewalk display of mums, cornstalks, gourds, and pumpkins, then set off for the newspaper office on foot. It was only a couple of blocks, but stretching my legs made me realize how little exercise I'd been getting lately, except for hauling Joe Riddley's wheelchair in and out of the trunk. I loitered a little, admiring fall window displays and taking deep breaths of the spicy fall air. One of the nicest parts of living in a small town is that you are near enough to farmers' fields to smell them right in town. That afternoon the light breeze carried a sweet blend of hay and cotton dust that made me forget all our troubles for a little while.

Then I heard an unearthly screech, followed by "Not to worry. Not to worry."

Hiram Blaine shot out of the newspaper office like a bullet, head thrust forward and fists clenched. Thank goodness he turned in the other direction without seeing me. Whatever rehabilitation Hiram had gotten in jail, he hadn't learned to wash. Even at that distance I could see that his long grizzled hair was greasy with dirt and flopped beneath a Yarbrough's cap so filthy it looked rose, not red. His jeans and shirt looked like they hadn't been washed since I last saw him.

His parrot, Joe, sat on his shoulder. For those who don't know, a red parrot is actually a scarlet macaw, and it's not just red. Joe spread a glorious rainbow of red, yellow, green, turquoise, and navy feathers down the back of Hiram's yellow T-shirt as he squawked a counterpoint to Hiram's rage: "Not to worry. Not to worry." Joe had a loud mouth, but he was a beautiful creature — a lot prettier than Hiram.

I slowed down so the stink would have time to blow away before I got to the door, but Hiram's memory still lingered on the air as I went inside. The little front office was empty, but I could hear Slade in the back giving somebody what Clarinda would call "up the country." I don't know the derivation of that expression, but it always involves a lot of self-righteous shouting. From what I could tell, somebody in circulation hadn't entered a subscriber's new address into the computer and they'd missed a paper or two. To hear Slade going on about it, you'd have thought Mr. Dean Witter himself hadn't gotten his *Wall Street Journal*. I could sympathize a little, of course — no matter how small a business is, it's important when it is *your* business. However, whoever made that particular mistake didn't deserve to be cut into tiny pieces and chewed up in public. I smacked the silver bell on the counter to say I was there.

Slade himself breezed around the corner, a welcome smile already plastered on his face. He had to know I'd overheard him fussing, but he didn't apologize — just leaned on the counter and said confidingly, "Half the world's people are below average. Did you know that? And I've got most of 'em working for me."

"You might be talking to one of them right now," I warned. I laid out the ad and my column. He read the column all the way through. To keep from watching his face, I looked at his hands. His left pinky was cut off below the nail and twisted at the end.

When he noticed me looking at it, he stuck that hand in his pocket. "I caught it in a car door when I was four. Took off the end and broke the knuckle." He set the column down on the counter. "This is fine. You write a good column, Judge. I've been told folks look forward to it."

"Thank you." Since we were so chummy, it seemed like a good time to get on with what I'd come to find out. I leaned on the counter like I was just being friendly and said, "Gusta says you're from North Carolina. What part? I have relatives there."

He hesitated just a second. "The Piedmont, but we had a house in the mountains, too, and one at the beach."

His folks must have had money if they had houses all over the state, but the Piedmont is a big place. "Not many mountains around here. Where in the Piedmont did you live?"

Mr. Rutherford was nowhere near as forthcoming about his heritage as a well-bred

Southern boy ought to be. "We moved around a lot with Daddy's business."

"You didn't go to Davidson, did you?"

He leaned over the counter and whispered, "Am I under suspicion for something?"

I could tell he was teasing, so I whispered back, "Should you be?"

He grinned and spoke normally, "Not that I know of."

"I was just wondering if you'd gone to college with our younger son, Walker."

"Sorry, no. By the way, did you hear that Augusta and Meriwether aren't coming back until next week?"

He'd dammed my stream. First, nobody ever called Gusta "Augusta." And second, "Where did you hear that?"

"From a primary source. I called Augusta's cook this morning to see if they needed me to pick them up at the airport tomorrow, and she said they're staying another week. She said Meriwether wants to do more shopping, so Augusta and Alice decided to stay with her." He sounded like extending a vacation was routine for him. If it was, he didn't begrudge spending pennies like Gusta. This was very puzzling.

I frowned. "I hope they'll be back before Joe Riddley's birthday party next weekend."

"They're coming Thursday, I believe."

Like Slade, I prefer primary sources. As soon as I got back to my office I called Florine. "I hear you're gonna have peace and quiet a few more days."

"Yes, ma'am, looks like it. You wouldn't believe what's happened. Miss Gusta called yesterday all the way from Kidnap or some such place."

"Shanghai?"

"Yeah, that was it. She said Meriwether's taken it into her head to stay over there another week, so they gotta stay with her. I don't know what's gotten *into* that girl. Just up and announced she was staying whether Miss Gusta liked it or not." I could practically see Florine flinging up the hand that didn't hold the phone. "Miss Gusta can't do a *thing* with her."

"I'll bet Gusta wasn't too happy about it."

"Fit to be tied. Said Meriwether dug her heels in like a stubborn mule. Decided to go on some old shoppin' spree and won't come home for nothin'. Miss Gusta said for two cents she'd abandon her over there with all them foreigners. But of course she can't rightly do that."

I could have, but neither Gusta nor Florine ever would.

"Did she say what Meriwether is shopping for? Is she buying clothes?" If Meriwether was buying a trousseau, my stock would soar in town when I found out first.

"No'm. Miss Gusta said she's took some notion of opening a store. She's buying up things to sell. Miss Gusta said if she wasn't right there, Meriwether might buy up the whole country."

"If they're in China, it would take her more than a week to buy it all."

"Well, Meriwether promised she'll leave Wednesday. I hope Miss Gusta holds her to it."

"I do, too. I don't want them to miss Joe Riddley's party."

"Oh, they'll be back for that. Don't you worry. Miss Gusta won't disappoint the judge." I would never be "the judge" to Florine.

We said all the polite things folks in the south use to oil the pain of parting, and I hung up. Then I propped my elbows on the desk, cupped my cheeks with my hands, and thought over what I'd heard. What on earth had gotten into Meriwether? First she didn't want to go on the trip because of her house. Now, instead of racing back to it, she was extending her trip. And opening a store? Surely she wasn't foolish enough to think she could make a go in Hopemore of a shop full of painted fans, cloisonne jewelry, and tea sets. Folks might pick up a pretty flowerpot, or maybe a little screen to set on a table, but a store like that could go broke pretty fast.

Yet, that's what folks said when her daddy, Garlon, opened his lawn and garden equipment place. They thought he was trying to compete with Yarbrough's, and predicted he'd go bellyup. Instead, he'd found a growing niche of the market we weren't covering, and our businesses helped each other. Garlon did real well. Maybe Meriwether inherited some of his acumen, or got his kind of inspiration. At least she could afford to gamble.

"There's no point in worrying about all that until she gets back," I finally told myself aloud. "You've got enough to worry about with Slade and Walker." When could Walker have ever known Slade? And why on earth had he disliked him so much?

# 7

During his last week on earth, Hiram had run-ins with several people. I personally witnessed two.

On Tuesday Pooh and Otis stopped by the store to buy some asters. Pooh came back to the office and stayed so long talking, I figured she was lonesome, missing Gusta. I offered to wheel her out to her car while Otis brought the flat of asters. He was fumbling for his keys — which, as usual, he'd left in the ignition — when we heard somebody call, "Hello, everybody!" Hiram sauntered across the parking lot wagging one hand like a frenetic queen.

Joe squawked from his shoulder and flapped his wings. "Hello, hello, hello."

Hiram smelled as bad as ever, and now had a gap where he used to have a tooth. His hair still brushed his shoulders in greasy tails and he'd grown a short, scraggly beard. It carried remnants of his last few meals. He wasn't much taller than me — maybe five-foot-five — so I had a good view of his squalid red cap. I shuddered to have my own name across its front.

He stopped smack in front of Pooh and gave her a little bow. "Hey, Granny."

Hiram knew as well as anybody that Pooh, who loved children more than anything, would never be a granny. She had volunteered at the hospital pediatric ward so long they gave her a plaque for fifty years of service. Even after her son, Zach, was killed, she kept going over to the hospital to read stories to sick and dying children, and still had Lottie bake cookies each afternoon so she could hand them out to children after school. When people wondered how she could do it, she blinked away tears and confessed, "I do it for Zachary, now. Whenever I hug a child, I pretend it's him." Joe Riddley said more than once that any child who came within three feet of Pooh went away a little more loved.

Pooh wasted no love on Hiram that particular morning. Her round face grew pink with distress. "You dreadful man!" Her lips trembled with indignation. "Otis, help me into the car right now!"

"I sure will, Miss Winifred. Don't rile her," he warned Hiram over his shoulder as he bent to set down the flowers. "She's taken up shootin' again. You'd best stay out of her road."

"You should have had more sense," I fussed at Hiram in a low voice. He shrugged and snickered.

When they got to the car, Pooh hoisted herself from her chair, turned awkwardly, and stood as erect as she was able. "I can't find my guns right now," she said while Joe regarded her with one cold white eye, "but if I do, you better watch out. I hit the birds I shoot at."

"You better not touch my bird!" Hiram's shout made Joe screech and hop onto his cap.

"Sic 'em, boy! Sic 'em!" Red wings flapped in zeal for a fight.

Otis helped Pooh into her seat and waited for her to draw her legs inside. Then he slammed the door like he wished Hiram's head was in it.

"Maggoty pig swill," Hiram muttered. He turned to me. "Mizzoner, you heard 'em threaten me. If she shoots Joe . . ."

Otis hurried around to the trunk with the chair. "She ain't gonna shoot anybody, 'cause the judge and I done confiscated her guns. But stay out of her road. That's all I gotta say."

"Help him get that chair and those flowers in the car," I commanded Hiram, more testily than I might have done if I'd known he'd be dead in a week.

Hiram sidled up reluctantly, it being, in his estimation, lowering to the dignity of a no-good white man to help an honorable old black one with manual labor. But he lifted the chair and lowered it into the trunk without another word.

When they'd driven away, I turned back to him. "Calling Mrs. DuBose 'Granny' was the cruelist thing I've ever known you to do."

He shrugged. "Not as cruel as Mr. Fayette used to be."

"What do you mean?"

"Helena went over there with Jed one day when she first got back to town. He ordered them off his porch like they was trash. Too big for his britches. He always was."

Zach had been killed just a few months before Helena came back with Jed. Had she hoped to offer Pooh and Fayette her baby to raise? Or had Helena and Zachary — ?

I squelched that thought. They'd known each other, and both had been at Warner Robbins at the same time for a few months, but Zachary was far too fastidious to get mixed up with Helena, who washed only slightly more often than her brothers until she came to work for me.

"Well," I told Hiram in what our boys called Mama's Lecture Voice, "Mr. Fayette's dead, and Pooh would never have hurt Helena's feelings. Remember how Jed used to love going over there to help her in the yard when he was growing up? You've no cause to hurt her."

Hiram shrugged. "Got no cause to *he'p* her, neither."

That conversation was going nowhere, so I asked about the only earthly thing we had in common. "How's Jed doing?"

"Doin' real well. Wears three-piece suits and shiny shoes and makes enough money to wipe his bottom with hundred-dollar bills. Makes more in most weeks than I'll see in a lifetime. But he gives me and Hector a bit now and then." That probably explained how Hector had managed to keep body and soul together while Hiram was away.

"Not to worry, not to worry," Joe assured me.

I reached over to stroke him, but he jerked back his head. "He don't like women," Hiram explained as I backed off. "Never did, much, but while I was away Hector left him with some old biddy who kept him in a cage. Since then, he's never found a woman he could like." He reached up and stroked the bird fondly. "Hey, Joe, this is Mizzoner. She's your friend."

"Hello. Hello. Hello." Joe fixed me with that large white eye to make sure I didn't get too close. I went back to our previous conversation.

"Jed's never married, has he?" It was a family of bachelors. Even Helena hadn't ever married, that I knew of.

"Nope. Miss Meriwether Wainwright was enough to turn him off women for life." Hiram spat into the bit of grass growing along the verge of our lot. "Just you wait. One of these days he'll come back and wipe his feet on this whole town."

Poor Jed, he'd have to come back sooner than either of us suspected.

The next evening, Wednesday, I stopped by the Bi-Lo grocery store on my way home to do Clarinda's shopping. I say "Clarinda's shopping" because I'm not much of a cook — a reputation I take care to maintain. Clarinda feeds us from Monday to Friday, we eat simple on

Saturday, and generally go to Ridd and Martha's on Sundays. That particular week, with the party on Saturday, Clarinda's list was pretty long. Even though most of the food would be coming from Dad's Outdoor BarBeQue and I'd ordered a special delivery of drinks brought to the house, she still needed butter and salt for the corn, mixes and stuff to make cakes and icings, plus paper plates, napkins, cups — things like that.

So, at that time of day when the sun is almost ready to set but hasn't quite made up its mind to do it, I wheeled a cart piled with Clarinda's groceries through the parking lot. Somebody shouted, "You needn't think you can fool me! I know who you are! You get back to where you came from, now! You hear me? Take your" — I don't repeat that kind of language — "right back to where you came from! We don't want you around here!"

"Sic 'em, boy! Sic 'em, boy!" screamed another voice.

A small crowd was gathering not far from my car. Forgetting that the world is different than it used to be, I abandoned my cart beside my closed trunk and headed in that direction.

Behind me, I heard a small boy shout, "Hey, that lady left her groceries. Grab 'em!"

A deeper young male voice replied, "You crazy or some'n? Them's the judge's groceries. You mess with *them* and you'll spend the rest of your natural life in jail."

I turned and saw Leon, a boy who played football on an after-school team Walker coached. "I'll watch 'em for you, Judge," he called, balancing on his beat-up bike.

Satisfied that my food was safe, I elbowed my way through the crowd. Hiram Blaine, cheeks scarlet above his little beard and dark eyes glittering with excitement, was shaking a fist at Darren Hernandez, Joe Riddley's physical therapist. He was egged on by a crowd of men who were obviously not fond of swarthy young men who prefer black shirts and pants, dyed hair, and earrings. Hopemore is not what you might call uniformly progressive.

Last week Darren's short spiked hair had been emerald green. Today it was bishop's purple. When we'd first met, I had been leery of that bright spiked hair and the silver hoop he wore in one ear. I'd also hated the way he shortened Joe Riddley's name to J.R. But after weeks of working together to encourage Joe Riddley to walk, I loved Darren almost like a son. His dark eyes twinkled with kindness and fun, his hands were invariably gentle with an obstreperous old man, and his saucy tongue could make Joe Riddley try things he didn't think he could do.

I arrived to see one of the men in the crowd poking a finger at Darren, who was trying to back away. Unfortunately, the crowd wasn't moving to let him through. A ring of men kept Darren where he was while Hiram had a public fit. From Hiram's right shoulder, Joe contributed his fight song, "Sic 'em, boy!"

I pushed my way to the front. "What's going on?"

"We don't like his kind here, Judge," one man muttered. "Hiram's telling him off."

Hiram looked around. "Where'd you park that dang thing you came in? Anybody see his spaceship?"

That's when the crowd realized Hiram thought he'd caught himself a real live alien. Immediately it switched its target, as Southern crowds are apt to do. We love a good show, and Hiram was suddenly better street theater than Darren.

"You're crazy as a coot," one man called to him.

"Looks like jail didn't do you one bitta good," jeered another.

I looked around for help, and saw Police Chief Charlie Muggins coming through the lot with two sacks of groceries. Now Chief Muggins might look like a cross between a polecat and a chimpanzee with the least attractive features of each, and he might have on a brown checked shirt with gray slacks, but most folks in that lot knew who he was and what: He was chief of police and mean as a snake. That was one of the few times in my life when I was glad to see him.

"You all break it up," I ordered in the same tone I used back when Walker's football team got a mite rowdy on our porch. "Hiram, if you

94

don't stop yelling I'm going to ask Chief Muggins over there to arrest you for disturbing the peace. Darren, go on to your car." I jerked my head in the direction of a sunshine-yellow Volkswagen bug a couple of rows away.

"He — he — he ain't got a car. He — he's one of them — them aliens I been telling you about." Hiram jigged with excitement. If he didn't calm down some, he'd wet himself. "See his hair? They got purple hair, due to the lack of oxygen in their atmosphere. You hold him here, Mizzoner, and I'll run in the store and get some vinegar. That'll shrivel him in a second!"

"Somebody better be shrivelin' you," taunted somebody from the back of the crowd.

"Vinegar?" sniggered somebody else.

"Sic 'em, boy!" contributed Joe with an angry flap of his wings.

By then Chief Muggins had caught the excitement and bustled over to where we were. Our mutual feelings for one another made him conclude immediately that I was causing the ruckus. "Evenin', Judge Yarbrough." If he sounded like the words tasted bitter in his mouth, they probably did. Charlie made no bones about the fact that he'd vociferously opposed my appointment. "What's all this commotion?"

The crowd oozed back a little, but stayed to see what would happen.

"Just a little misunderstanding," I told Charlie, not about to reveal how glad I was to see him.

"Hiram mistook Darren here for an alien."

Chief Muggins looked at the purple hair and earring. "Might not be far wrong. What you doin' around here, feller?"

I gave Darren a warning look and answered Chief Muggins myself. "He's a physical therapist in the new rehab center we're all so proud of." Since Chief Muggins helped dedicate the rehab center, that cut off his water for a second. "Darren has been working with Joe Riddley and I've known him for weeks. He's from Miami, not Mars."

"Same difference," somebody joked. Several people laughed nervously.

"Go on home," Chief Muggins told Darren as curtly as if he, not Hiram, had started the trouble. I'd have to explain to him the next day, and apologize.

Darren ran one hand over his purple hair. "You are *weird*, man," he told Hiram. With a little wave of thanks to me, he walked to his car with the fluid steps of an athlete, acting like he was merely taking a stroll. Once he was in the car, though, he screeched off and drove away a little faster than was legal.

"Did you see his hair?" Hiram insisted before the crowd of men could all melt away.

"Same color as your truck," one man teased, jerking a thumb to a decrepit old pickup not far away. Hiram had had that truck almost as long as I could remember, and it had been purple for twenty years. "Maybe you're an alien yourself."

"In Darren's case, it's dye," I informed Hiram. "It washes out. Since I've known him, his hair has also been pink, orange, red, and green. I think he mostly does it to see what other people will say. If he let it grow out, it would be as dark as yours."

Hiram shook his head and spat at a nearby tire. "You all just don't get it, do you? You just don't get it." He trudged away with the heavy tread of a man who alone in the universe knows the truth.

Charlie Muggins walked me to my car to make sure I got in it without causing another scene. I greeted Leon and, without thinking, handed him a dollar reward for guarding my car.

Charlie grabbed my elbow. "You giving that kid a bribe, Judge?"

"He's twelve years old, Chief. What am I supposed to be bribing him to do?" But I knew he was right. Public officials can't hand money to people on the street. In the past Joe Riddley would have walked on to the car and I'd have slipped Leon a dollar. Once again, the pain of Joe Riddley's accident sliced clear through me.

"Sorry, Leon. I can't give you that now, but if you stop by the store tomorrow and talk to the woman at the register, she'll have something for you then."

"You don't owe me nothin', Judge." Leon gave a flick of his hand. "You keep my folks from hittin' each other, and we'll be even." As he pedaled away, I wondered how many other children in the nation would gladly do a favor to keep their parents from fighting.

Charlie stood by the car while I loaded groceries in my trunk. I didn't expect him to set down his groceries and help. Charlie wasn't known for kindness to women. Ask his former wife, spirited out of town by a preacher after one too many visits to the emergency room.

"Who was that feller back there?" he asked as I hefted in paper plates and plastic cups.

"Hiram Blaine. He's been gone four years. Just got back this week." I put my last bag in the trunk and slammed it shut. "I wish he'd given up that alien nonsense while he was gone."

Charlie turned, ready to go. "If you all stop paying attention, he'll soon give it up."

Maybe Charlie was right, for once. I vowed I'd start ignoring Hiram when he talked about aliens.

Thursday, I missed seeing Gusta and Meriwether cruise into town. Joe Riddley and I were at occupational therapy, where they were trying to get him to scramble an egg. "I've been trying the very same thing without success for forty years," I told the therapist after their third failure.

Joe Riddley wasn't cooperating one bit. "Little Bit and Clarinda do our cooking," he raged. "I wash the dishes."

"Scrambling eggs teaches the brain how to sequence again," she explained. "Each step has to be done in order."

"Wouldn't washing dishes teach him the same thing?" I suggested.

She gave me the look medical people always give dumb family members who come up with alternatives to their professional methods. "We learn to scramble eggs."

"Good luck." I left them to fight it out and wandered over to physical therapy to watch Darren. He was trying to persuade a woman who'd fallen and broken her hip that she wouldn't fall again if she walked on the parallel bars. I sat in a chair at one side admiring the way he could cajole or tease people into doing what they should. Darren handled Joe Riddley far better than I, and I'd been honing my skills nearly sixty years.

About the time the woman took her first hesitant solo steps and Darren and I erupted into spontaneous applause, Gusta's old black Cadillac rolled into town with Alice at the wheel and the other two in the backseat. A stack of boxes sat between them while a mountain of boxes filled the passenger seat beside Alice.

Joe Riddley decided after therapy he wanted to go by the store for a while. "Write it in my log," he said, handing me the book.

"You write it," I told him. He had so much trouble writing in those days, just writing "go to store" kept him occupied the whole trip.

When we got there, everybody was talking

about the boxes Gusta and Meriwether had brought back with them. Gusta was too stingy to buy souvenirs, and Meriwether had always been on an allowance on previous trips, so they normally returned with little more than they had taken. "It took nearly half an hour to carry everything in when they stopped by Meriwether's house," one of my clerks reported. "What you reckon she's bought?"

"I guess we'll know soon enough," I told her.

Only Joe Riddley had a sensible suggestion when I mentioned it to him. "Finally found her wings," he said in his deliberate way, settling himself more comfortably in his chair and hanging his red hat on its hook by the desk. "Feathering her nest the way she wants it."

Speaking of feathers, later that afternoon I ran into Hiram and Joe again — and got my first and only chance to live up to my resolution to ignore Hiram when he got hipped up about aliens.

I needed to make a bank deposit, and Joe Riddley insisted that a clerk wheel *him* over and let him do it himself. I was trying to let him do anything he thought he could, and since he didn't have to do anything more complicated than hand a locked fabric bag across the counter and wait for a receipt, I decided to let them go without me. Seemed like more practical occupational therapy for him personally than scrambling eggs. But like a mother whose child is playing in the yard alone for the first time, I stood on our sidewalk, watching until they got inside. As I was finally turning to go, Hiram came sauntering down the sidewalk. Joe rode the Yarbrough's cap like a figurehead.

"Not to worry," the parrot greeted me with what looked like a shrug of his wings. "Where's Joe?"

I was startled, wondering if he remembered Joe Riddley. My husband always liked that parrot. They'd talk back and forth whenever Hiram came by the office, and Joe would hop off Hiram's arm and onto Joe Riddley's shoulder. "My namesake," Joe Riddley called him, after Hiram allowed as how he'd actually named the parrot Joe Riddley before Helena made him shorten it to Joe. We all knew darned well the name was to spite Joe Riddley; he'd just fined Hiram for painting a purple stripe down Oglethorpe Street one night. Hiram got the parrot the very next week. Joe Riddley always acted like it was an honor to have a parrot named for him, which took the air out of Hiram's tires.

That afternoon, I ignored the parrot and greeted the man. "Hey, Hiram. You doin' all right?"

Hiram's grin was full of crooked yellow teeth except for that one unexpected hole. He stuck out his hand, but before I could take it, he jerked it back and stuck it in his jeans pocket with a very red face. "Hey, Mizzoner. How's the judge?"

"If you mean Joe Riddley, he's over at the bank. He'll be back in a minute."

He shuffled his feet. "Think I could speak to him? I really hated to hear 'bout his accident. Feller who did that ought to be —"

"If you're about to use foul language, I don't want to hear it," I warned him.

He shrugged. "Well, it oughta happen, anyway. I want to tell the judge personal-like that they's no hard feelin's 'bout him signin' that warrant. He was doin' what he had to, and I know that." His daddy raised shiftless kids, but his mama raised polite ones.

"You can speak to Joe Riddley in a minute. He's just gone over to the bank."

"I'll do that. I surely will." He peered toward the bank, then gave me an anxious look from beneath the brim of his unspeakable cap. "You think you all might have some work I could do? I been workin' steady up in Atlanta, but I ain't found nothin' 'round here yet." He jerked his head back toward the corner. "Went down to the paper t'other day to see if they might need a story or two 'bout how to prepare in case of alien invasion, but that new feller —" He stopped and spat angrily into a clump of grass.

"Not to worry. Not to worry," Joe reminded him.

I felt a stab of pity. It's not always easy to come home. "You know how to use a riding mower, don't you?"

He nodded eagerly. "Yes, ma'am, Mizzoner!"

"I could use somebody to mow our yard tomorrow morning. We're having a birthday party for Joe Riddley Saturday, and I'd like everything looking nice. Could you come by early tomorrow?"

"I sure could. Sure could." He bobbed his head like it was going to fall off. "I'd like to do something for Hizzoner to show I bear him no malice —"

"I leave by eight-thirty, so you'll need to be there before then," I warned.

"I'll be there before eight. I surely will. Thankee, Mizzoner. Thankee." He stuck out his hand again, then jerked it back to his pocket before I could be so foolish as to shake it.

"Not to worry. Not to worry," Joe assured me.

"You know," Hiram continued, "that newspaper fellow, now, I wouldn't be surprised if he's not an alien. He's got that look in his eye." He stopped and froze, staring across the street with his mouth wide open. "My syphilis!" Hiram clapped his hand to his mouth.

"Don't talk like that," I said crossly.

"But omigosh, Mizzoner! Look at that! An alien, sure as shootin', and I can *prove* it!"

I turned to see what he was looking at. All I saw was Oglethorpe Street busier than usual, but not because of an alien invasion. Maynard Spence was hurrying out of the bank with a bag of change, probably for his daddy's appliance store down the block. He nearly careened into

Gusta as she stumped across the sidewalk with her silver-headed cane. Gusta wasn't looking where she was going because she was looking back at Meriwether, who was maneuvering her silver Mercedes into a legal parking space behind Gusta's Cadillac — which was parked, as always, in the handicapped zone. Poor Alice was sitting at the wheel looking straight ahead, probably trying to pretend she wasn't there. Vern, the bank guard, jumped up and down, yelling. Our clerk was wheeling Joe Riddley out just behind Maynard, and Joe Riddley was riled up about something. I couldn't hear the words, but I could hear the decibels.

Slade Rutherford had parked on our side of Oglethorpe and was crossing the street, headed for the bank. He had given me a quick wave with his left hand, but his eyes were clearly on Meriwether as he hurried her way. Otis Raeburn and Pooh had come to a dead stop beside Meriwether's car, holding up three cars behind them, because Gusta was parked in Pooh's handicapped spot. Darren's sunny Volkswagen sailed past in the other direction.

A lot of people, but not one single alien. I took Charlie's advice and ignored Hiram. "There's Joe Riddley. You can talk to him when he gets over here. Bright and early tomorrow, now, Hiram. You won't forget, now?"

He shook his head. "I won't forget. But listen —"

I had no intention of listening to him rave

about aliens. I left him standing on the sidewalk like he'd taken root.

Would he be alive today if I'd taken the trouble to listen?

# 8

Two hundred people showed up to celebrate Joe Riddley's birthday. I'd dubbed the event "Joe Riddley's Coming Out Party" because my ornery husband had finally believed Darren that he could stand on his own two legs with the help of a walker. He was actually walking a few steps at a time now, gingerly as a heifer on ice.

We were blessed with one of those glorious October Saturdays that always makes me glad to live in Middle Georgia. Poplars and dogwoods made yellow and red splashes against fuzzy dark pines. Warm, honey-thick sunlight smelled of ripe hay and musty leaves. Most folks preferred to stay outdoors, either at tables scattered under the oaks or up on the porch. Once they'd greeted Joe Riddley, some filled plates and carried them toward the band. Others took plates out under a pecan tree to watch Georgia play LSU on the television we'd set up there, or up on the front porch to cheer for Tech against Maryland.

Renting those two televisions from Spence's Appliance Store had been Walker's brilliant idea, so nobody would have to miss their game.

Folks take football seriously around here. I considered it a personal favor from heaven when I heard both Georgia and Tech would play out of state that weekend, so folks would be in town.

Of course Hubert Spence, who'd lived next door to Joe Riddley all their lives, wouldn't take a penny for the sets. "It's good advertising," he insisted, "but my sets have trouble picking up the University of Georgia." Hubert and Joe Riddley would either one do anything for the other — except vote the same way or root for the same football team.

A lot of people pitched in to make the party fun. Walker and his wife, Cindy, who grew up in a wealthy family up in Thomson and loves parties, circulated to make sure everybody was having a good time. Ridd made sure folks found the food and drink. His daughter, Bethany, drafted her cheerleading team and their boyfriends to oversee children's games in the side yard. Walker's Tad, nine, and Jessica, eleven, volunteered to keep the drink tubs full of cans and ice. Every time I looked up, I saw a towhead carrying drinks to the tubs. Martha, Ridd's wife and a registered nurse, offered to stay beside Joe Riddley in case he got tired or agitated. A swarm of kitchen help, overseen by Clarinda, made sure tables in the dining room and out on the side porch stayed piled high with barbeque and buns, cole slaw, corn on the cob, potato salad, baked beans, Brunswick stew, and even platters of raw vegetables for people related to rabbits.

I trotted between the house and yard having a good time. Once in a while, when I stopped by the kitchen to see how things were going, Clarinda handed me a bowl or platter with the order "Carry that out and fill a gap." I have, without a doubt, the bossiest cook in Georgia.

It was her fault I had the misfortune, around three-thirty, to carry a big platter of fresh-boiled, well-buttered corn into my dining room and catch Police Chief Muggins peering behind my Oriental screen.

"Don't look behind that screen," I said crossly. "You know good and well I put it there to hide things I don't want seen." I had enough to do without worrying about Charlie poking his polecat nose in corners where it didn't belong. I had set that particular screen, the biggest I had, between the oak sideboard and a corner to hide a mountain of magazines, catalogues, and junk mail I hadn't had time to sort through in the past two months.

Chief Muggins flung out one hand and grabbed my wrist in a way that suggested hand-cuffs would follow. "I can see why you wouldn't want this seen, *Judge Yarbrough,* but it's hard to keep it from being *smelled.*"

I wasn't bothered that he sounded like he'd finally caught me committing a crime. Charlie had suspected me of one thing or another since he came to town three years earlier. What annoyed me was his prying around my house when he was a guest. Mama always said you can take a boy out of the trash, but it's a whole lot harder to take the trash out of the boy.

And what did he mean "smelled"? Had Lulu taken advantage of an unsupervised moment that morning to drag in a dead squirrel? Worse, had she mistaken the magazines for newspaper and made an in-house deposit?

"What are you talking about?" I snapped with little grace.

With his free hand, Charlie moved the screen a little. "Your silent guest."

That's when I saw Hiram Blaine, sprawled across my unread mail with a small black hole in his head.

Have you ever noticed how the death of somebody you know stops your own breath for an instant? When I could finally breathe, I filled my lungs with air so ripe it made me cough. If Hiram hadn't been in the far corner of a huge room with a tableful of pungent food, all the windows wide open, and a ceiling fan on high, people would have smelled him long before. To his usual aroma was added the smell of bodily functions that give way after death.

Poor Hiram. He was never a lovely sight or a pleasant person, but he should have lived longer. He sprawled like a child who's found a quiet corner after a day of hard, dirty play, and spread out for a desperately needed nap. The red Yarbrough's cap was the cleanest thing on him.

As my eyes wandered back to the hole in his head, a crazy thing happened. My eyes blurred and I saw Joe Riddley's face right after *he* got shot. My dining room floor tilted, the walls whirled, my arms went limp. Clarinda's corn slid off its platter and bounced around my feet. Only Charlie's grip on my arm kept me from sliding to the floor after it.

"MacLaren, are you ill?" Gusta's sharp gray eyes saw me drop that corn, all the way from the throne she'd had somebody install in our big front hall so she could hold court without standing. Trust Gusta not only to *see* me drop that corn, but also to call public attention to the fact. I was the flower girl in her wedding and tripped, sprawling down the aisle in a fine display of ruffled drawers. She'd never forgotten, and always called attention when I was clumsy. Joe Riddley says Gusta has the memory of an elephant and the compassion of a peanut.

Next to Gusta, Pooh fluttered in her wheelchair. "Oh Mac, your lovely Persian rug! There's butter all over it!"

When Gusta and Pooh spoke, every blessed soul in my dining room and front hall hushed and looked at me. I flapped my arm — the one Charlie wasn't gripping. "I'm fine — just stumbled." Smiling was hard. Every muscle in my face voted against it.

"Let me help you." Meriwether started my way. Thank goodness Gusta grabbed her with one talon and pulled her back. Meriwether looked particularly long, lean, and lovely that afternoon in a silk pantsuit that exactly matched her eyes, and I didn't want her to see Hiram. He used to do odd jobs for her daddy when she was little, and made up knock-knock jokes that doubled her over in giggles.

Gusta peered around. "Alice? Where's Alice? Go pick up that corn." She gave an imperious wave. A ray of sun came in the open door, passed through Gusta's diamonds, and turned into little splashes of light on the far hall wall. Isn't it amazing the things you notice when you are trying not to notice a dead body behind your dining room screen?

Alice hurried our way. Even to the party she had worn a beige skirt and a baggy white top, but at least she'd put on a bright scarf that matched the green scrunchy holding back her hair. Maybe if she lived with Gusta long enough she'd develop a sense of style.

As she got near, she glanced toward the crack Charlie had left between the screen and the wall. I thrust my empty platter at her. "Here, honey, take this back to Clarinda in the kitchen and ask her to fill it with more corn, then take it out to the table on the porch." We didn't need Alice screaming the place down.

Worried about disobeying Gusta, she looked anxiously toward the corn on the rug. "What about —"

"Don't bother about that old corn." I tried to sound like having buttery corn smeared on a

Persian rug was normal around our house. "Just ask Clarinda to send somebody to clean it up." She obeyed without another word, but her hands trembled and I saw her give her employer one more anxious look. Working for Gusta can do that to people.

My head still spun and sweat trickled down my backbone. Breathing wasn't easy yet, either. I put one hand to my mouth and forced myself to inhale. My knees felt pretty rubbery. Gusta called in her gravelly old voice, "MacLaren, are you having a stroke?" Once again everybody in the room turned to stare.

I was particularly aware of Slade's dark eyes at Meriwether's shoulder. Any second he'd be sidling over, snooping for a story.

"No, Gusta, I'm fine. Can I get you anything to eat?"

"No, thank you." Disappointed I wasn't having a medical emergency, she turned to greet Sheriff Bailey Gibbons, who was coming in the door.

I took a step toward Buster myself. I was mighty glad to see him at that moment. But Charlie tightened his grip like he thought I was planning to escape and jerked his head toward the screen. "Did you kill him?"

I have told you that Charlie looks like a cross between a polecat and a chimpanzee, with the least attractive features of each, but I failed to say he is also pigheaded, prejudiced, and apt to make up his mind without reference to facts.

Having him smirk at me right then was not improving my nerves, nor did I deserve to be accused of murder in my own dining room.

I spoke indignantly but softly, so nobody could hear me above the din. "Of course I didn't kill him. Poor Hiram."

"He the brother of the kook who claims the Confederate treasury is buried on his property?"

"He might not be kooky." With Charlie, I was willing to defend even Hector. "There's been a rumor since the War that the treasury is buried around here somewhere."

"Well, this feller certainly ended your party with a bang." Charlie chuckled at his own bad joke, but didn't sound the least bit sorry about the party. "You need to send these people home."

It shows how overwrought I was — and how new to law enforcement — that I begged, "Can't you wait a little while? I know you want to get on with your investigation, but Hiram isn't going anywhere for the next hour or two, and you know how uncertain Joe Riddley's mind is right now. If he even suspects there's somebody dead in here —"

Suddenly I had a hopeful thought. Maybe Hiram wasn't really dead. His idea of a great practical joke would be to lie there for hours with dried ketchup on his head, on the off chance he could scare the pants off one nosy guest. Looking around quickly to be sure nobody was watching, I put my mouth close to the edge of the screen and called softly, "Hiram?" I waited for him to open one eye, give me a wink, and let out a guffaw they could hear in Macon. Seeing Charlie's expression, I explained, "Just checking."

"You're crazy. Any fool can see he's dead."

He was right. Death has a smooth, finished-with-life look nobody can fake.

Nobody could fake the signals my stomach was giving, either. I needed fresh air badly.

Clarinda bustled out of the kitchen already talking. "That child tells me —" What she read in my expression alarmed her. "You havin' a spell?" she asked softly.

I shook my head and gestured toward the corn on the floor, but she'd already noticed the shifted screen. "Who's been moving that? Folks know better'n to look back there." She turned a formidable frown on Charlie. Working for a magistrate all these years, Clarinda has lost any fear of officers of the law.

As she reached over to straighten the screen, he hissed, "Don't touch that!"

But she'd already seen Hiram through the crack and transferred her anger to him. "What you doin' back there, playin' the fool?" I tried to shush her, but she wasn't paying me one speck of attention. Clarinda tends to get a mite testy when she's got two hundred people to feed.

I grabbed her plump arm. "He's been shot," I whispered.

114

"Shot?" She whispered, too, but loudly, shocked wide eyes roving back to the crack. "You mean, he's *dead?*"

Several people looked our way. A couple of curious guests started drifting over. I shooed them away like late-summer flies. "Chief Muggins is making fun of all the junk mail in my corner."

"You know better than that," one man warned him with a playful shake of his forefinger. "Mac'll kill anybody who looks behind those screens."

At the moment, I could have done without that particular joke.

But the second man came closer, teasing, "What you got back there? Gonna let us peek?"

One of the reasons I value Clarinda is her common sense. "I'm gonna kill the first person to track buttered corn over my carpet." She glared at my guests, arms akimbo. They gave her apologetic smiles and retreated. She bent and started picking up corn.

"I don't want Joe Riddley to know," I pleaded with Charlie.

"Absolutely not," Clarinda agreed without standing. She reached over and twitched the screen back to its former position before he could stop her. "Just leave him be 'til folks go home. He's not goin' nowhere."

"I can't —" Charlie began.

"You leave him be 'til folks go home." She stood with two fistfuls of corn and spoke in a loud, reassuring voice. "I think we can get the grease out of the carpet, Miss MacLaren, but don't let nobody walk on it 'til I get back. And you go on outside," she added to Charlie as she headed for the kitchen. If Hollywood ever steals her from me, Clarinda is sure to win an Oscar.

Chief Muggins, however, tightened his grip on my arm and warned, "Don't you move. I'll be back in a minute." Before I could protest, he was worming his way through the crowd toward Sheriff Gibbons.

# 9

Sheriff Bailey "Buster" Gibbons and Joe Riddley met in kindergarten. Buster's one of our best friends, but law officers don't look like friends when you've got an unexplained corpse in the corner.

I was actually nervous as Buster sauntered my way. He looked like a bloodhound, but those sad eyes and hanging jowls went with the brain of a fine law officer. He asked as he reached me, Charlie at his elbow, "Something the matter, Judge?" In public and even in our offices, Joe Riddley and I always called Buster "Sheriff" and he always called us "Judge."

Before I could speak, Chief Muggins jumped in, pitching his voice to a low growl. "She's concealing a body behind that screen. May have killed him herself. Knows who he is, anyway. Since it's outside city limits, it's in your jurisdiction, but I stand ready to render any assistance you may require." Specifically, he stood between me and the door in case I tried to flee.

Buster peered behind the screen.

Clarinda bustled back with a thick roll of

paper towels and elbowed him in the ribs. "You all get outta the way, now. I gotta sponge up all that grease." She waved the two lawmen away like they were grandchildren. "Miss MacLaren, you look plumb pooped. Why don't you go over yonder by that window and sit down a while? Rest your bunions."

I don't have bunions, but my legs were wobbling. Buster noticed and steered me to a chair by an open window. I more fell than sat in it. Meanwhile Clarinda spread paper towels down on the rug and surrounded them with a wall of dining room chairs that guaranteed nobody else would touch that screen. Charlie watched her with a buzzard's stare.

Buster dragged over another chair and sat near me. "Rest a spell, Chief. I need to talk to the judge a minute before I call in my team."

I hoped he'd see reason where Charlie hadn't. "We've got to keep this from Joe Riddley. You know how unpredictable he still is. He rants at the dog, snaps at me and the boys, and sobs like a child if he spills peas off his fork. The doctor says it's all normal after a head wound, and he should get better, but I work so hard trying not to let anything upset him. And now, Hiram —"

At that moment I was glad buzzard Charlie hovered over me. At least nobody else could see me crying. "When did you last see the deceased?" he barked softly.

I reached in my pocket for the tissue I always carry, and blew my nose. "Day before yesterday.

He wanted to know if I needed any odd jobs done around here, and I said I could use him yesterday morning to mow for the party. He never showed up, though. Ridd finally did it yesterday afternoon, with everything else he had to do. I could have throttled Hiram —" I broke off, seeing the gleam in Charlie's tawny eyes. "But I didn't. Didn't shoot him, either. I am not in the practice of shooting people who disappoint me, nor am I dumb enough to kill somebody and hide the body in my own dining room where any fool could find him."

Buster put a hand on my shoulder to stop my tongue. "It's probably my fault Hiram didn't come. I pulled him over yesterday morning down near your turnoff for an expired sticker on his truck. After I pointed that out to him, we talked a little. He told me it was a real shame about Hizzoner getting shot, and he was on his way to your place to show Hizzoner and Mizzoner he still bore no malice about the warrant."

"Warrant?" Charlie's eyes positively glittered.

Buster stroked one jowl. "You don't know about that, Charlie? I guess it was before your time." Charlie had only been hired three years ago, a major mistake on the part of our town leaders. Buster said briefly, "An officer caught Hiram trying to pour vinegar in the town water to protect us from aliens. Joe Riddley signed the warrant for his arrest." He turned to me. "Didn't I hear that Hiram went up to Atlanta to be near Jed after he got out?"

119

"Drat!" I started to my feet. "We need to call Jed — and Hector, too."

"Calm down." Buster caught my arm. "We'll notify Hector and ask somebody from Atlanta to notify Jed."

"Ask if he owns a gun." That was another of Charlie's asinine suggestions. Jed couldn't come to town and kill Hiram without being recognized. But the word *gun* sent a cold poker up my spine. Joe Riddley had a case of guns in the back room. It was always locked, but what if somebody broke into it? As soon as I got everybody out of the house, I'd go check.

"What was this feller doing in Atlanta?" Charlie asked Buster.

"He told me yesterday he'd been doing yard work and maintenance for an apartment complex. Jed knew the manager and got him the job. But Hiram said the alien situation got so bad up there that he decided to come on home."

"Poor Hiram." I had to swallow tears. "He should have stayed in Atlanta."

Maybe Buster could tell I was about to bawl, because he gave a little chuckle. "Apparently the aliens followed him back. Hiram swore he saw one on Oglethorpe Street Thursday. He was so riled up about it, I had a time steering him back to his expired tag. But finally he promised, 'I'll see about that right away, Sheriff.' He turned the truck then and there and headed for the tag agency. Sorry, Mac. My guess is that he was so rattled about getting stopped he plumb forgot your mowing."

Charlie moved closer to my chair. "Thereby inciting Judge Yarbrough here to anger. . . ."

"I didn't kill him!" My voice was a hoarse, desperate whisper. I raised my eyes to Buster, stricken by a sudden thought. "I didn't even invite him to the party!"

"Somebody did." Buster's eyes roamed the crowded rooms.

"It's time to send everybody *home,* Judge." Charlie positively gloated at spoiling my party. "Get their names and addresses and tell them to go."

"I have their names and addresses," I said hotly. "But you don't think anybody killed Hiram since this party started, do you? This house has been fuller than a well-fed pup since before noon."

"So who was around earlier?" He waited for me to tell him who killed Hiram.

"Clarinda came at nine-thirty to get started in the kitchen. Walker and his kids came soon after to set up the tables and chairs he and Ridd brought from the church last night. We stored them in the barn in case there was a heavy dew. The florist came at ten to decorate the tables, and Ridd and Bethany followed her in with corn they picked real early. The kitchen crew came soon after that to start shucking. A lot of other people started coming around eleven, to set up the music system and televisions and to mark off the parking lots. Dad's BarBeQue brought the food at eleven-thirty, and the place has been a madhouse since."

"But until ten it was just you, Joe Riddley, Clarinda, and Walker."

I didn't remind him about Walker's two kids. Charlie was using the fingers of one hand to count on the other, and he doesn't have six fingers on either hand. But I wanted to smack him. "When the Sam Hill do you think any of us would have had time to kill Hiram? Besides, nobody was even *in* the dining room until the florist brought flowers for the table." I nodded toward them, a larger, nicer arrangement than I'd ordered, which she'd said was a gift.

"What about Joe Riddley? And what were you and he doing before Clarinda arrived?" Charlie's eyes drilled me like I was soft wood.

"I went to the beauty parlor at seven-thirty. Phyllis opened early especially for me. I got home a little before nine. Joe Riddley was still asleep, so I woke him and helped him dress. Then we ate breakfast. We were finishing when Clarinda got here." And fussed about us messing up her clean kitchen. I didn't mention that. I also didn't mention that I'd locked our kitchen closet. Mama always locked closets before a party, so folks wouldn't snoop. I didn't lock most of ours, but I didn't want folks seeing the ratty clothes we kept there for working in the yard.

"What did Joe Riddley do while you all were working so hard?"

Oh, he nipped in here on his walker and shot Hiram Blaine.

I didn't say it, but I came within a hair. "He

122

sat out on the porch and watched everybody work." And barked orders that didn't make sense, nearly driving us crazy. I didn't say that, either. I saw no point in clouding either Charlie's or Buster's mind with details that didn't have a thing to do with Hiram.

"So Joe Riddley was here alone the whole time you were gone, apparently sleeping."

"Not apparently sleeping, he *was* sleeping. I had the dickens of a time waking him up."

Buster spoke mildly. "We don't need to worry about who was where until we know when Hiram died. It's highly unlikely he died after eleven. It could even have been last night."

"No, it couldn't." I hated to correct him and help Charlie build a case against the rest of us, but I owed it to Hiram to be as helpful as I could. "I didn't set that screen up until just before I left for the beauty parlor at seven. Its paper was torn, so I glued it last night. Whoever killed Hiram had to do it while I was at the beauty parlor and Joe Riddley was asleep. He sleeps now in the den in back of the living room, with the blinds shut and an old wall-unit air conditioner on. It makes such a racket, he wouldn't have heard a thing.

"Two more things," I added. "I didn't lock the back door when I went to get my hair fixed, in case Ridd brought the corn or Clarinda got here early. And I left Lulu in the kitchen, but when I got home, she was out in the bird dog pen. I didn't think much about it at the time. It was just one less thing I had to do. But somebody *was* here while I was gone."

"Or the judge got up." Charlie was like a tenor who only knows one aria.

"The judge can't walk." I felt my blood pressure rising. "He could no more get that dog across the backyard and inside the pen than he could fly."

Buster looked at the press of people milling around the room. A few gave us curious glances, but at a party that size nobody cares who the hostess is talking to, so long as there's food on the plates and drink in the cups. "I'm sorry, but these rooms do need to be cleared, to —"

I've been around police work long enough to know what he needed to do. I even appreciated that we couldn't wait for my guests to decide to go home. But I couldn't help saying sadly, "It's been a *nice* party until now." I felt sorry for myself and a whole lot sorrier for Hiram.

Buster's hand was warm on my shoulder. "It's your best party yet, and Joe Riddley's had a great time. Can you tell folks he's getting tired, and ease them out?"

I had a spurt of hope. "If I get them outside, do we have to send them *home* yet? I wanted to plant a tree in Joe Riddley's honor."

"Where did you have in mind to plant it?"

"Down the drive where that poplar blew down last spring. And we haven't had cake and ice cream yet, either. Clarinda's been baking all week."

Charlie scowled. "We can't delay a murder investigation for cake and ice cream."

Buster, however, understood how important this party was. "Any outside evidence is wiped out already. Can you keep everybody out there so we can work in here? And will you head them home right after the cake?"

"Sure. Lock the front door and close off the front of the house. We'll serve cake and ice cream outside and steer folks needing a bathroom through the kitchen. With everybody who's been in that kitchen, it's unlikely you'd find any evidence in there, either. Fair enough?"

He nodded. I headed toward a brass gong next to the dining room door, feeling a hundred and five. I hit the gong with all the anger inside me. But when people looked in astonishment, I smiled brightly. I didn't feel any livelier than Hiram; I was just in better shape to pretend.

"Would everybody please come help plant Joe Riddley's birthday tree?"

When I heard the sheriff lock the door behind us, I shivered in spite of the sunshine.

# 10

I couldn't help looking suspiciously at our guests as I worked my way toward Joe Riddley. None of them looked like a murderer, but the last murderer I'd met was charming.

Before Joe Riddley saw me, I headed for Martha. Every family needs at least one calm, practical member, and Martha is also wise, funny, short, and comfortably round, with dark brown hair and eyes like a cocker spaniel's. There's not a mean or pretentious bone in her body, and when she walked into our house the first time, I felt like she'd been part of our family forever.

That afternoon I spoke to her low and fast. "Hiram Blaine's lying dead behind my dining room screen. Buster says we don't have to send people home until we've planted the tree and eaten cake and ice cream, but we need to move all the tables off the porches down to the grass and serve the cake outside. Will you tell Clarinda? She knows about Hiram — she'll understand."

Martha blinked a couple of times, but she's an emergency-room supervisor. She knows how to act now and ask questions later. Being a nurse, though, she had to ask one question. "You're sure he's dead?"

"Positive."

She hurried toward the kitchen.

I planted a kiss on Joe Riddley's head, glad somebody had managed to get him to leave off his cap. Probably Martha — she'd helped him get ready for the party. Joe Riddley has nice hair — thick and straight, another legacy from his Cherokee grandmother — and people were taking pictures.

He reached up to touch my cheek with one finger. "Hey, Little Bit," he said in his new deliberate way. "Doin' all right? Look a little peaky."

I was touched that he could still notice, but I would not worry him. "I'm fine, honey. Just a bit winded with all this."

"It's a fine party. I went over to the field and ran a race with the kids. Beat 'em, too. Not bad for an old man, eh?"

People with severe head injuries make up stories like preschoolers, based on whatever they happen to have seen recently. But I wouldn't nag him with reality on his special day. "I'm proud to know you, honey." I rumpled his hair fondly. Then I hailed Ridd and waved him over. "Ready to plant a tree, son?"

Joe Riddley frowned anxiously at me. "Is 'plant a tree' in my log?"

"I wrote it, remember? 'Have party, plant a tree, be nice.' "

"I been nice," he said proudly.

"You've been a sweetheart this whole blessed day." I bent to give his neck a hug.

Ridd came from behind a big oak-leaf hydrangea, carrying a shovel. "I'm ready, Mama. Round up Walker and the kids, and I'll fetch the tree in my truck." Ridd's a math teacher by profession but a farmer at heart. Joe Riddley always claims Ridd's yard and fields are our nursery's best advertisement.

Walker isn't a farmer, but he's a great public speaker with a loud voice. His brief speech about his daddy made his mama's eyes smart, and eased all thoughts of Hiram from my mind for a little while. After Ridd hefted the sturdy little oak from his truck and set it next to a hole he'd dug earlier that morning, Walker's Tad and Jessica poured in peat moss, Ridd's three-year-old, Cricket, poured in bone meal, and his big sister, Bethany, turned on the hose to fill the hole with water. Ridd stood the oak in the hole, then all the guests emptied small white paper bags of potting soil around it until the hole was full. Finally I unveiled a brass plaque mounted on a granite stone I'd had made for the occasion: THIS TREE PLANTED IN HONOR OF JOE RIDDLEY YARBROUGH'S SIXTY-FIFTH BIRTHDAY BY HIS FAMILY AND FRIENDS, followed by the date.

Joe Riddley glared at it. "Is that my tombstone?"

"No, honey, it's a sign saying this is your tree."

"They're all my trees."

128

"But this one is very special. It's your birthday present."

"Oh." He subsided as Ridd tamped down the dirt. I stood holding Joe Riddley's hand and tried not to think about the party we could have had if he hadn't gotten shot. He was right. It was a fine party, anyway.

Or it was until a sheriff's cruiser barreled up our road and coasted to a stop beside me. "Afternoon, Judge Yarbrough." The driver lifted his hat and settled it again. "Understand you've got yourself a murder."

The crowd hushed like they'd all seen their fourth-grade teachers walk in. Joe Riddley held his hand to one ear like he couldn't hear. "Whad'y say, son? Murder? We got no murder here. We're havin' a party!" He was getting excited, which was very bad for him.

I motioned to Ridd, but Ridd stood like a rock with a question in his eyes and one word on his lips. "Mama?"

Lightning might strike me dead, but I flapped one hand at him and said, "Don't be silly," then I leaned toward the car window and said as loud as that officer had, "That was Buster's little joke, to get you all here. He said you'd never leave your posts for a party. Go on to the dining room through the kitchen. You'll find him there."

The four men in the car looked at me like I was crazier than the Blaines. A forensics car pulled up behind them and the driver rolled down his window. "Where's the body, Judge?"

I forced myself to chuckle. "It's a large body of food. You all go into the dining room and get yourselves something to eat." Then I leaned close to hiss in the driver's ear, "Don't you dare spoil this party! Buster's in the dining room." I stood and waved. "Eat hearty, boys."

As both cars hightailed it toward the house, Walker's son, Tad, started giggling as only a nine-year-old boy can. "Eat Hardy boys? Eat Hardy boys? Eat Harry Potter, too!" He got so convulsed with giggles that everybody around him started to laugh.

Gusta was unimpressed. "Very poor humor, if you ask me."

Up by the house our kitchen workers were practically airlifting tables and chairs off the porch while Martha and Alice helped Clarinda carry cakes. "Are we done here?" I asked Ridd.

"Just one more thing." He dropped a hand to his father's shoulder. "We need you to put the last shovelful of dirt on the tree, Daddy, so we can stake it. Are you up to that?"

" 'Course I am. I'm up to anything, aren't I, Little Bit?"

"Sure you are, honey. Show us."

Sitting in a wheelchair, my once indomitable husband waved the shovel ineffectually over the dirt until Bethany knelt and lifted a handful onto the shovel in her cupped palms. Someone caught that picture, and I'll treasure it always. When Joe Riddley dribbled the dirt onto the base of the tree, everybody cheered.

Ridd tamped down the dirt and started staking the tree. I climbed on a chair so everybody could see me and shouted so they could hear, "Let's sing to our birthday boy, then there's a dozen kinds of cake and ice cream out yonder under the trees. It's nicer out here than indoors."

Mama used to say you can convince people of anything if you believe it strong enough yourself. That particular minute I *sure* believed it was nicer outdoors than in.

While they were getting dessert, I took a chair up on the porch by the front door to steer folks to the kitchen if they needed a bathroom. As I looked over the happy crowd, I felt a measure of contentment overlaying my worry. Except for Buster and his crew, our guests were still having fun. Joe Riddley was taking a few careful steps along the front walk on his walker to show off to Pooh, who clapped from her wheelchair.

As he lurched over a crack, somebody said proudly, "J.R.'s doin' real good." Darren lowered himself gracefully to the bottom step holding an enormous piece of Clarinda's red devil cake. Today his hair was bright yellow — a daisy center to his white pants and shirt. The silver hoop in his ear caught the sun as he jerked his head toward Joe Riddley and added, "Old J.R.'ll be walkin' on his own in no time."

"It's nice to hear him *laugh* at his mistakes," I said with an emphasis only he could appreciate.

We'd put up with Joe Riddley learning those skills. It had not been easy listening.

"How's your love life?" I teased. I kept telling Darren he could earn a fortune selling his on-going story to country music writers. One minute he had found the love of his life. The next minute he was down in the dumps because she'd done him wrong. "Have you been seeing more of that reporter I told you about?"

I'd seen Kelly wandering around the party, but hadn't seen Darren with her.

He wrinkled his nose. "We went out a couple of times, and she's a lot of fun, but she's short, redheaded, and doesn't *need* me. I like tall, dark, beautiful women who need me."

"Women who only need you don't make good partners. Look for a nice normal girl with pleasing looks and some intelligence."

He gave a Latin shrug. "What can I say? They bore me. But speaking of women who need me, do you think I could help that woman J.R.'s showing off for? The one in the wheelchair?"

"I doubt it. She's got bad arthritis, and she's been in that chair twenty years."

"Maybe I could loosen her up a little." Darren came from the brash school of youth that is sure all of us could be up and at 'em if we tried.

Just then Pooh clapped her gnarled hands like a child. "Very good, Bud! Very good!"

I sighed. "She gets more and more confused every day. Bud was Joe Riddley's daddy, and he's been dead twenty years."

"Don't you hate to see her gettin' like that?" Maynard paused at the foot of the steps, looking like young George Washington in a navy linen suit with his long blond hair caught by a navy ribbon at his neck. Beside him, Selena glowed like a soft yellow taper in a linen sheath with her mop of red curls blazing above. I checked out her engagement ring finger, but it was still bare. I could have shook Maynard. I didn't want to waste a perfectly lovely tea set.

Still I had to agree with what he'd just said. "Seems like ever since Fayette died and left her with nobody to tell her what to do every minute, Pooh's been lost."

Darren picked up a few stray crumbs with the tip of one finger. "What about the rest of her family?"

"She doesn't have any family," I told him. "Her only son was killed in Vietnam."

"Couldn't she go into a retirement home, or an assisted living facility?"

I shook my head. "The only ALF we have in the county is for indigent people. Pooh would need to move pretty far away to get into a nice place, and she wouldn't know a soul."

"That's so sad." Like Martha, even while eating peanut butter pound cake at a birthday party, Selena was still a nurse. "As confused as Pooh is here, she'd be worse somewhere else. She'd never understand where she was, or why. But she won't be able to live alone much longer."

"Pooh's not exactly alone. She's got Otis and Lottie." Maynard licked a last drop of ice cream off his spoon. "I just wish Miss Gusta would move and sell me her house."

"You want to add it to your old museum?" I teased. Maynard was not only the curator, he was also the secret benefactor of the Hope County Historical Museum. "Or buy it and live in it?"

When Maynard smiled, he was more handsome than I'd have ever believed back when he was a scrawny little boy. "I've bought Marybelle Taylor's old house, like I always wanted."

Marybelle Taylor had been one of my best friends when I was a little girl, and even though she'd been dead two years, I still missed her. "She's beaming at you from heaven," I assured him. But it wasn't Marybelle's spirit I felt. It was the Spirit of Charlie Muggins, telling me I needed to shoo people home.

Maynard finished up his own pound cake and answered my previous question. "What I'd do with Miss Gusta's house is open an antique store. A really good one. It would be a wonderful house for displaying antiques. I could rent out various rooms to dealers from all over the Southeast. She just rattles around in it, and it makes a lot of work for Florine. She's no spring chicken." Gusta's housekeeper and I were exactly the same age, but I didn't see fit to mention it. "Of course," he went on, "Miss Gusta will never move until Pooh does, and

134

Pooh worries me more than Miss Gusta anyway. I don't know how much longer Otis can keep on driving, and what will they do then?"

Darren snapped his fingers. "Are they the folks who drive that navy-blue Cadillac up and down the streets at five miles an hour?" When Maynard and I both nodded, he groaned. "Boy, they sure know how to clear the streets. I figure the driver gave up turn signals for his seventy-fifth birthday, and stoplights for his eightieth. He oughtn't to be permitted to drive. He even leaves his keys in the car."

Darren still had some acclimating to do to small-town living. Everybody in Hopemore knew Otis left the keys in the car. Half the folks in town had taken them to him at least once. But how else would Pooh get around?

Darren stood. "Are we allowed seconds?"

"Eat all you want." I spoke before I remembered: Buster wanted these people *gone.*

As Darren sauntered off toward the cakes, Meriwether and Slade came along the walk. He had one hand protectively at the small of her back, and she didn't seem to mind. "Joe Riddley's looking real good," she told me with her charming smile. I tried not to remember back when Meriwether's smile had been not merely charming, but radiant — back before what Joe Riddley called "Meriwether's Ice Age."

"The doctor says eventually he'll be up and attem like he used to. You're looking mighty good yourself. That's a gorgeous suit. Is it silk?"

"Yes. I got it in Hong Kong."

"Lucky you," Selena said enviously.

Meriwether and Slade made a good-looking couple, both tall and he as dark as she was fair. He was particularly handsome when he smiled, showing even, white teeth in a face that looked perpetually tanned. "You've had a lovely day for the party," he told me. He waved toward a poplar tree. "You even got a bit color, just in time."

"We don't get much down here, but we do our best," I told him.

"The mountains must be blazing now. I miss the annual week our family used to spend at our place up near Boone. But Hopemore's real pretty, too."

He was nice as could be, but I couldn't warm up to the man. It wasn't just because of Walker, either, although I'd noticed that a couple of times when Walker could have spoken to Slade that day he had gotten distracted in another direction. The real reason I didn't like Slade was that I loved Jed Blaine. I plumb hated seeing Meriwether with anybody else.

Besides, Slade made me nervous, the way his eyes kept flickering toward our closed dining room blinds. I was glad when Alice Fulton distracted us.

Alice scuttled down the walk, head down and eyes fixed on the ground. She carried a piece of cake and a cup of drink, and the ice cream on her cake was melting. She looked up at

136

Meriwether and said softly, "Your grandmother says she's ready to go."

"Fine. You all go on. Slade is taking me home." Meriwether took an inch-step closer to the protection of his arm.

Alice backed up one reluctant step. "But she said . . ."

Meriwether rested one fist on her hip. "For heaven's sake, Alice. You are competent. You proved that again and again on the trip. You drive as well as I do, and you were hired to replace me, remember? Tell her Slade's taking me home." She grabbed his elbow and practically dragged him away.

Alice looked after her, color high.

"You look lost. Can I help?"

That was Darren, carrying another wide slice of red devil cake with cream cheese frosting. As I looked at Alice through his eyes, I saw somebody tall, slender, brunette, and real pretty. And she certainly needed help right that minute.

She threw me an anxious look. "Mrs. Wainwright is going to be really mad."

I stood up. "I'll tell you what. You all sit on the steps and tell everybody not to use the front door, and I'll go tell Gusta that Meriwether has already gone."

"Why can't they use the front door?" she asked. Every pair of eyes in earshot roved curiously in that direction.

"Clarinda was trying to clean up the carpet and spilled a whole bottle of soap on the floor.

Now they're trying to get *that* up." I was becoming quite the liar. If I didn't watch out, it would get to be a habit. "Tell folks to go through the kitchen if they need a bathroom. If you'll do that, I'll go tell Gusta what Meriwether said, and I'll gussy it up a little." A smile twitched her lips. That encouraged me to suggest, "Darren, will you keep her company?"

She looked at him uncertainly. He grinned down at her and slowly she smiled.

As I left, I heard him asking, "Do you like athletics?"

"I like to run. Do you?" After that, I was out of earshot.

Predictably, Gusta was not pleased. "Ungrateful child! First she moves out and saddles me with a stranger, and now she's never there when I need her. Don't put your old-age hopes in your grandchildren, MacLaren. They are sure to disappoint you. And where's Alice? She ought to be where I can call her if I need her."

"I asked her to guard the front door while I came to find you. We've had a little accident inside and are having to steer people around to the back."

She fixed me with those steel-gray eyes. "It's not a murder, is it? That sheriff's man said it was murder." When I didn't answer at once, she glared. "MacLaren," she asked in an accusing tone, "whatever *have* you done?"

# 11

After the other guests had gone, Darren sat on the front porch steps, the late-afternoon sun setting his hair alight. "I thought I'd stay to help J.R. to bed and give him a good massage. His muscles are sure to be worn out with all the excitement and all that walking. My birthday gift," he added.

"Bless you," I said gratefully. "I think Ridd took him to his room." I walked him through the kitchen and pointed the way. "Behind the living room, in what used to be our den." I stayed in the kitchen to pay the workers. Clarinda had marshaled them so well they had already cleaned up every speck of the mess. She'd also put up food for each of them to take home. We waved them on their way, then she turned back to the kitchen. Seeing the slump of her shoulders and the weariness in her face was like seeing myself in a mirror. "We did it," she said.

"We sure did," I agreed, "and it was great." I fell into a kitchen chair. "But another day like this and I'll just go crazy and get it over with."

Clarinda wiped an invisible spot on the

countertop. "The sheriff says we can't get in there until tomorrer at the earliest. What time you want me here?"

"I don't want you here at all. I know you have church all day."

She nodded. "Sure do, and Otis is preaching."

I was surprised. "Otis Raeburn?"

"Yeah. He's real good. Quiet, now — not like some. But when he talks, something tingles deep inside you. You know you've heard the word of God for sure."

I'd seen Otis all my life driving Pooh around town or shopping for plants, and I'd admired his courtly gentleness, but I'd never guessed he was a preacher. "Life is full of surprises." I stretched and yawned. "You go on home. I'll do what has to be done tomorrow. You can finish the rest on Monday."

"Get that food out of the house, now. I don't want this kitchen smelling to high heaven." We heard the gentle toot of her grandson's horn in the backyard. Having given me my instructions, Clarinda tugged off the old blue cotton cardigan she wore in the kitchen and headed for the closet next to the back door.

"That's locked," I reminded her, "and the key's upstairs. I'll hang it up later."

She draped it carefully over a chair back. "Call me, now, if you need me tomorrer."

"I won't need you tomorrow."

She turned at the door, and I knew exactly what her next five words would be. "Oh, and one more thing." She never left without saying that at least once. "I made the police let me go to the livin' room for all the birthday cards and presents. I took 'em back to the study. Didn't want the boss takin' it into his head to go there lookin' for 'em."

The study was our fancy name for the paneled room at the far back of the house, behind the den. Furnished with odds and ends chosen for comfort rather than style, the room was a catchall for things we didn't know where else to put, and the space Yarbrough men had claimed as their own for four generations. Its desk was scratched and scarred. Its shelves sagged with books we never read but didn't throw out and *National Geographic*s we couldn't bear to burn. One corner was filled by the gun cabinet Old Joe Yarbrough had built and Joe Riddley still used to store his guns.

Clarinda put her hand on the knob to leave. "Cindy took the grandkids home, and the others are back there right now. I told 'em to list the presents so you can write folks later."

Tears stung my eyes and made my voice wobbly. "I don't know how you got this all cleaned up so fast. You did a heroic job today."

Her dark face crinkled in a grin. "Me 'n' you both, huh? More heroic than anybody knows. Workin' right on with Mr. Hiram lying dead in that other room —" She shook her head and pursed her lips. "Mmm, mmmm mmm! We oughta get medals, for sure."

I should have known my sons would have a different opinion.

As soon as I entered the study, I met three pairs of grownup eyes. Martha's were apprehensive. The men's glowered — Joe Riddley's black eyes in Ridd's olive face and my own lighter browns in Walker's fairer one.

"Okay, Mama," Walker started. "Tell us what's going on in the dining room. Buster and Charlie Muggins are both in there with a slew of officers and won't let us in."

Before I said a word I took the basket of cards out of Joe Riddley's red leather recliner, sat down, and extended the footrest. I laid my head back, took a deep breath, and closed my eyes. I didn't want to watch the expressions on their faces. "Hiram Blaine got shot sometime after seven this morning in our dining room. He's lying behind my Oriental screen with a hole in his head." I was so tired I could even say it without a tremor. "Charlie found him around three-thirty, but Buster kindly let us plant the tree and have our cake before we sent folks home."

"You knew this the whole time we were planting that tree?" Walker was scandalized.

Ridd had another gripe. "You lied to me, Mama. You flat-out lied to the sheriff's men and you lied to me."

I still didn't open my eyes. "Yes, son, I did. And I'd do it again to give your daddy that last hour of his party. Since he got shot, have you

142

ever seen him that happy, that alive . . ."

That last word undid me. Joe Riddley being alive got mixed up with Hiram being dead, and tears started pouring through my closed eyelids until I blubbered like a baby.

The boys didn't have a clue what to do. Ridd kept saying, "Now, Mama, it's gonna be okay. It's gonna be okay," when we all knew it was never going to be okay for Hiram again, and might never be okay for Joe Riddley, either. Walker kept patting my shoulder like I used to pat his when he was little. Thank goodness Martha is a nurse, and unflappable.

"You all go home." She handed me a wad of tissues. "Mac's plumb worn out, and she's carried this thing for hours. She and Clarinda. When we were trotting that cake down the steps, Clarinda told me she was proud as punch at the way your mama was bearing up, and here you are fussing at her."

I opened my eyes and lifted my head in time to catch Ridd drawing his brows together and frowning at his wife. "You knew about this, too?"

When Martha nodded, Walker pounded the arm of Joe Riddley's old leather couch and yelled, "You could have told us. We had a right to know."

His yell brought Ridd to his senses. He reached out and shook Walker's shoulder like he used to when he was eight and Walker three. "Cool it, bro, or Daddy will hear. If the women

143

made sure the old man had a good time, I guess the least we can do is act grateful. Stop crying, Mama, we aren't gonna fuss anymore. But if you get involved in trying to solve this thing —"

"Yes?" I jerked a tissue from a nearby box to rub my eyes. "Just what will you do?"

He stopped to think. "I guess the same thing you'd have done if we'd ever made you carry out that threat when we were little."

"What *would* you have done?" Walker sounded genuinely curious.

I shook my head and sniffed. "I don't know, but it would have been *terrible*." We all had a little laugh to clear the soggy air. "But don't worry," I added. "These days I'm too tired and busy to investigate anything. We'll leave this to Buster. You all go home — you, too, Martha."

After they left, I sat remembering the good parts of the day — until a howl from the dog pen reminded me that my day wasn't quite over. Lulu had become quite the little princess since she lost her leg, and wouldn't sleep outside anymore. No dog can match a beagle for outrage. "In a minute," I muttered. I couldn't move quite yet.

Lazily my eyes roamed the bookshelves and stopped with a pang at the very top shelf. I'd forgotten we had those five old books of Helena Blaine's. She gave them to us back when she first learned she was dying, to keep for Jed. "Give them to him when he turns twenty-one," she'd said. "If they stay at our place, Hector will use them to light the fire or Hiram will tear out pages to line his bird cage. Remember, now, give them to Jed on his birthday."

It was a pitiful little legacy, but we'd promised. Then Jed worked in Atlanta the summer he turned twenty-one, and didn't come back to Hopemore after that, and I plumb forgot the books. I'd need to remember to give them to him when he came for Hiram's funeral, but I was too tired right then to climb up. . . .

"Everybody else gone?"

I must have dozed, because Darren startled me, coming in with his soft fluid stride. He perched on a straight chair, hands dangling between his knees. His dark, dark eyes glistened in the dim room. "J.R. is sleeping. He may wake up wanting a bite of supper later, but let him sleep as long as he will. I gave his muscles a real good workout and you know what? His legs feel stronger. All that showing off today was good for him."

"I'm so glad. Thank you for his massage. Would you like to take some barbeque home with you?" I swung my feet off the recliner.

He grinned. "Don't want any barbeque, but I wouldn't say no to another piece of cake."

"The red devil cake is all gone. Some pig kept eating it. Will chocolate pound cake do?"

"It'll do fine."

While I was cutting cake and pouring iced tea, Darren roamed the kitchen. He touched my herbs in the windowsill and Joe Riddley's grandmama's old iron sitting up on the hutch. Finally he leaned against the closet door, hands behind him, and said, "How come you haven't told me about Alice before? She said she moved to town a *month* ago from Macon to work for Mrs. Wainwright, and you never mentioned her." His outrage was as keen as Lulu's.

"Sorry. I fell down on the job." I set a big slab of cake before him.

He sat down and hooked one ankle around the bottom rung of his chair. "And is the tall blonde the rich lady who moved into her daddy's house after he died?"

Darren once told me physical therapists are a bit like hairdressers: People gossip in front of them like they are mannequins. I wasn't surprised he knew about Meriwether's house.

"She's the one. She's Gusta Wainwright's granddaughter."

"She looks overworked," Darren said thoughtfully. I thought he meant Meriwether until he added, "Think she ever gets time off?"

I sipped tea before I replied, "I thought your heart was broken by that girl in Dublin."

He gave me an impish grin. "It could be mended by the right company. Wonder what she looks like with her hair down?"

"Better," I assured him. We sat in companionable silence enjoying our cake until Buster spoke from the door.

Our kitchen once had a fireplace in it, and the chimney wall sticks out so far it keeps anybody at the door from seeing all the way in. Because Darren was sitting at the far side of the table, Buster couldn't see him. Otherwise he wouldn't have said, flat-out, "We're taking the body out now, but of course that room's got to stay sealed a while."

Darren shifted slightly, like he wished he could disappear. But before I could tell them he was there, Charlie spoke from behind Buster's shoulder. "You ought to move out until we're done here."

"I can't move Joe Riddley right now, he's —"

Buster held up one hand. "No need to move out. We've put a seal on the room. I know you'll honor it."

I wrinkled my nose. "I hope you hurry. The food on the table's going to get pretty ripe."

"It looks pretty straightforward. He was shot right there with a twenty-two caliber gun. The mail beneath him stopped the bullet."

"Best use I can think of for junk mail," I said sourly.

A smile flitted over Buster's face. "No sign of a weapon yet, though. We'll search again to-morrow, and finish up in there. You want me to leave somebody out here with you?"

I shook my head. "I'm not scared. We've got the dogs."

Charlie Muggins piped up again. "You can't think of anybody around here with a motive, can you?"

"I hope by 'around here' you mean around

the whole county, and not around this property," I said tartly.

Charlie shrugged. "Whatever."

"No, I can't. Hiram's been gone four years, after all, and hardly been back long enough to rile anybody up that much."

"We want to take a look at Joe Riddley's guns." Charlie was practically salivating.

"Might as well." I struggled to my feet — neither of which was happy to be in use again after being overworked all day. Carelessly I flapped my hand toward Darren on his concealed chair. "You both know Darren, don't you?" Both men deserved the shock they got when they came into the room and saw him sitting there. They should never have spoken from the door.

The gun case in the den was locked, as usual, but up in the top right corner, one gun was missing.

"What was that one?" Charlie demanded, pressing far too close behind me.

"I don't know. I hate guns, hate having them in the house."

"But what kind was it?" Charlie persisted. "You gotta at least know that."

"I don't. The guns are Joe Riddley's. I leave them alone."

His voice was shrill. "You mean to tell me you live in this house and you don't —"

"What's goin' on in here?" Joe Riddley's voice was slurred with sleep, and he practically hung

148

on his walker. Darren moved to him and supported him with one strong arm.

"We're admiring your guns, old buddy," Buster told him. "There seems to be one missing. Know which one it was?"

Joe Riddley shuffled over and peered into the case. After a long minute's thought, he nodded, as if he'd come up with a satisfactory answer. "It's not missing, just mislaid."

"It was a small gun, wasn't it?" Charlie prodded.

Joe Riddley stared at him half a minute without saying a word, then nodded again. "Still is, far's I know. Guns don't generally grow." He turned back to Buster. "Quail huntin' season starts in a few weeks." Sometimes the things he remembered were more amazing than the things he forgot.

"Next month," Buster confirmed.

"Let's go. You and me, like we used to. I could do with some quail. You want some quail, Little Bit? Go write 'hunt with Buster' in my log for next Saturday."

I cleared my throat to be sure my voice was steady. "Not this fall, honey. Maybe next year. I'm not sure you're up to shooting yet."

"I'm plenty up to shooting! You hear me? Plenty up to shooting. I can outshoot anybody here. You know that. Buster, tell her! I don't ever miss. Don't you tell me I can't go hunting, Little Bit. Don't you tell me . . ." He broke down and sobbed.

Darren put one arm across his back and practically carried Joe Riddley down the hall to bed. I stood there with my mouth dry and my heart pounding. Charlie rubbed one stubby forefinger along his chimpanzee jaw.

I knew exactly what he was thinking.

"Joe Riddley was asleep this morning," I reminded him. "He gets confused, doesn't know what he's saying."

He nodded. "Might not know what he was doin', either." He turned to Buster. "Way I see it, Mac here could have killed Hiram before the party and shoved him behind that screen with the rest of her cluttered life, or Joe Riddley killed Hiram in one of those new rages he's gotten prone to since his accident."

I rounded on him, furious. "Joe Riddley didn't have an *accident,* he was deliberately shot. And if you repeat what you just said in a public place, I'll have you in court for —"

Buster put out a hand to shut me up, but his other hand was making circles along his temple, a sign he was thinking. "We need to call it a night and all get some rest. Want me to bring Lulu up to the house, Mac?"

"I'd be grateful."

"Come with me, Charlie, to hold the other dogs."

Joe Riddley's dogs knew Buster's scent. He could reach down and scoop Lulu up without any problems. But I appreciated his taking Charlie with him — although I suspected it was for Charlie's own protection. I don't like guns, but I do know how to use them.

Lulu came prancing in to greet me like she'd been exiled a month. As I reached down to quiet her, Buster touched his hand to his hat and said, "I'll get back to you in the morning."

"We'll both get back to you in the morning." Charlie made it sound like a threat.

Too keyed up to sleep, I sat in our bedroom rocker by an open window where I could hear country night sounds and catch a breeze. Lulu dozed contentedly at my feet.

Instead of Hiram, I found myself thinking about Helena. She'd never dated that we knew, and her only woman friend was another single mother who worked over at the courthouse and helped Helena get a birth certificate for Jed when he started school. It was typical of Blaines to keep worthless books and lose birth certificates. It was a wonder they survived.

Poor Helena didn't survive for long. She died of cancer when Jed was a freshman at Mercer. He must have inherited his grandmother's smart genes, because he won a full scholarship.

At the end, Helena started to ramble. She got all worried about Jed and a sackful of something, but we couldn't understand her. Jed finally remembered his one brief encounter with the law, when he'd stolen a pack, not a sack, of seeds off our rack. Joe Riddley made him work to pay for them. "Mama was real grateful you didn't take her job," Jed said ruefully.

Joe Riddley had cuffed him gently. "Our boys did worse things than that."

Suddenly Helena opened her eyes. "Watch over my brothers and take care of Jed. Give —" She squeezed Jed's hand, then she was gone, a lot more peacefully than her brother died.

Lulu stirred at my feet, raised her head, and whined. I listened but didn't hear anything. I wasn't *frightened* to be down at the end of a road by myself, but I'd have been a lot happier if Joe Riddley had been snoring gently in our bed instead of lying vulnerably downstairs. I started to get up and make sure he was all right, but when Lulu laid her nose down on her paws again, I took that for a sign that everything was all right. You don't get much past a beagle.

I took several deep breaths of clean country air and wondered if I'd seen Hiram's murderer when I went to get my hair fixed that morning. I'd met Ridd in his pickup with Bethany as I drove out, but he wasn't on his way to kill anybody. He'd rolled down his window and called, "Goin' for the corn." He'd experimented with a late variety of sweet corn, and wanted to show it off at the party. Ridd's always got an eye out for advertising.

Slade's green Lexus had been in front of the newspaper, and Pooh's Cadillac was creeping down Oglethorpe Street. Otis was alone and didn't see me. I hadn't recognized anybody else.

I left Phyllis's thinking about toilet paper.

How much could two hundred people use in one afternoon? I sure didn't want to run out. I decided to stop by Bi-Lo for two more eight-packs. As I turned into the parking lot, I nearly ran into an abandoned truck sitting smack in the driving lane. I meant to report it to the manager, but forgot.

I ran into Kelly Keane inside the Bi-Lo, and saw Alice Fulton sitting in her little white car when I came out. I figured Gusta had run out of something crucial, like butter for her grits. Gusta made up for being sparing with her money by being generous with other people's time.

As I drove away, I'd been in such a hurry, I nearly sideswiped the same truck —

Truck! That was Hiram's purple truck, with Joe on the dashboard. I'd muttered, "Next time you break down, Hiram, push the danged thing out of the way." Was the truck still there? Had anybody rescued Joe?

I wouldn't sleep until I found out, so I padded to the phone and called the sheriff's office. Nobody there knew a thing about a truck. "Would you send somebody to Bi-Lo's parking lot to see if it's still there? Especially see if the parrot's there. He could be suffering."

I finally climbed into bed, pulled the covers over my head, and slept like a baby.

Until I heard shots.

# 12

Lulu bayed at the bedroom window, a silhouette in the darkness. My clock said two-thirteen. Who the Sam Hill was shooting what in our yard?

I heard another shot, then a wild yell. "Hiya!"

Lulu bayed again. Joe Riddley's dogs answered frantically in their pen.

I flew out of bed and ran barefoot downstairs, muttering threats against whoever was bothering Joe Riddley at that hour.

A halogen security light between our house and the barn did funny things with colors and made us all look like creatures from Mars, but it also flooded the backyard with light. I hurried to the back door and peered between the curtains.

Joe Riddley stood in the brightest part of the light. He'd turned his walker around and propped himself against it like it was a seat. He had his shotgun on his shoulder, aimed straight at our barn. And he was naked as the day he was born.

He pulled the trigger and yelled again. "Hiya!"

We just used the barn for lawn equipment,

camping gear, and the fishing boat, so I wasn't worried he'd hit any living thing. But Lulu, who was trained to hunt and who would formerly have been in a frenzy to join the fun, cringed against my leg and trembled. That made me so mad, I forgot my training about treating Joe Riddley with care and patience. I flung open the door, dashed out onto the porch, and yelled, "What the heck do you think you are doing at this hour of the night? You're scarin' Lulu to death, and you're gonna bother the neighborhood."

Hubert and Maynard Spence were a quarter mile away, of course, but Maynard was a light sleeper. I didn't want him coming down to see my fool husband standing out in the backyard in his birthday suit shooting his own barn.

When he didn't even turn my way, I added, "Where's your pajamas?"

He looked down, uninterested. "I wet 'em." He turned back, propped against the walker again, steadied the gun on his shoulder, and pulled the trigger. A bullet whizzed, then plunked in the side of the barn. "See that, Little Bit? Who you sayin' can't shoot?" His dogs yelped their approval and excitement. For all they knew, they and Joe Riddley were heading after quail. He lowered the gun and peered toward the barn. "Can you see that? Right through the heart."

The heart he referred to was a red one Bethany painted on the old brown barn in a fit of teenage determination to fancy up the place before her friends came to the party. She'd painted a couple of flowers, too — one blue and one yellow — before the futility of the task caught up with her enthusiasm. Hitting that heart with a shotgun didn't take any particular skill. The thing was nearly three feet tall. But I didn't say so. I'd finally woken up enough to remember Joe Riddley's mind was sick and I was supposed to treat him gently.

I also remembered a year before, when Joe Riddley came in second in a county-wide shooting match. Despair rolled over me like an icy wave at the beach. "Oh, God help us," I begged, looking at my naked husband out in the chilly night with a loaded gun.

But you can't give in to despair when something goes on day after weary day. You have to buck yourself up and keep facing it. I brushed tears off my cheeks and took a deep breath to calm my voice. "That was good, honey, but you need to come in now. You'll have Buster's deputies roaring down the road. And it's a tad cool to be out there without a sweater."

He finally turned, angry. "Don't you tell me what to do, Little Bit. I gotta practice. Me 'n' Buster'r goin' huntin', an' I gotta practice. You go on back inside, now. You hear me?" The way he was slurring his endings was a dead giveaway he wasn't thinking straight. As if I needed more proof, the gun barrel made loopy motions in the air, and when it grew still, it was aimed straight at my breastbone. I was taller than the painted heart on the side of our barn, and Joe Riddley a lot closer to me. There was little chance he'd miss if he pulled that trigger.

When I faced down Pooh, I'd been mostly worried about the officer behind me. Pooh was forgetful, not malicious. But who knew what anger Joe Riddley harbored after forty-one years of marriage? Married folks do a lot of things to make their partners wish they could shoot them. Common sense, good manners, and breeding restrain most of us. But Joe Riddley's good sense, manners, and breeding were lost in a fog somewhere in the depths of his injured brain.

My feet stuck to that porch floor like it was a block of ice on a cold wet morning. I could never reach our door before he pulled the trigger. I'd have to talk him down, but I wasn't sure my lips would move.

They barely did. "Joe Riddley, put down the gun. You're pointing it straight at me."

"Then you get back inside. You hear me, Little Bit? Do as you are told. I gotta practice. Goin' huntin'." He looped the barrel in the air again, still facing in my direction.

"You're shooting real good," I assured him, backing slowly toward the door. "Why don't you lay down the gun and come on in for now?"

"Can't." He turned away again. I sagged against the doorjamb in relief, but his next words chilled my very soul. "Gotta practice. Like I told Hiram yesterday, I'm a good shot, but you gotta keep in practice." He propped his bare rear on the walker.

My knees grew so weak I had to hold on to the porch railing to keep from sliding to the porch's gray floorboards. "Hiram? When did you see Hiram?"

"Came by yesterday afternoon after my nap, lookin' for you. Said he'd promised to mow, but got detained. I told him I do our mowin'. He'll have to find another job."

"Oh." It came out a squeak of relief. "You mean Friday afternoon."

"No, I mean yesterday." He sighted along the barrel.

"Yesterday was your party, honey. You didn't have a nap. You must mean Friday."

"Don't you tell me what I mean." He started turning my way again.

Mindful of the gun, I scooted into the kitchen behind the screened door, ready to dash to safety if necessary. Lulu whined at my ankles. Still, I couldn't leave the conversation there. "But it *was* afternoon when Hiram came?"

"Morning, afternoon, I don't remember. What's the difference? Woke me up. I told him if them aliens bother him, I'll shoot 'em for him." He gave a chuckle that sounded wicked to my terrified ears. "Right in the middle of their foreheads."

I was so faint I scarcely noticed when he added, "Told him I do our mowin'. I do, too. Now go on back to bed and leave me be. I gotta practice." He sighted along the barrel and shifted his position.

"Honey," I persisted, "are you positive you saw —"

I didn't get to finish. Joe Riddley had miscalculated the walker's balance. It toppled, carrying him back with it. The gun flew from his grip, made two loops in the air, and landed on its butt in the grass not ten feet from the door where I stood. I dropped to the floor, arms over my head.

Hearing no shot, I climbed gingerly to my knees and peered out. Joe Riddley sprawled on his back, looking puzzled. "Gun didn't go off. Musta used both shots."

"You did," I remembered. My heart thundered a rapid *thankGodthankGod.* "Are you hurt?"

"No." Joe Riddley peered into his ammunition box. "Little Bit, run get me more shells. I'm out. You know the ones I mean?"

"I know the ones you mean, but I'm not getting them. You've done all the shooting you're going to do for one night." I held on to the door and managed to get it open, but my legs quivered like I was a hundred and fifty. I was pretty sure they wouldn't get me down the steps. I went down the ramp instead, holding tight to the handrail. By the time I reached the grass I felt stronger, but nowhere near strong enough to haul Joe Riddley to his feet.

"I'm going to have to call Ridd," I told him, panting.

"Call Maynard. He's closer. And get this infernal walker out from under me. It's lumpy."

I removed the walker and hurried in to dial the familiar number.

Maynard's voice was slurred with sleep. " 'Lo?"

"Maynard, Joe Riddley's gotten himself into the backyard and fallen, and I can't get him up. I hate to call you, but —" I stopped the way folks are apt to when they need a favor but don't like to come right out and ask.

"I'll be right there." Maynard dropped the phone into its cradle and I saw an upstairs light come on across the watermelon patch. I was grateful he hadn't demanded, "Was that him doing all that shooting?" Time enough for explanations later. First, I had something else to do.

It's amazing how embarrassment can strengthen and speed a person's legs. I managed to hurry in, find a fresh pair of pajama bottoms, and get back outside before I heard Maynard's car start. "Let's get these on you, honey. I don't want Maynard seeing you like this." I knelt and awkwardly tugged the pajamas over Joe Riddley's feet and ankles.

For a wonder, he didn't protest much. Oh, he gave a couple of kicks and grumbles, but he helped me by raising his hips so I could slip the pajamas up. I gave him a smile and smoothed back his hair. "I hear him on the road already."

He smacked my hand. "I'm not gettin' my picture made. Don't fuss."

I gave an exasperated huff and stood to wave at Maynard, who was out of his car almost before it stopped.

Maynard had come home months before from a good museum job in New York City to help his daddy after Hubert's heart attack. From the gentle way he raised Joe Riddley and supported him across the grass, I saw he had learned how best to help a feeble man without injuring either the frail body or the delicate dignity.

"Let's get you back to bed," he suggested, steering Joe Riddley toward the ramp. "Mac, you could do with a bathrobe and slippers. It's chilly out here tonight."

I looked down and was glad our halogen light did make colors funny. At least Maynard couldn't see how red I'd turned. I'd been so worried about Joe Riddley's modesty, I'd forgotten my own. There I stood in a flimsy gown without a robe.

Maynard tactfully turned away as I hurried up the steps and toward the stairs. That blasted gun could stay out there until it rusted, as far as I was concerned.

Joe Riddley was starting to snore by the time I got back downstairs. Maynard stood watching him at the door. When he saw me, he motioned me to follow him to the kitchen. "What were you all doing out there at this hour?" he asked softly.

"Didn't you hear him shooting? He's got some fool notion about going hunting with Buster this fall, and he was practicing. Woke me up. I'm surprised it didn't wake you, too."

"I've bought a white noise machine. I can stand New York, but I can't take the frogs down by Daddy's pond. I didn't hear a thing until the phone rang."

"I hope it didn't wake Hubert."

"It didn't. He doesn't hear much without his new hearing aids and I took the phone out of his bedroom." He gave me a worried look. "The way Joe Riddley is these days, you'd better get those guns out of the house."

"Especially after Hiram —" I stopped, appalled. I had no business talking about Hiram until the sheriff's office released a formal statement about his death.

Maynard gave a grunt of disgust. "I could shoot that old bugger. He came into the museum Friday afternoon eating a hamburger and got ketchup all over one of our upholstered chairs. I had the dickens of a time getting it out without leaving a stain." He shook his head at the memory.

I knew Maynard hadn't shot Hiram — or at least I was pretty sure he hadn't — but still, I warned him, "Don't go around saying you could shoot somebody. It can get you in trouble."

He chuckled. "Spoken like a new judge. But seriously, you need to get rid of those guns."

I heaved a frustrated sigh. "I don't know where to take them. Neither Walker nor Ridd has a safe place to keep them, with their children around."

"Want me to take them to our house? I can put them in one of our spare rooms upstairs. Daddy doesn't climb steps anymore, so he won't mess with them." What he meant was, Hubert wouldn't be tempted to think he could go out in the woods alone after a squirrel or rabbit, like he used to before he had a bad heart.

"I'd be very grateful," I admitted.

He got a sudden gleam in his eye. "Any more antiques among them?"

When Maynard first got home, he nearly drove everybody crazy asking for things we used every day and claiming they had "historical value." He'd slacked off some, but he still kept his eyes and ears open for antiques for that museum.

I owed him, though, for getting him out of bed. "I don't think so, honey, but you take a look. If there's something you want for the museum, I'll see what I can do. Ridd and Walker sure won't mind. None of us but Joe Riddley has ever cared a thing about guns. It used to be a real sorrow to him that the boys refused to hunt, but he finally accepted it."

I unlocked the case, and together we gathered all the firearms and took them to his car. Then I went back and got the ammunition as well, then the shotgun in the backyard. "When he gets better, you let me know when you want these back," he said as he stowed the last one in his trunk.

I shuddered. "I could do without them ever

coming back. Particularly the way Joe Riddley is now."

Maynard leaned over and gave me a hug, the privilege of a boy who'd known me since he was in diapers. "He's gonna be all right. He's getting better every day. You maybe can't see it, because you're with him all the time. But just now he was perfectly lucid when I was getting him into bed. Thanked me for coming and apologized for hauling me down here at this hour. Said he hates to be a burden on you and other people."

Tears stung my eyes. "You don't know how it cheers me to hear you say that. Seems to me like it goes on and on. It helps to get a fresh perspective. You want a cup of coffee or something before you go?"

I offered automatically, but found I really hoped he'd stay. "You got the makings of hot chocolate?" Maynard used to come down on chilly Saturday afternoons when he was a kid and I'd make hot chocolate with marshmallows. I didn't know at the time that his mother was trying to cut back on his sugar because she thought it made him hyper. Looking back on it, and on how well he'd turned out, seemed to me what made Maynard hyper as a little boy was being fussed over so much.

I made hot chocolate and put three fat marshmallows in each cup. We went out onto the porch and sat rocking gently, listening to night sounds and letting the steam warm our noses. The darkness made me bold. "Tell me something. When do I get to wear my wedding hat? You've bought Marybelle's house and are having it fixed up, you've got a good job and a legacy from your uncle, Selena's got a good job, so what's holding you back?"

He looked out toward where an owl was calling. "I don't see my way clear quite yet."

"You love her, don't you?"

"Oh, yes!" His thin face broke into that smile that made him so surprisingly handsome.

"So what's got hold of your suspenders? You can't live with your daddy forever."

He twisted his mouth, like he was trying to decide whether to tell me. Finally he drained his cup and held it, turning it around and around in his hands. "I can't see getting him to move, can you? And he can't stay out here by himself, but he has a fit if I suggest looking for somebody to live with him." He stood up before I said another word. "That was good. Thanks."

I wished I were charitable enough to have Hubert move in, but we couldn't live with Hubert. Still, I hated to see Maynard and Selena putting off their marriage because of him.

I watched his taillights grow small up the road and found myself thinking, *How blessed a person is who has good neighbors.*

As I turned to go in, I saw another set of lights coming down our road.

For a terrifying moment I remembered Ridd's truck barreling down to say his daddy had been shot. But these headlights were lower than Ridd's truck and not as blinding as Walker's Infinity. I hurried to the kitchen and latched the screen, wary since I'd inadvertently let in a murderer. With relief I saw a sheriff's cruiser pull to a stop under the light.

A deputy got out, pausing to take off his hat and smooth back his hair before he shut his door. "You need me to sign a warrant?" I called, unlatching the screen.

"No, ma'am, I brought you something." He put back on his cap and opened his back door. I heard a raucous shriek. "Sic 'em, boy! Sic 'em!" The yard dogs started a trio on the theme that we didn't need any parrots. At my ankles, Lulu made it a quartet. I fully agreed, and so, apparently, did Joe. His wings flapped angrily as the deputy reached into the backseat and struggled to grab a parrot who did not want to be grabbed.

Fighting an impulse to slam the door and go back to bed, I padded to the yard in my slippers. "Don't overexcite him. Give him a minute to get used to you." Then I turned to the dog pen and yelled, "Quiet, there! Quiet!" like Joe Riddley used to. To my utter amazement, the dogs hushed. Even Lulu subsided after a brief solo.

"You and who else?" the parrot shrieked as the deputy made another grab for his tail. The next minute the man backed out, rubbing the back of one hand with the other.

"Dang bird bit me! Maybe you ought to try,

Judge. I don't know much about birds."

"I don't know much about birds, either. Why didn't you take him to Hector, or back to your office?" I felt as disgruntled as the parrot.

"Hector wouldn't take it, and we don't have holding facilities for a bird. Besides, I thought you wanted him."

"Your nose is going to grow five feet long. Have you fed him?"

"No, ma'am."

"Wait a minute." I had no idea what parrots liked to eat. The only thing I'd ever seen Joe eat were bits of Hiram's hamburgers, buns, fries, and pizza. I ran into the kitchen, grabbed a bun left from the barbeque, and filled a bowl with water. I opened the car door. Joe perched on the steering wheel looking like any minute he'd drive away. No such luck. He gave me a disdainful glare, then turned around to show me his back. "Hungry, Joe?" I asked. "Want some roll?"

He twisted his head this way and that, but didn't move. As I continued to stand quietly and hold out the bun, though, he turned and hopped onto the seat, then inched my way. I also offered the bowl of water and he ducked his head for a swallow. After he'd had several, he arched his neck and pecked off a bite of bun.

I stood there while he ate bread and water, then held out my arm like I'd seen Hiram do. I was as frightened of his claws as Joe was of me, but when he hopped onto my forearm, they felt like tiny feathers on my skin. I was surprised how light he was. He felt no heavier than an orange.

I nearly dropped him, though, when he side-walked up my arm and climbed onto my shoulder. "Sic 'em, boy!" he called to the dogs, flapping his wings in my face.

They tuned up again. The deputy at least was good for something. He got them quiet.

"I'll take him in for tonight," I agreed grumpily, "although how I'll keep him and Lulu in the same house I don't know. Could you take her upstairs and shut her in a bedroom until I get Joe settled?"

We went to the kitchen together, and the deputy picked up the beagle without any trouble. He had two of his own from one of her litters. He nuzzled her gently as he took her up the stairs. "There you go, girl. Happy dreams."

Behind the closed door, Lulu started another aria. I hoped Joe Riddley's air conditioner was turned on high.

As the deputy clomped back downstairs, Joe started climbing from my shoulder to my head. "No!" I said crossly, but he hopped up and perched in my hair. "If you mess in my new hairdo . . ."

I didn't complete that sentence any more than I used to with the boys, but as I shook my head crossly, Joe hopped back to my shoulder. "Good boy," he croaked. "Good boy."

The deputy took off his hat, smoothed his

curls, and replaced his hat. "He says a lot of words."

"Why don't you take him home with you? Your kids would love him."

He grinned. "And my wife would kill me. Good night, now."

"Well, Joe, I hope you are housebroken," I muttered as I closed the back door. "If you tear up my house while I'm asleep, I'll positively kill you."

Then I remembered that his owner was already killed, and I felt so bad I gave him another bun. I left him perched on a ladder-back chair. muttering parrot obscenities to himself.

# 13

I stared in dismay at my kitchen. Morning sunlight streamed through the window over the sink, which was full of broken flowerpots, loose dirt, and fresh herbs that used to decorate the sill. Plastic containers and lids Clarinda had left in the drainer littered the floor. A red potholder dangled from the top of the refrigerator. Dish towels were strewn here and there. Clarinda's blue kitchen sweater was nothing more than a shredded mass of yarn covering the stove. Up near the twelve-foot ceiling, Joe perched on the curtain rod over the sink, a splash of scarlet against the creamy wall, and preened himself like he'd been grooming all night long.

Lulu stood below the sink and barked a warning that as soon as she learned to fly, Joe was dead meat.

"You filthy animal!" I raged. "As if I have nothing better to do than clean up after you."

"What'sa matter, Little Bit?" Joe Riddley spoke behind me.

I turned in astonishment. "You walked to the kitchen by yourself?"

"Me and my helper here." He steered the walker through the door.

I'd been too upset the night before to realize he'd made it all the way to the backyard alone. Now I found myself with the same jumbled emotions a mama feels when her infant first toddles across a room. Of course I was delighted Joe Riddley could walk by himself. But what if he wandered off, or went somewhere and couldn't make it back?

Sometimes life got too much for my legs. I sank into the nearest chair. Lulu pranced nervously at my feet, waiting for orders. With me out of the way, Joe Riddley finally saw the kitchen — and Joe. He laughed so hard he had to push himself over and take the chair beside mine. "Hello, Joe! No point pleadin' innocent. You left an evidence trail." He pointed to the overturned sugar bowl and large prints in the mess.

Joe flew straight to his shoulder. Joe Riddley gently stroked his bright red chest. "Always wanted a bird. Mama kept sayin' no."

"Your wife says no, too." I picked up dish towels, then reached for a sponge to clear the table. Joe squawked his displeasure.

"She's destroying your masterpiece, isn't she, feller?" Joe Riddley continued to stroke his bright chest with a large forefinger. Joe picked at something under one wing.

Lulu yipped her displeasure at not getting Joe Riddley's attention. I bent to pet her, then wiped sugar into my cupped palm. "Have you ever known a dog to make this big a mess in one night?"

Joe lifted his head and gave me a cold stare. "Not to worry. Not to worry."

Joe Riddley gave me a smug grin. "Ever know a dog who could talk?"

"This bird belongs to the Blaines. It's going home as soon as I can get Hector over here to pick it up." I couldn't rinse the sponge until I cleaned dirt and herbs out of the sink, which involved getting a bucket from the utility room. I went to fetch it, calling over my shoulder, "Heaven only knows what germs that animal has left in this kitchen."

"Not an animal. Birds are not animals. I don't think." Joe Riddley held up his arm and peered closely at the parrot. "Hello, Joe. Why are your cheeks so pink? Are you blushing?"

He was right. Joe's cheeks were normally white. Today they were bright as a flamingo.

"Blushing with shame for making such a mess." I finished picking plants and dirt from the sink and rinsed it. Then I rinsed the sugar-coated sponge. As I wrung the sponge, I half wished it was that bird's neck.

Joe fixed me with one big white eye with a bottomless black pupil. "Hello! Got a burger?"

Joe Riddley laughed. "Get him a cracker, Little Bit. Bird's hungry." He drew his log toward him and reached for the pencil. "Feed bird," he said as he slowly wrote the two words.

His sprawling letters were much larger than his handwriting used to be.

"I'm hungry, too," I said crossly. "Up half the night with you, and now feeding a bird. I don't even know what they eat."

"Call Cindy." I was astonished he could remember that. Our second daughter-in-law looked like a fashion plate, but she grew up with animals.

Fortunately, her family menagerie had included parakeets and cockatoos. "Feed him anything fresh and crunchy," she told me. "Apples, carrots. Also oatmeal and sunflower seeds."

Behind her, I heard Walker demanding, "What's Mama up to now?" so I said a hasty good-bye.

While I was retrieving carrot sticks and broccoli spears left over from the party, Joe spread his wings, flapped them a couple of times, and swooped back up to the curtain rod. In a second, a stream of bird doo streamed down to the sink.

"Get him out of here!" I was shaking with disgust.

"Hey!" Joe Riddley stuck out his arm. "Come down here." Joe obligingly flew down to the top of his head, then hopped down to his shoulder and walked down his arm. "Wanna be my bird?" It had not occurred to Joe Riddley to ask where Hiram was.

"You are not keeping that bird," I informed him shortly, cleaning up the latest mess.

"Sic 'em, boy," Joe urged him.

Joe Riddley put up one fist. "Wanna fight, Little Bit?" He gave me Joe Riddley's old, normal grin. I turned away. I would *not* soften on this. I didn't need a bird to clean up after, with all the rest I had to do.

"Here. Eat this." I held out a carrot stick. Joe arched his neck, then turned away.

"You have to cut it up," said Joe Riddley, Mr. Ornithologist U.S.A.

When I thumped smaller pieces down on the bare table, Joe Riddley picked up a few and held them on his palm. Joe ate like he hadn't eaten for a week.

I went to a phone out of earshot to call Hector. After I'd told him how sorry I was about Hiram, I said, "We've got Joe. You need to come get him."

"Wring his neck," Hector said brutally, making me ashamed I'd thought the same thing a little while ago. "I hate that animal. Messes up the house and uses the whole place like one big toilet. You keep him." He hung up before I could protest.

I came back to find Sheriff Gibbons and a couple of his men talking to Joe Riddley in the kitchen. Joe Riddley explained, "Sheriff and his men came to help you clean up from the party. Right neighborly, I call it."

I threw Buster a grateful look over Joe Riddley's head. He clapped his old friend on the shoulder a couple of seconds before he led his men toward the dining room. I needed to get Joe Riddley and myself fed and ready for church.

Joe Riddley didn't object when I said Joe had to go to the barn while we were gone. "Birds can't go to church," he explained to Joe. "You'll like the barn. Room to fly. Go to Little Bit." The bird hopped willingly from his arm to mine, surprising me again how light he was.

The dogs set up a racket as soon as I carried the parrot out on my arm. I half hoped Joe would fly away in terror, but he clung to my arm and taunted the dogs with squawks. When we got to the barn he hopped onto the handlebar of the lawnmower like it was a new kind of perch. I left him looking around to see what kind of mess he could make.

We had a crisis after Joe Riddley got dressed. I couldn't find his cap. He usually hung it by the kitchen door, but before the party, I'd hung it on the ladder-back chair by his bed. Now, it wasn't there.

"I can't go without my cap," he insisted.

"You don't need it for church."

"I need it to" — he searched for the word — "blind my eyes. From the sun." He sat stubbornly on his chair, waiting for me to find it.

"Shade your eyes," I corrected him. "And this isn't Miami in July." I'd already looked everywhere I could think of, and we were running late.

Suddenly he flapped one hand. "Not to

175

worry." He sounded like the parrot. "It's mislaid."

"Mislaid?" This was the second time in two days he'd used that word, which I couldn't ever remember him using before.

He explained as if I was the one with an injured brain. "Mislaid means you put it somewhere else and forgot. But now I remember. I gave it to Hiram."

"Hiram?" I was so startled, I blurted the word loudly. I hoped Buster hadn't heard me.

I also remembered what was different about Hiram. His cap had been clean.

"Hiram Blaine. You remember him?" Joe Riddley still sounded like I was the one with memory problems. "It was his birthday. He had a dirty cap, so I gave him mine. A present."

"Hiram climbed the water tank on his birthday, honey, and that was in April." This could be another of Joe Riddley's confabulations, but if so, where did Hiram get that clean hat? "Where were you when you gave Hiram the hat?"

"We were on his birthday."

"Hiram wasn't here on his birthday. Was it on the sidewalk Thursday, when you all were talking? After you went to the bank?" If I sounded desperate, I was. Desperately trying to recall if Joe Riddley had worn a cap since Friday. I couldn't. Maybe he was right. Maybe I was having sympathetic memory loss, like a husband who gets nauseated when his wife is pregnant.

He gave me a perfectly lucid frown. "My mind's not what it used to be. You know that. You'll have to ask Hiram."

Then his gaze slid toward the space under his bed and he started flapping his hand again. "Don't worry about it!" he shouted. "Don't worry about it. Don't worry about it!" He pulled himself to his feet and balanced on the walker. "Come on, we're going to church." He moved faster than usual toward his door, barking orders over his shoulder. "Get a move on. Come on, now. Come on!"

I'd seen that guilty look often enough to know there was something under the bed he didn't want me to see. As soon as he was through the door, I knelt, hoping I'd be able to get back up without calling for help. My knees aren't at their best in the morning. In the dimness near the wall, I saw something red.

One of the handiest things they gave Joe Riddley in rehab was a reacher — a long stick with a handle on one end and a claw on the other. Short women ought to be issued one at birth. Fishing under Joe Riddley's bed, I pulled out a filthy Yarbrough's cap streaked with white bird doo.

I knelt in that warm bedroom and shivered. My teeth chattered so hard I had to clench my jaw. My ears roared. With a hand shaking so hard I could hardly make the muscles obey orders, I picked up that unspeakable hat between two pinched fingers and carried it at arm's length, hoping germs weren't swarming up my hand. "Where did this come from?" I asked in a shaky voice.

Joe Riddley hadn't gotten far at the speed he traveled. He stopped, turned, looked at the cap, and glared at me. He spoke each word so carefully you'd have thought he was teaching me English. "That is not my hat."

"How did it get under your bed?"

He gave a huff of impatience. "I don't have time for whatchamacallits. We are going to be late." He moved the walker a baby step ahead. "Are you coming or aren't you?" As if he could get there without me.

I shook his elbow fiercely. "I'm coming, but first you have to tell me. Was Hiram in your room? Or did you bring this hat back with you?"

His answer, excruciatingly slow, lasted at least one lifetime. "I told you. He came to see me. It was his birthday. His hat was dirty. That's not good for the store. It doesn't matter. I can get a new hat."

"But why was this one under the bed?"

His lips trembled and I knew he was close to tears. "Don't fuss. I couldn't get it off the floor. Scared you would fuss, so I kicked it. Now you're fussing anyway. Don't fuss. Let's go to the ballgame."

I was ashamed of myself. Had I become such a tyrant that he was afraid of me? I reached around him from the back and held him close. "We're going to church, honey, and I'm not fussing. I'm glad you gave Hiram a present. Let's go to the car."

He resumed his turtle crawl toward the back door.

As much as I hated to, though, I had to show that hat to Buster. I tossed it back into the bedroom and followed Joe Riddley out, but as soon as he was in the car, I told him I'd forgotten something and ran back in. I went to the dining room door and said formally, "Sheriff Gibbons? I have something you need to see."

I do not know how I forced my legs to walk down that hall. They certainly had other ideas. My mouth struggled to form the words, and they came out sounding like Joe Riddley. "That is Hiram's cap. I found it under Joe Riddley's bed. Hiram had on Joe Riddley's when he died. Joe Riddley says this morning that he gave his hat to Hiram, but he can't remember when — or how this cap came to be here." I simply could not repeat Joe Riddley's words about Hiram coming to see him. Not until I'd had time to question Joe Riddley more closely. The way his mind was working, he could be remembering some time four years ago. But if so, where did that hat come from?

Buster took my elbow and escorted me to the back door. "We'll check the room for prints while you're at church. Don't worry, Judge Yarbrough. Don't worry about a thing."

That was easy for him to say. I'd seen Charlie Muggins at my dining room door. He'd heard every word I said. From the look on his chimpanzee face, if it was up to him, Joe Riddley and I wouldn't be heading to church. We'd both be heading to jail.

# 14

I called our house as soon as church was over. Sheriff Gibbons said they had dusted Joe Riddley's room for Hiram's prints and found them on the ladder-back chair, on the night-stand, and on the doorknob. "Oh, Lord," I breathed.

Buster knew me well enough to know I was praying, not swearing. "We're still looking for a weapon. Do you think it would do me any good to talk to Joe Riddley?"

"He's just finished telling Martha it was a shame she had to keep the nursery today, be-cause Hiram staggered down the aisle in the middle of the sermon, confessed all his sins, and got baptized. Do *you* think it would do you any good to talk to him?"

The way Buster sighed, I felt ice water creep through my veins. "Is he mobile at all on his own?" he asked. "Could he have gotten himself to the dining room without your help?"

"Joe Riddley didn't kill Hiram. He didn't!"

Buster was not given to raising false hopes. "We'll know more after we find the weapon. Keep asking him about the missing gun. And do you have the key to your kitchen closet? It's locked."

"I locked it for the party, and the key's here in my pocketbook. Do you need it now? We were going to Ridd and Martha's for dinner."

"Go ahead. We'll check it later."

After dinner, little Cricket asked, "Pop, can you build a tower? I got new blocks."

"I'm the best tower builder in the world," Joe Riddley informed him slowly. He looked at me anxiously. "Is 'play with Cricket' in my log?"

Joe Riddley and Cricket had always been real close, but that fall they were getting along especially well. Joe Riddley was like a three-year-old in a lot of ways, and if Pop said or did something silly, Cricket didn't get upset, he got tickled — so tickled he made Joe Riddley laugh, too. I reached out and gave Joe Riddley's hand a squeeze. " 'Play with Cricket' is in your heart, honey. You don't need it in the log." The two of them moved contentedly to Cricket's room while we grownups went to the porch to let our dinner settle. While we rocked and enjoyed the breeze, I brought them up to date.

"You mean Hiram's hat was under Daddy's bed but Daddy can't remember when Hiram was there? And Daddy was out in the backyard shooting in the middle of the night, claiming he showed Hiram how well he can shoot? And one of his guns is missing?" Ridd's voice rose in greater disbelief with each question.

"Hush!" I looked toward the open windows.

"I don't want your daddy hearing this."

"My daddy is going to get arrested for murder, Mama. They are going to put him away for the rest of his natural life, and you want me to hush?"

"I don't suppose you can identify all his guns, can you?" I asked hopefully. "Maybe the one that's missing is an entirely different kind than the one that killed Hiram."

"I might have recognized them back when I still lived there, but he's added some and gotten rid of others."

"Well, last night he told Buster and Charlie this one isn't really missing, it's 'mislaid' — whatever that means to his poor fuddled brain. He said it again today, about the cap. It's not a word I've ever heard him use before."

"Oh, dear." Martha bit her lip. "That's my fault. Yesterday when I was helping him get dressed for the party, he wanted to wear a particular tie, but I couldn't find it. He was getting so agitated that I told him it wasn't really missing, it was only mislaid. Then I explained that 'mislaid' means it was put somewhere else, we just couldn't remember where it was at that moment."

I gave a sigh from the bottom of my toes. "That man is a marvel. He can't remember whether he's had dinner half the time, then at the precisely wrong time he remembers something complicated like that."

Ridd glared. "Don't make jokes. What if

Daddy did it? What if he got mad at Hiram and shot him? If he could get to the backyard by himself, he could get to the dining room."

"Your daddy is not a killer. Hang on to that thought, son. We are all going to need it."

Martha never could stand for Ridd and me to fuss. "Did you see Selena and Maynard this morning, coming out of the Episcopal church? They're so cute. I don't know why he doesn't go ahead and ask her to marry him."

"Maynard says he can't leave Hubert." I sketched out what Maynard had said the night before.

Martha thought that over. "Why don't they take Hubert with them?"

"Maynard doesn't think he'd go. Old men get real set in their ways."

Ridd gave me a surprised frown. "I thought Hubert was the same age as Daddy."

"Old is a state of mind, honey. Hubert was born with it. Heck, it's hard enough to get him to change his underwear, much less his ways."

"Well," Martha said with determination, "I think we need to work on Maynard. If he and Selena move into Marybelle's house, there's plenty of space downstairs to fix Hubert up an apartment. We'll have to put our minds to it."

"I'm not going to put my mind to it until somebody buys the Pickens place," I told her. "I don't want to be down that road without a single neighbor."

"Have you and Pop ever thought about

moving?" She asked the question idly, but from the quick look Ridd gave her, I knew they had already talked about it.

"Not yet." I wasn't any readier to think about that than Hubert.

Martha stood. "Didn't you tell me you needed to go back to the store for an hour or two? Go ahead, and leave Pop here. You can come get him when you're done."

I kept my windows down as I drove toward the square. The courthouse clock chimed two, its voice deep and quiet as befitted an autumn Sunday. The air was tinged with that certain smell that says the earth is gently decaying and getting ready for winter. Birds celebrated their homecoming from northern summer vacations with excited chirps and whistles.

On a whim, I decided to run by to see Meriwether's new house. I hadn't had a reason to drive down Liberty Street lately, and I was dying to see how it had turned out.

Liberty Street isn't as fancy as Oglethorpe, but is lovely in its own way. Most of the houses were built in the eighteen hundreds, and many have recently been bought by couples with growing families. Unlike on Oglethorpe, children on Liberty Street played ball, rode bikes, and skated while parents read papers or chatted on their porches.

I pulled up to the curb and stopped to look. Meriwether's house had always been pretty — a white one-story Victorian with gingerbread trim at the eaves. But her choice of soft cream paint with subtle accents in slate blue and dark burgundy had transformed it into a beauty. Just at the gable of the roof I saw the touch of dark green Phyllis had mentioned.

Two huge white-and-gold ceramic planters decorated with dark green Chinese characters flanked the steps. "Burgundy mums sure would look gorgeous in those pots," I called as Meriwether waved from the swing where she'd been studying an enormous piece of paper.

"Come in and take the tour," she invited.

Slade was reading a paper in one of three porch rockers, long legs stretched in front of him like he owned the place. He was stunning in tan slacks and a dark brown sweater. Meriwether was gorgeous as usual, even in jeans and a plain white shirt. She lay down her paper and met me on the steps. "I'm real proud of it," she said happily.

I admired lace curtains in the front windows and a shining new brass mail slot, then followed Meriwether from room to room, cooing like a demented creature over oak kitchen cabinets, Italian bathroom tiles, newly refinished heart pine floors, and restored high ceilings.

"You're a tad short on furniture," I pointed out. The rooms were almost bare.

"Candi took almost everything. I'm going to Augusta tomorrow for some basics."

"You could always shove a few boxes together for sofas and tables," I suggested, peering into

186

the back bedroom. "You've got enough of them." The room was littered with cardboard cartons stamped with Chinese characters.

"Those are my secret," Meriwether said conspiratorially. "But before I tell you about it, let me get you some tea. Grab yourself a rocker and I'll be right out."

While I waited, I peered at the paper she'd been reading, an architect's rendering. "Is she planning to build another house?" I asked Slade, who was working a crossword.

He answered without looking up. "No, she's got a bee in her bonnet. She'll have to tell you about it. Do you know the French word for summer?"

"I think it's e-t-e."

"That's right. You'd think, after all the times I've been there —" He penciled it in as Meriwether brought iced tea in enormous plastic cups. "Sorry about the size." She set them down on a glass-topped table. "The Bi-Lo was out of smaller ones."

"They sold them all to me." The tea was cold and sweet, but weak. Meriwether hadn't mastered good tea yet. "What's that big paper you were so interested in when I got here?"

That was the only nickel her jukebox needed. "The plan of Granddaddy's warehouse, down by the railroad. I'm going to have it fixed up for my business."

"What kind of business?" I asked encouragingly.

"A pot business. On our trip, I started noticing different kinds of pots. Flowerpots, yard pots, kitchen pots, bathroom pots —" She turned a delicate pink and gave an embarrassed laugh. "I mean the kind you can put cotton balls in, or pretty soaps. I started buying some for my house, like those planters by the steps, then I thought, why not get some to sell when we get home? Every woman in the world needs pots."

"You think you can sell enough in Hopemore to make it worth your while?"

Her laugh pealed over her yard. "Heavens, no. I'll have a small store here, but mostly I'll sell by catalogue and on the Internet." She couldn't have looked any prouder if she'd been Columbus sighting land. "I'm going to call it Pots of Luck, and offer pots from all over the world. Pretty pots for scrubbers by the sink. Pots to hold finger towels in your bathroom."

"Not to mention flowerpots," I agreed. "I've been wishing we could get rid of the pottery side of our business. You are welcome to it, if you like."

"Thanks. The only thing I'd worried about was competing with you all."

If she thought that was her only worry, she had a lot to learn. But she was prattling on. "The ones in the back are just what I could send or bring back with me. I have several more shipments coming. I'm going to renovate Granddaddy's warehouse to hold the stock, and I've got a consultant coming next week to talk about how to get started. I think it will be fantastic. I'll have things for every pocketbook, from almost every country in the world. I figure I'll hire at least twenty people eventually." Meriwether's cheeks were flushed and her eyes sparkling. Slade seemed a bit sour on the idea — possibly because pots had given her an animation his own company hadn't yet achieved.

"Hopemore can certainly use that," I admitted. "I don't know if I've ever seen a catalogue just for pots, either, and if I don't get it, it doesn't exist."

I was just about to mention Hiram when Gusta's Cadillac purred to a stop out front. "Don't talk about pots now," Meriwether warned. "Nana's not real happy about the idea."

"You still talking pots?" Gusta demanded, pushing her walker up the front walk. Even though she hadn't been at church, she had dressed up for dinner in a gold silk blouse and her black Sunday suit. Alice looked like a quiet mole behind her in a dark brown skirt and sweater. She offered Gusta an arm to help her ascend the front steps. Gusta clutched her hard, but Alice didn't flinch. I might have to join the town betting pool and place my nickel on Alice staying. Most folks thought she'd hightail it back to Macon by Christmas.

Gusta took the rocker Slade offered and said icily, "My granddaughter can't even boil water, yet she fancies herself the queen of pots. If my brother the senator had known our family would one day be selling pots —"

I winked at Meriwether. "Pot wasn't his problem." Gusta gave me a frosty gray glare. Meriwether managed not to laugh, but barely. Alice and Slade were the only people there who didn't know that Gusta's brother was such a drunk his aides had to hold him up when he went to the Senate to vote. Why he served three terms had always been another mystery of the universe. But at least that shut Gusta up about pots.

Alice took the rocker beside mine. When Meriwether didn't move over to make room on the swing, Slade leaned against the porch rail, still clutching his puzzle.

"Were you all right this morning, Augusta? We missed you at church, and I hoped you weren't ill." He beamed his lovely smile straight at her. Gusta thawed. That man could charm cats down from trees.

"Jet lag," Gusta replied with dignity. "And all that gallivanting at MacLaren's yesterday."

"It was a great party," Alice told me shyly.

"Thank you, honey. My husband's physical therapist was certainly smitten with you. He asked me to find out if you get time off."

"Of course she gets time off," Gusta snapped. "She goes for a run every morning."

"That doesn't count," I informed her. "Darren meant a day off, or an evening."

190

"All she has to do is ask. But isn't he the one with bright yellow hair?"

"This week. Sometimes it's green, or purple. But he's charming," I told her firmly, "and very good at what he does."

Alice looked at the porch floor, but she wore a secret little smile.

Gusta had bigger things on her mind than her companion's love life. She glared at Meriwether, looking like thunderclouds had permanently settled on her forehead. "I see you are still serving in plastic cups. You know a lady does not serve guests in plastic."

"This lady serves in plastic until I can get to Augusta in the morning."

"Augusta? What do you need in Augusta?"

Slade threw back his head and laughed. "Oh, just furniture, dishes, a table and chairs, a sofa — a few necessities."

Gusta's old lips pinched together. I could almost hear the struggle going on inside her. Finally she clutched the arms of her rocker to sustain her, and demanded, "Why didn't you ask? I probably have some old stuff lying around the attic you could use."

It was a major concession. Maynard had been permitted one brief glimpse of Gusta's attic and had been drooling ever since.

"Come over tomorrow," she said with a grand wave. "Take what you want. It'll all be yours one day, anyhow." She gave Slade, not Meriwether, a frosty smile.

Meriwether's eyes widened in astonishment, but she was smart enough to only say, "That would be wonderful. Thanks."

If I was going to ask any questions about Hiram, it was time. "I'm surprised you sent poor Alice out so early yesterday," I told Gusta. Seeing Alice's equal surprise, I added, "I saw your car in the Bi-Lo parking lot around eight-thirty, when I was leaving the beauty parlor."

"I didn't hear you go out," Gusta said severely.

Meriwether laughed. "When have you gotten up before nine? We could all go out and come in a hundred times, and you'd never know a thing."

Alice flushed. "I had to — uh — get something personal from the store." She shot Slade a quick, embarrassed look. He didn't look up from his puzzle, but I regretted bringing it up. Trust me to call attention to a person's private needs in public.

Gusta must have felt as sorry as I did about it, because she leaned over and gave Alice a pat. "Never mind. You have to get a breath of air from time to time." Meriwether gave her a skeptical look. She'd been at her grandmother's beck and call twenty-four hours a day.

"This girl has such a good head for business," Gusta boasted. "She's saving me time these days, and time is money. Have you ever used a stamp to sign checks you're going to deposit, Mac?"

"All the time, Gusta." I was wondering how to ask Meriwether and Slade whether they'd seen anybody or anything suspicious early Saturday. But Gusta wasn't through with rubber stamps.

"I'd never thought of such a thing. But Alice ordered one before we left, and it was waiting when we got back. Now, instead of writing my name on every check, I just stamp 'For deposit only to the account of Augusta Wainwright' on everything." She made a stamping motion with one hand. "It even has my account number on it, so they can't make a mistake."

"That's a great idea," I told her. "Next Alice will be suggesting you get a computer to keep your bank accounts straight."

"Not just my bank accounts," Gusta announced triumphantly, "but all my lists, too. Remember all those envelopes we used to have to hand address, Meriwether? Alice says we can put the lists on the computer, with phone numbers and addresses for everybody, then when we need to send out a mailing, we can print out just the labels we need. The computer will sort out who's in hospital auxiliary, or the Garden Club, the D.A.R., the A.A.U.W. —"

"That's great." If I hadn't interrupted, Gusta might have listed every organization in town, and it's amazing how many groups a town as small as Hopemore can have.

"She even says we can put my rents ledger on the computer and know exactly who has paid and who hasn't," Gusta finished proudly.

"Fancy that," I said, as if I hadn't been using computers for the past umpteen years.

"Are you planning to buy a computer?" Meriwether didn't believe it any more than I did.

"She brought one with her." Gusta reached over and patted Alice on the knee.

"It was my sister's." Alice sounded apologetic for owning something so modern.

"If you can bring Nana into the computer age, I'll buy you a dinner," Meriwether offered. But I noticed her eyes had narrowed a bit while they were talking. Could Meriwether possibly be jealous? The little I'd seen of Alice, she wasn't competing with anybody for anything.

Slade looked at his watch, and I knew I ought to go. But I hadn't found out what I'd come for. Maybe the best thing to do was shake everybody up and watch for a guilty reaction. "Did you all hear Hiram Blaine got shot yesterday?"

Meriwether gasped. Alice froze. Slade asked, "Who?" Looked like perfectly normal responses to me.

Gusta got pink and her gray eyes glared at me. I knew she was mad because I hadn't told her first. To pay me back, she said, "I don't suppose Walker Crane Yarbrough had anything to do with it, did he? He's got a whale of a temper."

I opened my mouth to speak more hotly than I should to an elderly woman, but Alice jerked her foot and kicked over my tea.

"Sorry! I dropped my paper," Slade apologized, retrieving it from Alice's lap. "Do you want another glass, MacLaren?"

I drew my feet away from the running tea. "I've already drunk enough, but we ought to get some water and wash this up, or you'll have ants."

Slade caused the accident, but Alice went for the water. As soon as she'd gone, Slade griped, "I don't know why they haven't informed me about his death. We'll need to cover it in the *Statesman*. Our lines of communication with law enforcement agencies leave a great deal —"

I didn't want to listen to a diatribe about the informal way our former editor gathered news, so I interrupted. "Be sure to interview folks about Hiram, to get his whole story. He lived here most of his life, even if he's been away a few years." I paused, then added, "He told me he went by the paper and offered to write a weekly column, but you turned him down."

I watched closely for his response. He looked merely puzzled until I prodded, "A filthy man in a red Yarbrough's hat, with a big red parrot?"

"The one who thought aliens were heading for Hopemore any minute?" When I nodded, he slapped his paper against his leg. "Yeah, he came in. Offered me a column a week about aliens — how to prepare for invasion, how to tell them from other people, things like that. When I told him we weren't interested, he stomped out furious. At the door he warned me I'd be sorry when they landed."

"Poor Hiram," Meriwether said softly. "He told great knock-knock jokes."

Slade transformed himself before our eyes from a Sunday porch potato to a working man. "Honey, do you mind if I go over to the police station?"

"Go ahead." Meriwether looked like she minded being called "honey" in front of her relatives and friends a whole lot more.

He headed down the walk.

"You'd do better to go to the sheriff's," I called after him. "The crime was committed in his jurisdiction."

He turned. "You know where he was killed?"

"In my dining room, yesterday morning. Police Chief Muggins found him behind one of my screens in the middle of the party."

"Oh, no!" Meriwether gasped. Alice, who was coming out the screened door, stayed inside. Maybe she was worried she might be in danger just being around me.

"I'll want to interview you later." Slade pulled keys from his pocket. "But I want to talk with the sheriff first."

"Anytime." I waved him on his way.

Nobody on that porch had a thing to hide that I could see. I stood. "I need to be going, too. I'm supposed to be down at the store while Cricket baby-sits Joe Riddley. Your house is beautiful, Meriwether. *Southern Living* ought to be around any day with cameras."

"The loony bin will be around any day with

their truck," her grandmother replied testily, "unless we can get her to give up this catalogue business notion."

I left them to their wrangling. On the way back to the store, though, I tried to figure out what made Slade drop that paper. He looked to me like he'd seen a ghost.

# 15

Since I had to pass Pooh's house on the way to the store, I decided to stop and tell her about Hiram. I hated for Gusta to know more than Pooh.

"She's in her Cozy," Lottie informed me, leading me to a back room with ruffled curtains, flowered fabrics, and a small desk with inviting pigeonholes overflowing with envelopes. Photographs filled every surface — a diminutive blond bride and groom beaming at one another, the same couple holding an infant, Zachary at seven or eight with a hose pouring water over his freckled face and into his wide-open mouth, Zachary in his graduation tuxedo with his hair slicked back with so much water it looked dark, Zachary in his Air Force uniform looking far too young to die. Pooh sat in an electrically powered chair that tilted to help her stand, situated next to the back window where she could look out and see birds. A good reading lamp stood behind it and a little mahogany table beside her held a glass of tea and a plate of Toll House cookies. She'd been reading the Bible and listening to Chopin etudes, but her face brightened when I came in. "MacLaren! How nice to see you! Lottie, bring her some tea, please."

Lottie trudged back to the kitchen with such a worried look that an uninformed guest might have wondered if there was enough in the larder to feed us. But Lottie wasn't worried about that any more than she was worried we'd tell Pooh the cookies and tea were made without sugar. Pooh lived in blissful ignorance of most things Lottie did to control her diabetes.

Lottie looked worried because she'd looked worried all her life. Joe Riddley claimed she took one look at her no-good mama, knew she'd have a lot to worry about in life, and decided to get on with it. As a child she'd had a small worried face that gradually settled into permanent worry wrinkles. Worry in no way soured her disposition or her cookies.

I settled on the love seat across from Pooh. "You had such a nice party yesterday." Pooh leaned forward and beamed. "I doubt anybody ever did a nicer thing for Bud."

"For Joe Riddley," I reminded her. "Bud's been gone twenty years."

Pooh smacked one cheek with her small palm. "How could I forget that? He had the loveliest funeral." She lowered her voice. "Sometimes I get the tiniest bit confused. Otis gets very angry with me, but I tell him by the time he gets to be my age, he'll know so much he'll have to forget some of it, too." I pictured Pooh's mind as a small computer — pink, of course — so full that programs couldn't move. She wasn't forgetting, her hard drive was just freezing up.

"Otis doesn't get mad at you very often, does he?" I reached for one of Lottie's good cookies. If I hadn't known better, I'd have sworn they were full of sugar and calories.

Pooh sighed and shook her gray curls. "He got *very* angry one day. I went for a little walk, and he thought I was lost." Her eyes snapped with indignation. "Looks like a person could have some time alone once in a while without everybody havin' a fit."

"It certainly does." I stood up. "Excuse me a minute. I need the powder room."

"Of course, dear. You know where it is."

Otis must have still been at church, but Lottie sat at the kitchen table watching a nature program on television. "When did Pooh get lost?" I demanded, propping against a cabinet.

Lottie slewed her eyes my way. "Who's been telling tales out of school?"

"Pooh herself. She said she got lost and Otis got angry with her. When was that?"

She scratched a scab on her arm. "Yesterday, real early. When I went to help her get up, she was gone, power chair and all. She mostly uses the power chair in the house and yard, because Otis can't be liftin' it in and out of the car. Once in a while I take her for what we call 'a little walk' down the block and back, but she never took it off the property alone before." Lottie made little clicking noises with her tongue and echoed my worry about Joe Riddley. "If she can get out of the house by herself, there's no tellin' where she might end up."

"Where did she end up yesterday?"

She shook her head. "We don't rightly know. Otis drove up and down every street in town lookin' for her, thinkin' she couldn't have got far. But we didn't know when she left, see. And the way that chair can go, she could have gone clean out to your place."

Fear clutched my heart, but I forced myself to stay practical. "Not down the gravel road."

"Oh, she could make the chair go on that road, all right, as good as you keep it. I'm not saying she didn't, either. Her chair was pretty dusty when she got back."

I had to pull out a chair and sit down. "Where and when did you find her?"

"We didn't. Sometime past nine-thirty she showed up back here at the house, on her own. Otis had been out combin' those streets for nigh on two hours, checkin' by here every now and then. I was gettin' real worried, because she was past time for her shot. He came back to report to me that he couldn't find her, and there sat Miss Winifred pert as anything, right here in her own backyard like she hadn't ever left the place. Her face was red and hot, and she was sweatin' some, but she wouldn't say a word about where she'd been or what she'd done. Said 'twas none of our business." She twisted her mouth in what passed for her smile. "She said maybe she'd been courtin'."

"This could be very serious, Lottie. Otis told you we took all the guns out of the house, didn't he? But there was one missing."

"That little bitty one? I think Miss Gusta's still got it."

"Gusta said she *might* have it." I sighed. "Which means she might have given it back to Pooh. I want you to search this house again, as carefully as you know how — the downstairs, at least. Hiram Blaine was shot yesterday morning early down at our place, with a little gun."

Lottie pressed a thin hand to her equally thin chest. "Miss Winifred never!"

"I hope not, but he'd been deviling Pooh earlier in the week, and if you think she could navigate our road, we need to be absolutely sure. You look for that gun, all right?"

"I'll look," Lottie agreed. "I haven't seen that little gun around here for some time, but if Miss Winifred wanted to keep it from me, she's got her ways."

"Let me know if you find out anything," I said as I left her.

I went back into the Cozy and sat down on the love seat before I remembered I'd passed up my chance to visit the powder room. Pooh looked up and offered, "Would you like another cookie, dear?"

"No, I don't want any more cookies. But I want to know where you were yesterday morning. Lottie says you went out for awhile all by yourself."

Her eyes slid from one side to the other, then she looked down as if fascinated by her enormous engagement diamond. "I went out to get fresh air."

"But why didn't Otis see you? He drove up and down all the streets."

She giggled like a little girl. "I hid. I watched very carefully, and when I saw him, I pulled behind a bush. He passed me several times, but he never knew I was there."

Poor Otis. Poor all of us, if this got any worse. But I simply had to know where she had been. "He said maybe you'd been down to my house. I was over at Phyllis's getting my hair fixed. Did I miss you?"

Her lips closed up as tight as a drawstring bag. "I'm not going to tell you, so you needn't ask." Pooh waved me away. "Can I have Lottie bring you some more tea?" A doubtful expression began to gather on her face. I could tell she wasn't quite sure now how long I'd been there or how much tea I'd had. In another second her eyes took on the blank look we had all come to know and dread.

As I left, she leaned forward and gave me her hand. "Thank you so much for coming." She might not be real sure at that moment who I was or why I was there, but courtesy would be the last part of Pooh's mind to go.

# 16

I'd been gone so long, I stopped by the store just long enough to get Joe Riddley a new hat, then went back to Ridd and Martha's. "Wanna see something cute?" Ridd greeted me with a finger to his lips.

We tiptoed to Cricket's room. Joe Riddley lay on the bed in white shirt, gray pants, and black socks, snoring. Cricket lay beside him in gray pants, white shirt, and red socks, gently patting his chest. A beagle pup slept on the floor, curled beside two pairs of black Sunday shoes.

Cricket sensed our presence, looked around, and put one finger to his own lips. "Shhh," he warned. We smiled and backed out.

I heard Cricket slide to the floor and pad after us. "I put Pop down for his nap."

"That's wonderful, honey. I wish you'd put Me-mama down for one, too."

"Want to run on home?" Martha offered. "Ridd can bring Pop when he wakes up."

"I'll follow you," Ridd informed me. "I want to have a look around for the missing you-know-what while Daddy's not there."

"I doesn't know what," Cricket said. "What?"

I don't believe in keeping secrets from children unless absolutely necessary. They are so apt to get things garbled. "We're missing one of Pop's guns, honey."

"De deer wifle? Or de shotgun? Or is it de twenty-two wifle he got when he was ten?"

The grownups stared in surprise. "How do you know so much, Little Britches?" Ridd ruffled his son's soft brown hair.

Cricket shrugged. "Pop tole me. I know of all de guns." His chest stuck out with pride.

"Do you know which one goes where in the case?" I asked, hardly daring to hope.

"O' course. Dey all has special places."

"Do you think he does?" Martha gave Ridd a worried frown. They didn't approve of guns.

Ridd's shrug was very like his son's. "Only one way to find out. Let's go for a ride, Little Britches. We're gonna follow Me-mama home and you can tell her what you know about the guns. Okay?"

"Okay." Cricket headed happily for the door.

"Get your shoes," Martha reminded him.

Buster and his men were gone and had taken the crime tape from the dining room door. They'd left a legacy of fingerprint dust Clarinda was going to love, and the barbeque and potato salad on the table were as pungent as I'd predicted. What repelled me most was the memory of Hiram. It would be a while before I served a meal in there again.

At least they'd taken my junk mail as evidence.

When we stood in front of the gun case, Cricket shook his head in disbelief. "Somebody stole *all* Pop's guns! He's gonna be *so mad*. . . ." He pursed his lips and shook his head, speechless for once.

I put a hand on his shoulder. "No, honey, Memama sent them away while Pop is sick. I don't want him getting into the guns and hurting himself."

He nodded wisely. "Guns is berry dangerous if you doesn't use good sense. And sometimes Pop doesn't *have* good sense right now. He's berry sick."

Ridd and I exchanged smiles over his head. Mine was full of gratitude that they'd made things so blessedly clear and unfrightening to that little boy.

"Do you really remember which gun used to go where?" Ridd asked dubiously.

"Sure." Cricket's small forefinger pressed the bottom of the glass. "Dis one was de deer wifle. Pop will take me huntin' when I'm big enough. And dat" — he moved his finger up a notch — "was de wifle Pop got when he was ten, from his daddy." His eyes slid sideways to me, a sure sign he was talking to Ridd as well. "My daddy doesn't gib me guns, 'cause he doesn't like dem. But Pop will gib me one when I gets ten."

"Oh." I didn't dare say more than that. I pressed my own finger up at the top of the case. "I'll bet you don't know which one went way up here."

Cricket flung back his head and gurgled at my silliness. "Co'se I do. Dat was de derringer twenty-two." He looked up to explain to his daddy, "Twenty-two means it's got a little hole." Then he looked seriously back at me. "It's silber and berry old, and it looks like a toy, but it's *not*." He shook his head solemnly. "Boys must not touch guns, eben if dey looks like toys. I can't touch *any* guns 'til Pop says I'm old 'nough, or he'll gib me a *hidin'!*" He gave his head one short nod. Ridd and I both burst out laughing. Cricket looks like Martha, but that minute he was the spitting image of his granddaddy.

"It's not funny," Cricket warned, fist propped on hip. "Guns is serious bidness. Pop says so. Pop says nebber touch a gun wifout him standing right dere and saying 'okay.' "

I knew Ridd was seething inside at how much his father had taught his son. I hoped he also appreciated how very much Cricket had absorbed about safety. Joe Riddley had been very thorough in that respect.

Ridd suggested, "Why don't you two go get Lulu out of the pen and play with her a little bit? I've got one more thing to do before we leave."

Cricket ran happily toward the kitchen. "I'll search for the gun, if you'll keep him outside a few minutes," Ridd promised.

"The police have already looked, but go ahead."

I went out to help Cricket let Lulu out. They

greeted one another with mutual raptures and neither paid a speck of attention when I said, "I'm going to run inside and get my slippers. My feet hurt." I headed toward the kitchen closet, where I kept yard clothes, coats, boots, and house slippers. When I got the door unlocked, I kicked off my shoes faster than a fat goose sheds water. My freed toes wiggled for joy, but only found one slipper when they fumbled on the closet floor. I bent over to have a better look and saw the mate hiding in the far back.

As I reached for it, I knocked over one of Joe Riddley's cowboy boots, the old ones he wore to mow the lawn. They'd been standing unused so long they were gray with dust.

I picked up one dust-fuzzy boot and held it to my cheek, wondering if he'd ever need it again. Then, angry at myself for being silly, I shoved it to the back of the closet. "There's no point in you taking up space near the front when he's not using you." When I picked up the second, it was heavier than the first. Puzzled, I shook the boot into the empty wastebasket, in case it harbored a mouse. What fell out was a small silver gun.

A wave of terror took away my breath. Only two people in the world knew where Joe Riddley kept the key to his gun case. Before Ridd even began to crawl, Joe Riddley came in one day with a scruffy old book. "Look, Little Bit. What I've been wanting."

I examined the title. "*History of the Etruscans?* You're pretty desperate for reading matter, aren't you?"

"Look!" He opened the cover and showed me hollow pages, glued to make a box for hiding things. He took the key to his gun case from his desk drawer and dropped it into the box with a satisfying clunk. "Now nobody will open that case by accident." He put the book up high on his shelf, along with others that were read as seldom as they were dusted. "Let's make a pact, honey. Don't ever tell or show anybody where that key is. That's the only way I'll ever have peace of mind."

Peace of mind. As I knelt before my waste-basket, those three words bounced around in my suddenly empty brain. "Oh, honey," I whispered. Only Joe Riddley could have opened that gun case. And I could think of only one reason why he'd take out a gun and later hide it. Joe Riddley was, as I have said, in some ways a little like Cricket just then. He probably thought if he hid the gun, nobody would ever know what he'd done.

I should have called Ridd, but I couldn't. I wanted to pull that gun out, wipe it so shiny clean nobody would ever know it had been handled since the day it was made, and dump it in Hubert's cattle pond. However, being an officer of the law has certain disadvantages. I knew better than to tamper with evidence. Still, Buster wasn't going to get this evidence quite yet — not until I'd had time to think.

Hearing Ridd moving toward the kitchen, I carefully lifted the gun with a fork and dropped it back in the boot. Then I relocked the closet and hurried out to our backyard swing. When Ridd arrived I was watching Cricket chase Lulu around the birdbath.

Ridd settled his long frame onto the other side of the swing. "I looked in the study and Daddy's room. Even looked in the bathroom. But I could tell the police searched already." He pushed the swing to move it gently. In the maple overhead a mockingbird sang, then flew into the sky. "Have you and Daddy ever thought about moving out of this isolated place?" There it was again, that casual tone that meant he and Martha had talked about it already.

"Not recently. Our minds have been rather otherwise occupied."

"This place is a lot of work. Why don't you look for a smaller house closer to town?"

Cricket shouted from the birdbath. "If you moves, Me-mama, I can come live here."

Ridd gave a grunt of embarrassment.

"Little jugs have big ears," I reminded him, rubbing his own closest ear. "He takes after somebody we both know and love."

"Hello! Hello!" A squawk from the barn reminded me of somebody I certainly didn't love. Lulu scampered toward the door, barking furiously. Cricket hared right behind.

Ridd stopped the swing. "What on earth?"

210

I pulled myself to my feet. "Come meet our guest."

When I opened the barn door. Joe swooped down and landed on my head. Cricket danced and giggled. Lulu put her paws on my knees and griped noisily. Ridd stared in disbelief. Joe must have seen his resemblance to Joe Riddley, because he flew to his shoulder.

"Scat!" Ridd backed away, swatting air. "Get off me! Get off!"

"I wants him!" Cricket jumped up and down. Lulu leaped and yelped. Joe squawked. The yard dogs tuned up for a chorus.

I thought for a second about hightailing it to the house, locking the door, and going for a nap, but there are responsibilities never mentioned in the motherhood manual.

I reached up my arm. "Come here, Joe!"

For a wonder, he obeyed. He hopped onto my arm, and then back to the top of my head. Cricket shrieked with delight. Lulu started another aria.

"Put Lulu back in the pen and go on home," I told Ridd. "Bring your daddy when he's ready to come. And don't ask any questions, just go!"

For a second wonder, Ridd obeyed me, too, without a word.

I took Joe to the lawnmower and nudged him until he hopped onto the handle. He perched on one foot like he'd lived there all his life. "I'll get you some food," I promised. I headed to the kitchen, figuring the dogs could hush when they were ready. They weren't bothering anybody but me. "Just what the doctor ordered," I muttered. "A day of quiet rest."

When I bent to get a water bowl from the lower cabinet, my knees went off like little firecrackers. A voice spoke in my head, clear as could be. *You and Joe Riddley are ten years older than his parents were when they moved into town and gave you this house. You're almost exactly the age Joe Riddley's grandparents were when they died and left the house to Joe Riddley's daddy and his family — who had already been living with them for over ten years.*

"People live longer these days," I answered out loud, getting Joe some vegetables.

*That's no reason for standing in your children's way. If Ridd and Martha lived here, they'd be near their fields. Bethany and Cricket would love having the pool and all this space to run around. And you know how Martha's been wanting to adopt a couple of children with special needs. They can't put any more children in the house they've got.*

"I don't have time to stand around here like Joan of Arc, listening to voices. I've got a bird to feed and water." The voice didn't reply, but I had a suspicion it was biding its time.

When I got the barn door opened, Joe huddled up on the far rafters, a splash of bright in the dimness. "Dinnertime," I told him. I set the bowl down on a dusty shelf and held out my palm full of broccoli. He fixed me with a baleful eye and didn't budge. "Then starve. I've done the best I can." I put the food beside the water.

"Back off. Back off!"

"Gladly. See you later."

I left him on the rafter, cheeks pink and tail feathers drooping. He shrieked behind me, "Good *morning*, Hiram! Good *morning*, Hiram!" It was almost enough to break my heart. But not enough to waken Hiram.

I heard a car on the road. Surely it wasn't Ridd back already. When I saw Darren's little yellow Beetle, I couldn't help a groan of dismay.

"Hey!" he called, climbing out. He wore white shorts and a bright blue shirt. Alice sat beside him, in white shorts and a white top. "We're going over to the high school track to run, but first we thought we'd come see how J.R.'s doing today."

I knew darned well he just wanted to show me he'd gotten her to go out with him. Boys are the same in every generation. I hoped I could keep my eyes open long enough to speed them on their way. "He's fine, but he's over at our son's. I was heading up for a nap."

"We won't keep you, then. Just wanted to say hello. You know Alice, don't you?"

"Sure. Hey, Alice. How're you doing?"

She gave me a little wave through the windshield. Neither of us mentioned we'd been drinking iced tea together earlier that day. Let Darren enjoy his triumph.

"Have fun." I hoped my feet weren't sending

down roots where I stood. Another day, I'd have offered a piece of cake and some tea. Right now I wanted to stretch out and sleep for hours.

Alice opened her door. "Would you mind — could I —" She gave me a look women always recognize.

"Sure, honey. It's right inside at the back of the hall. I'll show you."

I nearly had a heart attack, though, when she tripped just inside the kitchen door and grabbed at the closet doorknob to steady herself.

While she was in the bathroom, I sat at the kitchen table and looked at that door sourly. What was I going to do about that gun?

I was so deep in sleep I don't know how long Joe Riddley was calling before I heard him. "Little Bit? Get down here right now! Little Bit! Did you hear me? Get on down here, now."

Just as I was thinking maybe I ought to try to open my eyes and see if my legs could still function, a small sharp finger pried open one of my eyelids. "Me-mama? Pop wants you."

I pushed away his hand and sighed. "So I hear." I reached for my robe. As we clumped down the stairs, I felt so heavy and tired I made almost as much noise as he did.

"Little Bit!" Joe Riddley growled as I rounded the newel post of the landing. "Call Buster. Somebody's stolen all my guns!"

He was sitting enthroned in his wheelchair, facing the stairs. Ridd, behind him, apologized.

"I'm afraid Cricket let the cat out of the bag that they're gone."

Cricket plunged down the last few steps and went to press against his daddy's leg, afraid he'd be punished. When Ridd cupped the small head in one hand, Cricket relaxed a little, but his brown eyes met mine anxiously.

I tied the belt on my robe and rubbed my eyes, hoping to persuade them to join me in waking up. "He'd have found out soon anyway," I reassured Cricket.

"Where are those guns?" Joe Riddley demanded. "I need them to go hunting."

I stifled a yawn. "I, uh — I sent them to be cleaned."

"Nobody cleans my guns but me. You know that. Where'd you send them?"

I thought fast. If I told him Maynard had them, he'd find a way to demand that Maynard return them. If I lied —

I was tired of making up stories and pussy-footing around, treating Joe Riddley like he was no older than Cricket. I pulled the chair Gusta had used the day before so it faced him, and bent over so my hands rested on his knees. Leaning over so we were eye-to-eye, I said, "I'm not telling you where they are until you get better. I don't want you accidentally hurting yourself or somebody else."

He gave a huff of disgust. "I'm not going to hurt anybody, and you know it. I want those guns back and I want them now!" He pounded the arm of his wheelchair. "You hear me, Little Bit? I want those guns back *right now!*"

I covered my ears with my hands. "Don't you shout at me! You're not getting those guns until you are well."

"I am well. I just can't walk. There's nothing wrong with my aim."

The old Joe Riddley was as calm as a barn owl on a dark night. It was me who got excited and raised my voice. Having him yell at me now enraged me.

"There's something wrong with your *head!* Going out in the backyard stark naked at three A.M. to practice shooting the side of the barn. Who knows what you might have hit? Or who? You even aimed that gun at me. Don't tell me how well you are!" All my anger gathered in one big cloud and burst in a torrent of tears. Heaving with sobs, I didn't even try to stop the words pouring out. "You scared me to death last night. I don't ever want to go through that again. You're not getting those guns back until I say so."

Out of the corner of my eye, I saw Cricket pressing his face into his daddy's leg. Ridd put one hand on Joe Riddley's shoulder. "Mama's trying to protect you, Daddy."

Joe Riddley smacked him away. "I don't need protecting. Get off my property. You hear me? Get off and don't come back. I don't need you telling me what to do, or your mother stealing my things." When Ridd didn't move, he shouted, "You hear what I said, boy? Get out.

Now! I never want to see your ugly face again."

Ridd threw me an anxious look. I shoved my chair away from his daddy's and flapped one hand at him. "Go on home," I said wearily. "You know he doesn't mean it."

"I damn well do mean it, and I mean it now!" Joe Riddley seized one wheel of his chair and jerked it. "Get!" Ridd had to jump back to avoid being hit by the whirling footrests.

"You not 'posed to say dat word, Pop," Cricket admonished in a scared little voice. "Dat's a bad word."

I couldn't bear for Joe Riddley to swear at Cricket. "Go home, Ridd," I said quickly, though tears nearly choked me. "Go home and take Cricket. I can deal with this. Go!"

Ridd pushed Cricket ahead of him down the hall. We heard Cricket start to ask, "Is Pop —" and heard Ridd reply before he'd even finished, "He's real sick, honey." The kitchen door slammed. In a minute Martha's car started and headed down our drive.

They'd brought the car because Joe Riddley wasn't up to climbing up into the truck yet. Joe Riddley wasn't up to so many things. . . .

I looked his way, braced for another tirade. Instead, he sat with his head bent and hands clasped in his lap. Tears fell from his eyes onto the backs of his large dear hands. With difficulty, he formed the sentences in phrases, with pauses in between. "I'm not good . . . for nothin'. Might as well . . . take me . . . out back

. . . and shoot me." His whole body heaved with sobs.

Tears streamed down my own cheeks and fell warm onto the backs of my hands. I knelt by his chair and reached out one wet hand to cover his. We sat in the dimness and sobbed together.

# 17

Sheriff Gibbons didn't come back that night to open the closet, for which I was grateful.

I didn't sleep well, but at least Joe Riddley woke as if he didn't remember anything about the day before except one. "Where's Joe?" he demanded as soon as he plodded into the kitchen.

"In the barn where he belongs."

"Go get him. I want Joe." He pushed his walker to the table and sat down, waiting.

Half an hour later, Clarinda surveyed the ruin Joe had made of her old blue sweater and tightened her lips. "Mmm-mmm-mmm. I ain't cleaning up after no parrot."

"Me, neither," I agreed. "He's going to stay in the barn until we get rid of him."

At that very minute, Joe was sitting on Joe Riddley's shoulder at the breakfast table, sharing his toast and tiny bits of bacon. Clarinda was sweeping up oatmeal where Joe had knocked over the box. I was scrubbing parrot doo off the faucets.

"You got any other sweater I can use?" Clarinda moved toward the kitchen closet.

"Not in there!" I spoke so emphatically I startled us both. "I forgot where I put the key."

"In your pocketbook." She started to hand it to me from the counter.

"It's not there," I assured her. "I mislaid it." Mislaid it in my skirt pocket, where nobody would get it except over my dead body. "I'll find you another sweater upstairs."

Joe Riddley reached for his new red cap and put it on. Joe pecked the red bill joyfully. "Good morning, Hiram!"

"Where is Hiram?" Joe Riddley looked around like the man had left a minute before.

Clarinda and I exchanged a glance. "He's gone away for a while," she explained.

"And we're keeping the bird until Hector comes for him," I added.

"Or hell freezes over." Clarinda turned to her dishpan and started running hot water.

When we were finally ready to leave for physical therapy, the danged parrot refused to let me take him to the barn. "Take him with us. He's no trouble." Joe Riddley ran one long finger down Joe's rainbow back. Joe nibbled his ear. "I won't go without him."

"Go away! Go away!" Joe squawked at me.

"Great. Now instead of folks talking about crazy Hiram with his parrot, they can talk about the crazy Yarbroughs." But I didn't really care what people thought. People could say what they liked, so long as stroking Joe brought that look of quiet satisfaction to Joe Riddley's face.

When I helped them both into Joe Riddley's big gray Towncar, Joe obligingly hopped down onto Joe Riddley's thigh for the ride.

Joe Riddley's smile widened to a grin. "Crazy Yarbroughs. Can you say that, boy? What all can you say? Hello, hello, hello?" I had never seen Joe Riddley so animated since he got shot. When Joe repeated "Hello, hello," Joe Riddley threw back his head and laughed like he used to.

While we slowly made our way into the physical therapy center and toward Darren's daffodil hair, I called to make sure nobody thought the bird was my idea. "Joe Riddley wouldn't leave the parrot home, and barring surgery, I don't know how we can separate them. We're just keeping him for a few days."

"I don't mind him." Darren's dark eyes sparkled. "And if somebody asks, we'll say, 'Parrot? What parrot?' Come on, J.R. You showed everybody Saturday how well you can walk. Today you're gonna walk the whole length of the parallel bars. Ready for that?"

"I can't walk," Joe Riddley told him grumpily. "You know that."

Darren gently steered him toward the bars while Joe peered around the room from Joe Riddley's cap. "Sure you can walk. Your legs weren't shot, just your head. You'll walk fine once your brain decides you can. The reason we do therapy is to train your brain."

Darren might be right. I had noticed that if I said, "Right foot, left foot," like he did, Joe

221

Riddley walked on the walker with a lot more confidence. But he was a long way from taking a stroll downtown. His poor brain had its wiring mixed. Right then it was telling him to scratch his bottom in public. "Stop that." I gave him a nudge. People with head injuries have no more inhibitions than tiny children.

Darren positioned him on the parallel bars and commanded, "Step with your right foot. Now your left. Right foot. Left foot."

"Did you have a good run yesterday?" I asked as Joe Riddley snail-walked along the bars.

"We sure did. Alice is fast! Then we went up to Augusta and danced. She's a great dancer, too. We're going to play miniature golf tonight after supper." He had a spring in his step as he went to nudge Joe Riddley along. Poor Kelly Keane.

Out of the corner of my eye I saw the head of the physical therapy department heading our way. Quickly I went to intercept her. "We won't bring the bird every day," I assured her. "My husband was being obstreperous this morning, and I couldn't make him go to the barn —" I stopped, flustered, hoping she knew it was the parrot and not my husband I wanted to make go to the barn. I was getting as bad as Joe Riddley. Sentences perfectly clear in my head got garbled on their way to my tongue.

She looked over to where Joe Riddley was actually cooperating with Darren for a change, and smiled. "The judge is like a different man.

If the parrot doesn't bother the others, you can bring him."

Since Joe Riddley didn't seem to need me right beside him, for a change, I headed to an empty seat next to a pretty young woman with a blond ponytail and a pink sweat suit. I'd have thought she'd wandered in looking for a gym except for the thick medical shoe on one foot. "That's a fine scarlet macaw," she said. "But why is he grieving? Has he lost his mate?"

I stared in surprise. "He lost his owner. How'd you know?"

"He's blushing. Macaws are the only animals except humans who blush. For them, it is often a symptom of grief." Seeing my surprise, she added, "I'm Marge Grafton, a veterinarian from Roanoke." She held out her foot ruefully. "A clumsy veterinarian. I came down to visit my folks and fell off a chair cleaning off my mother's closet shelf. Broke my foot in three places. But hopefully they'll release me today and let me get back home. Oh, there's my therapist." She stood, then turned. "Don't worry about your bird. Just give him a lot of love."

There was one doctor's order I couldn't follow. But I could love Joe Riddley and tolerate the parrot for his sake. I hoped that would be enough.

# 18

By Monday afternoon, radio announcements and white notices around the county urged people to come forward with anything they saw in the region of Yarbrough Farm Road between seven and nine the previous Saturday morning. Two days later I was out at the nursery checking a delivery of roses when Clarinda called, her voice deep and troubled. "I hate to bother you —"

My heart thudded. "What's the matter? He was fine when I left."

"It's not the Judge. He's sleepin'. It's that therapy feller. He called here looking for you. The sheriff's taken him in for questionin' about killin' Mister Blaine."

"Let me hang up and call the sheriff."

His office said the sheriff wasn't there, but about the time I got back to my desk, he pulled into a parking space outside my window.

*Are you going to tell him about the gun now?* I'd have smacked that voice if I could.

"Afternoon, Judge." Sheriff Gibbons came into the office turning his hat in his hand, a sure sign he was anxious. He'd stood turning his sack lunch just like that when he was ten, standing by to lend moral support while Joe Riddley asked me to go steady. I had no idea what "go steady" meant, but I'd have gone anywhere with Joe Riddley. When I said yes, Buster flung his sack into the air and yelled, "Whoopee!"

*He isn't gonna yell "whoopee" today when he hears what you have to say.*

I greeted him like a normal adult who doesn't have voices in her head. "Good afternoon, Sheriff. I hear you're interviewing Joe Riddley's physical therapist about that shooting."

He nodded, still turning his hat. He was also shifting from one leg to the other.

"Sit down. You're making me antsy. And tell me what this is about."

He perched on the edge of Joe Riddley's leather chair at the desk, still turning his hat between his hands while he spoke in legalese. "He and the deceased had a major altercation Friday evening concerning the alleged perpetrator's —"

I held up a hand to stop him. "We're all alone here. Give it to me in everyday language."

"Okay." He laid the hat on the desk and propped one ankle on the other thigh. "This is from three witnesses. Friday night Hernandez was over at Hardee's with the Keane woman from the paper, having a burger. Hiram went in with his parrot and started hitting on the girl. Hiram could be pretty offensive, you know."

"We both know," I agreed. "But Darren works

225

with disturbed people all the time. He's used to handling them."

"He tried to handle Hiram, but Hiram wouldn't be handled. Hernandez asked him to leave, very politely. Hiram said something else offensive. Hernandez started to get out of the booth. The witnesses say he wasn't at all threatening, but Hiram shoved him before he could get out. Then Hiram spat in Hernandez's face. As he turned to leave, he shouted so everybody could hear, 'If that was vinegar, you'd be dissolved by now.'"

I let out a breath I hadn't known I was holding. "Hiram came home crazier than he left."

"Seems like it. Never used to be trouble, before he took up with old Amos out your way."

"I refuse to take credit for Amos just because he lived on my road. But that's not all, is it? You've got something to link Darren with Hiram Saturday morning."

He shifted unhappily. "Afraid so. Several folks saw Hiram push his truck off the highway into the Bi-Lo lot and start down your road around seven-fifteen. Two testify that a yellow Beetle went down your road around eight-fifteen, and two others say it came back around eight-fifty. Hernandez presently owns the only yellow Beetle in Hope County."

This did not sound good. But there was one possibility. "Are your witnesses reliable?"

"One of the ones who saw Hiram heading

down your road is the Bi-Lo manager, who was checking his lot for trash just before opening. Miss Keane herself saw the Beetle turn into your road as she was going to the paper at eight-fifteen, and a bag boy at Bi-Lo noticed it because he's saving for a red Beetle. He also noticed the time, because as he was heading back to the store, Pooh DuBose stopped him to ask what time it was."

"Pooh?" Startled, I spoke without thinking.

"Yeah. She was apparently in the lot in her motorized wheelchair. I'm going to speak to Otis about that. She could get hit."

"Otis will be delighted to know where she was. She sneaked out, and was gone quite a while that morning." Had she been gone long enough to motor down to my house and shoot Hiram? Our road comes into the highway less than fifty yards from the Bi-Lo. "I take it you didn't question Pooh?"

"We tried, but she isn't exactly with it today. She told us Hiram Blaine is a dreadful man who ought to be banned from the streets, but she not only didn't remember seeing a yellow Volkswagen at the Bi-Lo, she couldn't remember what a Bi-Lo is. When I explained it's the grocery store, she said her family shops at Tribbles' market. How long since Tribbles' closed?"

"It was right after Walker was born." We shared the look of two people desperately unhappy about what was happening to one of their favorite people. Then I got back to business.

"Does Darren admit he was down at our place?"

"Oh, yes. Says he had to go count tables. Claims he didn't go in the house, though, and didn't see Hiram Blaine. Counting tables sounded pretty thin to me, but he lives next to the florist who made centerpieces for your party, and he said she called saying she'd forgotten how many centerpieces she needed. He said they do each other favors from time to time."

"You'll talk to her, I suppose."

"I sent a deputy while I finished interviewing Hernandez, to be sure he didn't get to her before we did. She corroborates his story. Says she had worked all night and around eight she realized she couldn't remember whether the thirty-five you ordered included the one for the dining room table. She called Darren and asked if he'd run down to count the round tables."

I nodded. "We had thirty-five round tables. She brought a gorgeous arrangement for the dining room."

He chuckled. "She gave you something she'd made for a hotel up on I-20, and went back after she finished decorating at your place to make them another." He picked up his hat and turned it again. "But she said she had to do that because Hernandez took his own sweet time getting back to her. She'd figured on it taking him no more than fifteen minutes to get to your place, count the tables, and call on his cell phone. It took him more than thirty."

"What did he say to that?"

"Says he found Lulu out in your road and your car gone, so he chased her and put her in the pen." He grinned. "Says he never imagined a three-legged beagle could run that fast."

I didn't feel like smiling. "I told you I found the dog in the pen when I got home, and I'd left her in the house. Darren didn't say he saw Hiram at our place?"

"Says he didn't. Says he didn't go inside, either."

"Maybe somebody came after Darren left."

"The schedule's too tight. Besides, Maynard took his pup out just as Darren went by, and he saw you come in less than ten minutes later. Between the two of you, nobody went up or down the road."

"I saw Maynard playing with his dog." I was jotting down notes, trying to fit all the pieces together. "Let's see. Just after seven, I left home. Around seven-fifteen, Hiram started walking to our house. That would take — what? Fifteen minutes?"

"More like twenty, I figure. He wasn't what you'd call a real dedicated walker."

"Okay, he gets there around seven thirty-five. Around eight-seventeen Darren gets to our house, counts tables, chases Lulu, pens her, and leaves around eight-fifty. Nine o'clock I get home. And nobody went down the road between Darren and me. Sounds like Hiram had to be killed before Darren got there. There's plenty of time."

The sheriff's bloodhound face looked sadder than ever. I knew he was thinking what I was: The only suspect we had for that time slot was Joe Riddley.

"Hernandez must have done it," he said, almost hopefully. He wasn't a friend of Darren's like I was. "Your dining room screen didn't have any prints except smudged ones of yours and Clarinda's, but we'll check his prints against others from the dining room. I don't suppose you remember whether he was in the dining room during the party, do you?"

"I don't have any idea who all was in there during the party." What I did remember — a memory that was making me sick — was Darren leaning against the closet door Saturday night after everybody had gone, his hands behind him, asking about Alice. Was he leaving prints in case he'd left others there before, when he'd dropped the gun in Joe Riddley's boot?

As if reading my thoughts, the sheriff asked, "By the way, I haven't gotten by yet to check your kitchen closet. I presume you still have it locked?"

"I certainly do. But getting back to Darren, he seemed his normal perky self at the party."

"You know you can't go by that. Maybe shooting Hiram released his tensions."

"I don't want to believe Darren did it, Sheriff."

"You prefer the alternative?"

"You don't have any evidence linking Joe

Riddley to this!" Terror spoke more hotly than I intended. "You might as well arrest *me* and get it over with."

"Phyllis vouches for where you were." My mouth dropped open. He settled his hat on his head. "Have to check on everybody, Judge. You, especially, with Chief Muggins assisting with this investigation. But the truth is, we don't have one piece of hard evidence against anybody. Best way in the world to get rid of evidence is to have a party for two hundred people."

"I didn't do it deliberately," I said grumpily.

"I never for an instant thought you did." He stood. "I came by because I figured you'd kill me if you heard about Hernandez from anybody else."

"You got that right." I rose to see him out, almost deafened by an argument in my head.

*Are you going to tell him about the gun?*

*No. He'd just think Darren got it and used it.*

*You could point out Darren had no way of knowing where the key is kept.*

*Not without saying Joe Riddley and I are the only ones who do.*

*Maybe Joe Riddley told Darren. These days he blabs secrets to whoever will listen.*

*He's never alone with Darren. I'm right beside them all the time.*

*You're just trying to protect Joe Riddley.*

*Durn tootin' I am.*

It made me shiver when Buster turned at the door and said, "I think we ought to protect Joe

Riddley. We're not making an arrest as of yet, so don't mention this to him."

That minute, I missed the old Joe Riddley more than ever. He'd never liked my looking into murders, but we'd talked about everything else. I needed to talk to him about Darren so bad I could taste it. Joe Riddley, however, had gone far, far away.

Wednesday's weekly *Statesman* was lying on my desk, Slade's most ambitious edition to date. He had devoted the entire front page to the murder. He'd interviewed Hector, written a piece about Hiram's history of warning Hopemore about aliens, and dredged up a real good picture of Hiram with Joe on his head.

Slade himself had written the stories. I had to admit the man could write. I resented, however, a big picture of our house on page one labeled "The site of the crime," followed by a boxed appeal from Sheriff Gibbons:

> Anybody knowing or seeing anything which might pertain to the murder of Hiram Blaine at the home of Judge MacLaren Yarbrough, please call the sheriff.

Slade had deemed Kelly's article on Joe Riddley's party important enough for half of the second page. Photos included not only a close-up of Joe Riddley and me while the tree was planted and several clever, amusing shots of our guests (including one of Slade and Meriwether),

232

but one of the house with the yard full of people. Anybody would know it was the same house, and presume we'd gone ahead with our party even though Hiram got shot.

It was a good thing I was an appointed judge. With friends like Slade, I'd never win an election.

I generally took the paper home. Joe Riddley didn't understand what he read, but he liked to look at pictures and have me explain certain stories. He had made me write "read paper" on every Wednesday page in his log. But I had no intention of dealing with his questions about the pictures in that particular paper. I threw it away.

After supper, Joe Riddley pointed angrily to his log. "It says right here, 'read paper.'"

"I know, honey, but I didn't bring it home. Maybe I'll remember tomorrow." By tomorrow he would have turned his page. He wouldn't think about it again.

But by tomorrow, Darren could be in jail for murder.

# 19

Thursday, Lottie called right after I got to the office. "Miss Winifred is in a state and we can't do nothin' with her. Her bank statement just arrived, and she thinks they aren't honoring her checks. Could you come over?"

I decided to walk from the store, but when I got onto the sidewalk, I was glad I'd worn a light jacket. Gray clouds banked overhead, and a stiff breeze came from the west. I eyed the clouds, hoping I wouldn't get soaked walking back to the store. The television predicted rain, but we'd had such a long spell of nice weather I hadn't believed it. *Any more than you believe Joe Riddley may have shot Hiram.* I held my head into the wind so I couldn't hear.

Pooh was in her Cozy with a steaming drink beside her. "You want I should bring you a cup?" Lottie asked in her mournful way. She didn't specify what would be in it.

"That would be wonderful," I agreed, hoping I wasn't accepting a cup of stewed grass some people call tea. I needed something more stimulating than that. I took a seat and asked Pooh,

"What's going on? I hear you've got some trouble with the bank?"

Pooh's blue eyes were wide with worry. "It's dreadful, MacLaren. I try to pay my bills, but the bank won't let me. They keep sending all the checks back." She took an envelope from the table by her chair. "If my lights and water get cut off, I don't know how we'll live."

Normally I'd no more look at another woman's bank statement than read her diary, but Pooh looked so bewildered, I thumbed through the checks and perused the balance. "They honored all these."

"They sent them back. Now I have to mail them all out again."

I reached out and touched her arm, hoping to bring her a little closer to reality. "No, honey, these have all been used to pay your bills, then returned to the bank. The bank sent them back to you along with the statement saying how much money you have left."

"I have enough for now. I call every little while to be sure I have enough to pay my bills."

She had enough to buy a couple of small countries. I was surprised her financial advisor let her keep so much in her checking account. "Who helps you with your money, Pooh?"

"Fayette did all that." She waved her plump hands as if her financial problems had been taken away by her husband when he died.

I had turned the checks over as I laid them in my lap, so now they rested back-side up. The one on top was endorsed with Gusta's new red stamp, and her account had the same last three digits as my telephone number. That's the kind of dumb fact that tends to stick in my brain. But I was puzzled about the check. "Why are you writing checks to Gusta?"

Pooh shrugged. "Maybe she needs money?" Like I needed another head.

"Let's see. It was for a hundred dollars, written last Friday right after she came home. Did Gusta pay your way somewhere, maybe?"

Pooh looked bewildered.

Lottie came in with a steaming cup of coffee, strong and black, just the way I needed it, and overheard my question. "Remember, Miss Winifred? You forgot to take your pocketbook when you went to the Friends of the Library meeting, and they wanted donations for new computer equipment. Miss Augusta wrote her check to cover your share and stopped by here on her way home for you to write her a check. It was last *week*," she added, as if that ought to make a difference to Pooh's poor addled brain.

I waited until Lottie left, then turned to Pooh. "I want to talk to you about two things. Pay close attention, now."

"Of course, dear." Pooh leaned forward like she was memorizing every word.

"First, I want you to give your lawyer the power to pay your bills. You don't need to be worrying about this. Your lawyer needs to take this off your hands. May I call him and ask him to come see you? And will you sign the papers he gives you?"

She fluttered her hands. "Why, of course, dear. If you say so." She'd have trusted anybody.

"Who's your lawyer?"

"I don't think I have one."

Lottie would know who'd handled Fayette's affairs. I moved to the next question. "Sheriff Gibbons says you were down at the Bi-Lo Saturday morning. What was it you wanted there that morning?"

She cocked her silver curls, listened carefully to be sure Otis and Lottie's television was going in the kitchen, and leaned forward to whisper, "Twinkies. Lottie won't buy Twinkies. That old doctor claims I have too much sugar in my blood." With a wave, she consigned serious diabetes to the realm of a medical fairy tale. "I went down myself and bought a whole box. Then I brought them home and hid them."

She was so proud of herself you'd have thought she'd won an Olympic medal. Come to think of it, it was no small feat to get herself into that chair and out of the house, travel nearly a mile each way by motorized chair, elude a determined pursuer, and remember what she went for and how to get home. Maybe they ought to make it an Olympic event for arthritic, forgetful octogenarians. But Twinkies could be dangerous for Pooh. "Where did you hide them?"

She hesitated, but couldn't resist bragging.

"In my high-heel shoes. I don't wear them any-more, and they are too small for Lottie." She held out a tiny foot complacently.

I managed not to gasp. "Have you hidden things in shoes before?"

"No, somebody —" That train of thought vanished into a mist. She looked down at her hands in distress.

I could have sworn. "Who told you to put Twinkies in the shoe?"

Pooh looked at me like I had said something particularly silly. I wanted to shake her. But you can't shake a damaged mind any more than you can shake an open feather pillow. I leaned closer to her and asked, "Do you remember lending a gun to Gusta once?"

Pooh had no trouble remembering the distant past. It was just the present that gave her trouble. "A twenty-two," she said promptly. "Faye bought it because he had to be out of town so much. Silly man," she added. "I didn't want a little old pistol. So I gave it to Gusta and got a dog. Remember Bowser?"

"Sure I do." Bowser was a St. Bernard straight from *Peter Pan*. He was so huge and so tame that elementary school children used to stop by after school to ride on his back. "Was Bowser sup-posed to protect you? He was such a pussycat, I don't think he could."

Pooh put back her head and laughed merrily. "No, but if I left him in the yard at night, he'd bark if anyone came near our fence. What he

238

wanted, of course, was for me to let him in so he could hide under my bed, but burglars wouldn't know that." She looked around uncertainly, but with a perfectly clear eye. "I had a box of old pictures — there. Hand them to me. You're so much younger than I."

When you are over sixty and somebody tells you how young you are, you jump to do anything they ask. I brought her the old square box and set it in her lap. She opened it and rummaged through it. "Here he is. Remember?"

I smiled fondly at the familiar huge head and lolling tongue. Pooh rummaged in the box again and brought out a yellowed letter. Her lips trembled and her voice was odd as she said, "You are so kind, MacLaren. I want you to see this. I want you to know."

I unfolded the letter. When I saw who it was from, I nearly dropped it. "Are you sure you want me to read it?"

Her face crumpled like a child's before it cries. "I'd have told you before, but Fayette wouldn't let me."

I scanned the single sheet, written from Vietnam:

*Dear Mama,*
*Prepare yourself for a shock. I am married! She is a wonderful girl, and I know you will love her as I do, but Daddy will give us some problems. I wasn't going to tell you until I got back, but I just found out we're going to have a baby, and I have*

*to tell somebody or burst! If it's a girl, I will name her Winnie. You know I hate to write, so that's all for now.*

*Love,*
*Zach*

If my memory served me right, the letter was written just a week or two before Zach was killed.

"I would have had a grandbaby, but Zach died." Tears rolled down Pooh's cheeks. She brought a flowered handkerchief out of her pocket and wiped her eyes.

I don't know how Lottie knew she was needed, but I have seldom been as glad to see anybody coming through a door. "What you crying for?" she demanded.

"Bowser." Pooh held up the photograph. "Bowser's dead."

"Sure he is. He's up in heaven with Mr. Faye, running and playing like he used to down here. So what you crying for, when they're so happy?"

"Is Zach there, too?"

"He sure is. He and Mr. Faye spent the whole morning throwing sticks to old Bowser."

Pooh's eyes were like a rain-washed sky. "Really?"

"Really. Why don't you let me take you to lie down a little while before dinner? Miss MacLaren can come back another day."

"Please," Pooh said, holding out one hand like she was begging me not to forget her.

"Sometimes Pooh nearly breaks my heart," I told Otis in the kitchen a minute later.

He nodded his grizzled head. "Might near breaks mine, too."

I laid the letter on the table. "You know anything about this?"

He held it up, turned it around, and laid it back down. "You'll need to read it to me. I don't have my glasses about me right now."

I looked at him sharply. "Otis, can you read?"

He shook his head and grinned sheepishly. "No'm, not to say —" He paused, then admitted, "No'm, I can't."

I am always astonished and filled with admiration when I find someone who maneuvers in this complicated society without being able to read. "How do you manage?"

"Lottie reads real good. Between us we make out all right."

I picked up the letter and read it to him. "Did you know anything about this?"

He hesitated, then nodded. "Yes'm, I knowed about it when it happened. We had a right smart dust-up 'round here the afternoon it came. Reason nobody heard about it is, Mr. Fayette told Miss Winifred not to mention it to *nobody* 'til he'd had time to check it out. Then, not much more'n a week later, the telegram came saying Zach was gone." Otis's voice faltered, and he had to clear his throat before going on. He had loved Zachary very much.

"War or no war, Miss Winifred wanted to call

241

Vietnam itself to try and find that woman, but Mr. Faye said he wasn't interested in findin' a foreigner who'd tricked Zach into marrying her so's she could get into this country. He wouldn't even let Miss Winifred tell a soul. She might nigh went crazy, losing Zach plus knowing there was gonna be a baby in the world that belonged to her and she couldn't look for it."

"I'd never have thought Fayette could be so mean!" I remembered Hiram Blaine saying something like that.

Otis nodded soberly. "He could be a hard man at times." Then he sighed. "To tell the truth, though, I think his grief was so big right then he didn't want to share her with anything or anybody. And you know Miss Winifred and babies. If she'd had a baby around here, the rest of us could have packed our bags and left. She'd never have noticed."

I handed him the letter. "Put it back in the box in her Cozy when she's asleep. Did you ever hear from the girl?"

He shook his head. "Mr. Fayette tol' me, 'Just give her time, she'll be writin' for money soon enough.' But we kep' waitin' and waitin', and that letter never came."

Our church is around the square from Pooh's. I stopped by on my way back to the store and sat in the chapel alone. Soft light streamed through creamy stained-glass windows. The small room was dim, cool, and very quiet. I wasn't so much praying as feeling the presence of God and admitting that no matter what I was bearing right then, there were others who were bearing things I never could. Was it Socrates who said if they put all the troubles in the world in one big pile and told us to pick some, we'd choose our own?

One by one I pictured my grandchildren, and gave thanks for them. What if I had never seen their dear faces, heard their baby laughs? No wonder Pooh's mind had finally gone. I was surprised it stuck around as long as it did.

I took a minute to pray for Pooh, that somebody would take care of her. "But not me," I added in a whisper. "You know I've got my hands full with Joe Riddley right now."

I prayed for Darren, and that the real murderer would be found.

I ambled back toward the store, thinking about Zach, Darren, and Pooh. Oh, if Joe Riddley were only well and could talk to me! I was so busy thinking I ran smack into Kelly Keane.

"I'm so sorry," I told her. "My head was somewhere else."

"Don't apologize. I've been wanting to see you." Her eyes were anxious behind her glasses. "Are they going to send Darren to jail?"

"I hope not, honey. Sure he went down to my house Saturday morning, but he had a good reason for being there, and there's no evidence yet to connect him to the murder."

"I feel so bad about saying I saw him." She nibbled one thumbnail.

"You did what you had to. And there were

other witnesses. Besides, he isn't arrested yet. So far the sheriff's just asking him questions."

She shifted her shoulder bag from one shoulder to the other as if shifting her troubles. "I'd hate for him to suffer because of me."

I patted her arm. "Don't worry yet. Oh, and thanks for the party article."

I hadn't gone half a block when I heard somebody else call, "Judge Yarbrough?" I turned and saw Alice Fulton jogging toward me. Sweat beaded her upper lip, but otherwise she looked fresh and a lot livelier than usual. "I got the car put in my name," she greeted me, jogging in place.

"Good. That will save us sending you to jail," I joked.

She jogged slower, then stopped. "May I ask you something? Something real important? I don't know who else to ask."

I expected it to be something to do with how many hours she worked, or benefits. I never expected her to blurt, "There used to be a gun in my room, and it's gone." I must have looked as shocked as I felt, because she put three fingers over her mouth like she was sorry she'd said anything, and backed away. "It may not be important."

"It could be real important. Whose gun was it, and what was it doing in your room?"

"I don't know whose it was. It was small and silver, and it was in a shoebox on the shelf in my closet. I found it when I put my suitcase up there. The suitcase wouldn't go all the way to the back, so I climbed up on a chair to see why. That's when I saw the box. I — maybe I shouldn't have opened it, but I did, and all that was in it was a gun."

"Was it loaded?"

She hitched up her shoulders in a shrug. "I don't know. I don't know anything about guns, so I wouldn't know how to tell, except by shooting it. I didn't even pick it up. I didn't want it to go off accidentally or anything."

"Did you ask Gusta about it?"

"No ma'am — I thought about it, but then I decided maybe that's where they kept it and she might not have wanted me poking around."

"Florine should have cleaned off the shelf before they put you in that room."

"She's not very tall, and the gun was back in the far corner of a real deep shelf."

"When did you notice it was gone?"

"Last night. I wanted to get down some sweaters I'd left in my suitcase, and when I got up on a chair to get the suitcase, I saw the box was gone. Do you think I ought to tell Mrs. Wainwright?"

"You need to tell the sheriff. They are looking for a small gun that killed Hiram Blaine."

She took a step back and covered her whole mouth with her hand. "Oh, no."

"I'm afraid so. Who has been in that room besides you?"

She hesitated.

"Florine, to clean," I prompted. "Anybody else?" When she didn't speak, I guessed. "Was Darren ever up there?"

I couldn't imagine how he could have been, given their short acquaintance and Gusta's gimlet eyes, but she nodded and looked down like a confessing child. "He came by Monday evening to go play miniature golf. Mrs. Wainwright was at a meeting and Florine had gone to see her sister, so when he said what a neat house it was, I showed him around."

"But he wasn't alone in your room, was he?"

"No more than five minutes, while I went to the bathroom to brush my hair and put on lipstick."

"I don't think he could have found that gun in five minutes."

Her dark eyes were full of misery. "I'd told him I'd found it, the afternoon before. I wanted to know if it could go off accidentally, and I didn't know who else to ask."

A bird called from a nearby bush. Seemed to me we stood there long enough for the bird to mate and build a nest before I finally could speak. "You're going to have to tell the sheriff, honey. And the sooner the better."

She nodded and turned to go, shoulders drooping and her head down.

# 20

I arrived at my office to find Hector Blaine propping up my filing cabinet, talking to Walker. "Here she is now," Walker said with obvious relief. "Mama, I need to get back to my own office." He practically bolted.

I understood. The place reeked.

Hector was taller than Hiram, and bigger, with a shaven red face and greasy grizzled hair cut just below his ears. As soon as I sat down at my desk, he reached up one hand to take off a gray felt hat like most men stopped wearing around 1970. If Hector got his then, he'd certainly not cleaned it since. He might have washed his hands a year or two later, but the pores were black and he had great half-moons caked under each nail. "Got a minute, Judge?"

"Sure, Hector. I've got a parrot, too, I'm still waiting for you to claim."

"Well, now, I can't rightly claim that parrot. It hates me, and I hate it. Just wring its neck. That's the best thing. I don't think you can eat 'em — never heard of anybody doing such — but if you fling him in your pasture, the buzzards'll take care of him."

The thought of all that glory, those incredible feathers, lying on the grass waiting for buzzards made me cringe. "You didn't come to talk about the parrot, I guess. So what did you want?" The office was getting riper by the minute. He shifted from one foot to the other. Although it went against my better judgment, I invited, "Why don't you sit down?" But I pointed him to Joe Riddley's desk chair instead of my slip- covered red one. Leather is easier to clean.

He hitched up his crusted denim pants on the chair and chewed his lower lip. From a rim of scabs on it, I suspected he chewed it pretty often.

"It's about Hiram." For one heart-leaping second I thought he'd come to confess. But as he went on, my heart plopped back into the cold waters of reality. "I think he was killed on account of — you know what I mean." He gave me a knowing little nod and looked anxiously toward the closed door between us and the store.

"The Confederate treasury?" The Blaine brothers were tediously consistent.

"That'd be it. I think he told somebody where it is, and they done for him. They'll be after me, next. I need protection, Judge, in the worst way." He hooked one bare ankle around the shaft of the chair and leaned so close I nearly gagged at his rancid breath. "It's not anybody local, you know. It's that criminal element he got mixed up with."

"Criminal element?"

"Yeah, you know. Folks he met in jail."

If I didn't immediately respond, it was because I was remembering that Hiram had been in jail only once, while Hector had served three long sentences for various offenses. "Who, exactly?"

"Oh, I don't know their names, but I know they're out to get me. Want to drive me off my land so's they can take it over. I saw a man with binniculers walking through my watermelon patch not two weeks ago."

"Could have been a bird watcher. They carry binoculars."

"Naah. He was looking for the treasury. Just pretended to look at birds now and then. What I think is this. While he was in the pen, Hiram musta told somebody about it. Now they're out, and they want it. You gotta help me, Judge. You gotta."

I could tell he was scared. His right cheek twitched, and his hands couldn't be still. But neither Bailey Gibbons nor Charlie Muggins was going to spare anybody to baby-sit Hector through this fantasy. "I'm not sure what we can do, exactly. You know our police force is pretty small. But so is the town. If there were strangers here, we'd know it."

"They's lots of people I don't know."

"Sure, but you know their faces, don't you? Somebody new stands out a mile. If you see somebody you don't know following you, make a note what they look like and go tell Chief

249

Muggins." I felt like a snake, but a happy snake. That ought to fix Charlie for suspecting Joe Riddley of killing Hiram.

*So long as Joe Riddley didn't do it.*

I ignored that dratted voice and made another suggestion. "Maybe you ought to take the parrot after all. He could warn you if somebody tries to break in at night."

"Too much trouble, Judge. Birds are *dirty*," he said, virtuous as Mr. Clean.

"Well, you tell Chief Muggins if you notice anybody hanging around your place. That's the best I can suggest."

I expected him to stand up, but he hunched forward a little and said in a soft voice, "I don't suppose you and t'other judge could see fit to help me with the funeral, could you? Seein' how's he died at your place 'n' all? I'd like to lay him out real nice, but I can't rightly come up with the money to do it. They'll bury him like a pauper lest somebody kin he'p out. . . ." He trailed off and wiped a tear from his eye. Hector could cry at the drop of a pin. As a child, it had been his most outstanding accomplishment.

It made me mad that he thought we owed him a funeral. Seemed to me the Yarbroughs had done our share by providing a handy spot for the murder and a foster home for the parrot.

"Jed will take care of that. Let's wait until he gets here," I stalled.

"Could you just give me twenty dollars or so, to get a tie to wear to the funeral?"

"No, but I'll call Taylor's Department Store and tell them to charge one to me."

"Don't bother." We both knew he hadn't been planning to buy a tie. "I sure hope nobody does to me what they done to Hiram. You'll feel real bad, not helping me 'n' all."

"I sure will," I agreed, showing him to the door. I hurried to open the window and spray some air neutralizer, thinking, That has to be the craziest man in town.

Then Jed Blaine arrived, sounding as crazy as his uncles. He claimed Hopemore might actually have aliens.

Jed didn't look crazy. In a three-piece charcoal suit, pale gray shirt, gray-and-blue tie, gold tie tack, and highly polished black shoes, he looked like a prosperous young lawyer. To my surprise, I saw he'd filled out into a mighty handsome man. As fair as his uncles were dark (his mother had brown hair and blue eyes), he'd been an adorable but gawky child with a face full of freckles, light blue eyes framed by white lashes, and a shock of snow-white hair. Now the freckles were almost gone, and he wore his thick sandy hair parted precisely on the left side. He still had that engaging grin full of strong white teeth and a chuckle that made you want to chuckle along. If he stuck around a while, the single women and their mamas would be holding another series of parties. Meriwether might even reconsider her earlier decision.

He came into my office already talking. Joe Riddley always said Jed Blaine could talk ears off corn. "Meant to get down here sooner, but had to be in court all week until noon today."

We hugged, he slung his coat across the extra chair, and we exchanged the kind of news people do when they are fond of one another and haven't been together for a while. Then he leaned forward like we were fixing to do serious business, and started talking crazy.

"You aren't gonna want to hear this, but I think Hiram was killed because he found an alien living in Hopemore." Seeing my expression, he held up a hand. "Wait. Listen to what I have to say. He called me Friday evening, all excited. At first I couldn't make heads or tails of what he was saying. A lot of 'They're here! They're here! I've seen one with my own two eyes!' When I finally got him calmed down a bit, he said he'd seen an alien on Oglethorpe Street that very day, and we could prove it legally."

Jed waited for me to say something, but my vocal chords were on strike. I was glad to be interrupted by a deputy, bringing in a warrant for me to sign. Jed waited until he'd gone, then shook his head. "It ought to seem funny seeing you do that, but it doesn't. Now, to get back to this other thing —" He leaned back in his chair and stretched out his legs. "I'm not saying you've got people from Venus." He waved that idea away in the air. "But what Hiram said was, an alien is living in Hopemore disguised as somebody else, that there was absolutely no doubt, and he'd be wanting me to get legal documents to prove he was right. He wanted to watch the situation for a week or two, then he'd get back to me. Now I know and you know that most of the time Hiram was nuttier than pecan pie. But this time — I don't know, something rang true. I haven't the foggiest notion who he was talking about, or what kind of legal documents he wanted, but he truly believed somebody here isn't who he seems to be."

Jed waited for me to say or do something smart, but all my smarts seemed to be flitting somewhere out near Venus. I shoved my fingers through my hair, finishing the wreck Joe had made of Phyllis's good work.

"He'd worked in Atlanta long enough to know there are illegal human aliens as well as extraterrestrial ones," he pointed out when I didn't speak.

"And you think whoever it is found out Hiram recognized him or her, and killed him?"

He shrugged. "Have you got a better idea?"

"Not at the moment. Have you talked to Hector?"

"No, I thought I'd stop by here first. Then I'm going over to Miss Hubbard's Bed and Breakfast to get a room, so when I go by home I'll already have a place to stay."

I didn't blame him one bit. "I'd ask you to stay with us, but —"

"Thanks. I really appreciate that, but you've

got enough on your plate without having company. And I may be here a while. I've told my office I won't be back until I scout around a bit. I owe it to Hiram. What were you going to say about Hector?"

"He thinks Hiram talked in jail about the Confederate treasury, and somebody — the criminal element, he called them . . ."

"That old jailbird?" Jed sounded both fond and disgusted.

"Yeah. He's sure the criminal element is after the treasury and planning to kill him to get it. The reason I mention it is, if anything does happen to Hector, you're next in line for the inheritance, so watch your back."

"I'll do that. Right now, I thought I'd run over and see Pooh. She doin' okay?" His eyes were a bit anxious, like eyes always are when asking about an elderly friend we haven't seen in a while.

From the time he was four or five, Jed and Pooh had been special buddies. He'd stop by her place for cookies after school and we'd see them chattering away like equals up on her big porch. He used to help Otis around the yard some, too, and after he went to college and law school, he used to write long funny letters Pooh would bring by for me to read. She confided once she had a special fondness for freckle-faced boys. Her hand touched the big silver locket with Zach's picture she wore next to her heart.

"She's gone down real bad this past year," I

warned him. "Her mind comes and goes."

As he stood and reached for his coat, I hoped he'd ask about Meriwether, but he merely rolled his sleeves down and slipped on his jacket.

I never imagined I'd get to witness their meeting, but as I walked Jed out front, he nodded across the street and said, "Nice car. If I didn't have a BMW, I'd like a Benz."

The Mercedes was Meriwether's silver convertible, parking in front of the bank. The day was chilly enough that she had the top up, which meant Jed and I couldn't see who was in it. First Slade swung out of the passenger seat, looking especially nice in a light tan suit with his dark hair ruffled by the wind.

"That's the new editor of the *Statesman*," I told Jed, since he hadn't asked.

Was it coincidence, or something stronger, that made Meriwether glance across the street as she opened her door? As far as anybody in Hopemore knew — and what we don't know in Hopemore is generally not worth knowing — that was the first time those two had laid eyes on each other in twelve years.

Oglethorpe Street has only two lanes plus parking on each side, so the two of them weren't very far apart when their eyes met. Meriwether climbed out of her car, showing more knee and leg than was absolutely necessary, and stood as haughty as a Viking princess in a navy skirt and brightly embroidered sweater. "What are you doing here?" she called coldly.

"My family lives here," he called back, "in case you hadn't noticed. And my uncle got murdered, so I came home for the funeral. *You* certainly know how important family can be."

Meriwether lifted her chin and slammed her door so hard I fully expected the window to break. "Come on, Slade." She marched toward the bank.

Jed threw back his head and laughed.

# 21

I didn't have time to stand around watching those two put on a performance. I had to decide what to do about the gun in my kitchen closet and talk to Sheriff Gibbons about the one missing from Alice's shelf. Which should I do first?

When things are in a real muddle and I don't have an earthly idea what to do about them, I do what Joe Riddley calls "real straight talking with the Boss." I went to my office, told my workers I did not want to be disturbed, and sat at my desk. "Things are in a real mess right now," I said out loud. "I don't know if the gun in my closet is Joe Riddley's or Pooh's, and I don't know a good way to find out. If I ask him and it's his, that probably means he shot Hiram. I'll have to tell Buster. And Joe Riddley's gonna want to put the gun back in his cabinet, and I don't want him having a gun in the house right now. Even if I ask him and it isn't his, he'll be reminded of his and want me to start looking for it. And if it's not Joe Riddley's, chances are real good it's Pooh's, and Darren put it there. I can't believe he shot Hiram, either, because he's a nice kid, in spite of his hair. . . ." I stopped. I was heading off track, fast. "Anyway, what I need to know is, how do I go about this? What should I do first? Any help will be greatly appreciated, and I'm open to suggestion. Thank you. Amen." Having delegated responsibility, I turned on my computer to start working on accounts.

Answers to prayers come in many forms. Mine came in a very small package that bounded into the office, flung its arms round my neck, and squeezed so hard I couldn't breathe. "Not so tight, Crick," Ridd admonished. "We want to keep Me-mama around for a few years."

"What's he doing here?" I reached in my bottom drawer for the lemon sucker Cricket knew was there.

"I told him I was going to use the forklift, and he wants to drive. Did you check on the Christmas trees?"

"Yeah, they'll be here in three weeks. Say, could I borrow Cricket for a little while?"

"Sure. For what?"

"It's a secret." I couldn't think of a single explanation Ridd would accept for why I'd hidden a gun in my closet for nearly a week without telling the sheriff. I couldn't think of an explanation the sheriff would accept, either.

Cricket chattered happily as we headed to the house, and he let Lulu give his face a good washing when we got there. "Where's Pop?" he demanded.

"Pop has occupational therapy Thursday afternoons."

"What's pational therpy?"

"He's learning to scramble eggs, cook bacon, and wash dishes."

Cricket chortled at the silliness of grownups. "Dat's not pational therpy, Me-mama. Dat's cookin'."

"Yeah, but you have to do one thing at a time, in order, and Pop's not real good at that right now." I felt a sudden surge of anger that Cricket wasn't getting to know the same granddad the other grandchildren had. No point thinking about that right now.

I got the boot from the closet and put a dishtowel on the table. "I want to show you something and I want you to tell me if you ever saw it before."

"O' course I saw dat before. Dat's de boot Pop wears to mow de lawn and clean de dog pen."

"Yeah, but there's something in it." I gently turned the boot upside down and the gun fell onto the dishcloth.

"Don't touch," I warned, afraid he'd mess up prints.

Cricket shook his head. "I doesn't touch guns 'less *Pop* says so."

I took a deep breath to steady my voice so I could ask, "Is this the gun Pop lost?"

"Pop didn't lose any guns. You gibbed dem to Maynard."

"But what about the little missing one? Is this it?"

He looked at me, obviously baffled. If he'd already forgotten the small gun, I had little hope he'd be able to identify it, but I made one more try. "You told us there was a little gun that went up in the top of Pop's cabinet. Is this it? Can you tell?"

He gave a big sigh of disgust. "O' course dat's not it. Pop gibbed dat little gun to Maynard, to put in the me-see-um. It's weal old."

I stared. "Are you sure?"

"O' course I'm sure." His brown eyes flashed with indignation. "I went wif him. Pop tole Maynard he can hab it now, but if I wants it when he's dead, Maynard must gib it back."

I sent Cricket and Lulu to the backyard and called Maynard. Waiting for the ring, I remembered something he'd said as we loaded the guns in the car late that night: *Any more antiques among them?*

"Hello, Maynard, it's Mac. I need to ask you a real funny question. Did Joe Riddley give you a gun for the museum recently?"

"Not real recently. It was before he got shot — about a week before. Why?"

I sank into a chair in relief. "What kind was it?"

"A silber derringer twenty-two," Cricket told me at the kitchen screen, still indignant.

"A silver derringer twenty-two," Maynard echoed. "Joe Riddley said his great-grandpa carried it in the War. Is there a problem? He was fine when he signed the donation papers."

"No problem. I had just missed it, and Cricket said Joe Riddley gave it to you."

Maynard chuckled. "Gave it to me with the written stipulation that if Cricket wants it when he grows up, he gets it back."

"That's what Cricket said, too. Thanks a lot. Oh, any more news on your house?"

"They're working on it. It's going to be real pretty." Poor Maynard. Who wouldn't sound discouraged to know the house of your dreams would soon be ready for you, and you couldn't live in it with your sweetheart?

I gave Cricket a cookie, locked the gun back in the closet in the boot, left Lulu in the pen, and drove to the store feeling about fifty pounds lighter. Ridd was driving the forklift, loading sod into a waiting pickup. He, like Joe Riddley, really enjoyed the hands-on part of the business. Walker and I preferred the clean-hands part in the back office. I didn't know if the boys would run the store when we were gone, but it was nice to know they would make a good team.

"You said I could do dat!" Cricket clamored even before I let him out. Ridd stopped and took him onto his lap.

"One mystery solved," I informed him before he restarted the motor. "I found a gun in your daddy's yard boots, and thought it was the one we were missing, but Cricket says that's not ours. He even told me where the missing one went. Tell Daddy, honey."

"Pop gibbed it to Maynard for his me-see-um." Cricket was far more interested in the forklift levers.

Ridd held his hands away from them. "Why didn't you tell us that before?"

"You didn't ask." Cricket pushed his hand away so he could play with the levers.

I mentally ran over the conversation we'd all had by the gun cabinet. "We didn't. We asked if he knew which gun went there, but we didn't tell him it was missing."

"Dey were all missing," Cricket reminded me. "Now Maynard has dem all."

He happily helped Ridd restart the forklift. I went back to my office, walking very slowly. Maynard didn't have quite all the guns. I still had one in a boot in my closet.

I dialed the sheriff's number, wishing I was calling to make an appointment for a root canal. "Hey. It's Judge Yarbrough. Have you talked to Alice Fulton this week?"

"No."

She must have chickened out. "Well, I've got something in my closet you need to see, and something you need to hear."

When he got there, I pointed to the old boot and stood back so he could examine it. "Look inside. And don't put all the dust in your report."

He grunted and shone his flashlight into the boot. "Got a dish towel handy?"

He gently lifted the boot and tested it for weight, then dumped it onto the dish towel. The silver gun lay between us. He shone his light over it. "It's been wiped clean of prints."

"I didn't do it."

"Didn't say you did. Is this the one Joe Riddley is missing?"

"No, he gave his to Maynard for the museum before his accident and forgot he'd done it. When I found this one, I brought Cricket over this afternoon to see if he could identify it. He couldn't, but he said Pop gave his own little gun to Maynard. Maynard verifies that." It was all true, if you allowed for a week between some of the events.

Buster took a pen from his pocket and poked the gun, lifting it to examine it. "Got any notion whose this is?"

"From something Alice Fulton told me, I think Pooh gave it to Gusta years ago. Pooh said Fayette gave her the gun for protection when he was away, but she bought Bowser and gave the gun to Gusta."

"Bowser — you mean that old St. Bernard they had?"

"That's what Pooh told me this afternoon."

He shook his jowls with a mournful frown. "If that gun's been lying around Wainwright's all these years, anybody in town could have taken it at one of their parties or meetings."

"No, it was there a few weeks ago." I told him what Alice had said. I still didn't tell him Darren could have taken it. There was absolutely no proof that he had.

He took a plastic bag from his pocket and carefully put the gun in it.

"At least you know Joe Riddley didn't kill Hiram." There, I'd finally spoke my fear out loud.

"Never thought he had." Buster stood and reached for his hat. "You never went hunting with him, did you?" I shook my head. "He won't shoot anything he can't eat, and he's the only man I ever hunted with who whispers before he pulls the trigger, 'Forgive me, fellow.' "

My lower lip began to tremble. "Will he ever hunt again, Buster?"

His hand was warm and firm on my shoulder. "Believe it, Little Bit. Just keep on believing it. That's all we can do right now."

He hurried out, but not before I'd seen his own eyes were shiny with tears.

# 22

Sheriff Gibbons called the next morning. "It's the gun that killed Hiram. It's also Pooh's gun. She, Otis, and Meriwether have all identified it. Meriwether confirmed she kept it on the closet shelf, and Miss Fulton gave us the dates when she saw it and found it missing. The way Miss Gusta locks up even when they are home, it had to be taken by somebody who has been a guest in the house this fall."

"She's had umpteen meetings and at least one chamber-music party," I reminded him. "Anybody could have nipped up there and taken it."

"Only if they knew it was there. Miss Fulton reluctantly admits Hernandez knew it was, and had opportunity to take it. He did it, Mac. I firmly believe that. But proving it could be hard. He was smart enough to come back to your kitchen after the party to make sure his prints were all over the place."

I hated to think about that. Thank goodness I was too *busy* to think much right then. Our chief magistrate was down with flu, so I had to hold a lot more probable cause hearings than usual as well as sign more warrants and go to the jail for more bond hearings. The store was holding its pre-Halloween sale, doing a brisk business in pumpkins and cornstalks. The nursery was getting ready to receive hundreds of Christmas trees and poinsettias. And Joe Riddley still went to therapy twice a day. I spent so much time in my car, I kept expecting to meet myself.

I ran into Otis at the grocery store one day and told him I felt guilty for neglecting Pooh. "Why, she's doin' fine, Miss MacLaren. Jed Blaine has been coming by to see her every afternoon, and it's doing her a world of good. A world of good."

I wished somebody could do Darren a world of good. Shadows were developing under his eyes and his smile was a little more strained each day. He hadn't dyed his hair in a while, either. It was electric blue with brown roots.

"Are you still going out with Kelly and or Alice?" I teased halfheartedly one morning.

"Mostly Alice," he said with a faint grin. "She's a lot of fun when she gets out of town. Keeps me from thinking about — you know." He gestured with one hand. I could tell she hadn't told him what she'd had to tell the sheriff.

I hated to think he could kill a man, though. He was so dedicated to helping people get better. Joe Riddley adored him, and even Joe now greeted him with a squawk — which was more than I got. Joe still had no use for women, merely tolerated me as a necessary evil. The feeling was mutual.

Speaking of mutual, Jed and Meriwether seemed to have a mutual attraction just then that neither sought or wanted. Granted, Hopemore isn't very big, but I can go days without running into members of my own family. It was uncanny how Jed and Meriwether kept running into each other. Every meeting, of course, was faithfully reported around town.

Jed went to buy a paper at the drugstore. Meriwether ran in for a new lipstick and didn't see him until they were both heading to pay. He asked if she'd followed him in. She got so mad — she paid, then stomped out without her lipstick.

Meriwether stopped by the Bi-Lo for paper towels, and only one register was open. Jed came to the line to buy a candy bar just as she discovered she had forgotten to bring her wallet. When she rooted around in the bottom of her purse, she was a dime short. Jed handed the cashier a dime with a wide smile. "Here, I've got plenty of money." The cashier said later she thought Meriwether was going to level him with the towels.

Jed wheeled Pooh into church to sit with Gusta, and sat down beside her. Meriwether, coming in late, made Slade take her to a different pew.

Ridd took Jed to play golf over at the country club and reported, "You'll never guess who was playing ahead of us, Mama. Slade and Meriwether. Slade offered to make it a foursome, but I've got at least a little bit of sense."

"How was Jed's game?"

"Terrible. He bogeyed almost every hole. Meriwether was better, but over par."

"How do you know?"

He grinned. "Jed jotted her shots on our card. He swore she was missing shots to let Slade win, and it made him furious. You should have heard him."

A couple of nights later, Walker and Cindy took me to her birthday dinner at a new restaurant down by the river. Sadly, we all agreed it would be an easier occasion without Joe Riddley, so I asked Darren if I could pay him to come down for the evening. Joe Riddley was delighted to write "Darren coming" in his log. As I climbed into Walker's Infiniti, I hoped I hadn't asked Darren to return to the scene of his crime.

There were twelve of us at dinner, including several single friends of Cindy's. Jed had been invited, too, and I could tell that two young women, at least, could fancy themselves as an Atlanta lawyer's wife. The only time I got to speak to him alone was briefly while we waited for the hostess. He sidled over to me and said, "I want to talk to you sometime about Pooh. She needs a legal guardian. Do you know who her lawyer is?"

I pressed one hand to my mouth in dismay. "I meant to find out, but I plumb forgot."

"I wish you would. Somebody has to take care of her. I wish I lived close enough."

The hostess arrived then to show us to a large reserved table by a big plate-glass window overlooking the water. I was already in my seat before I noticed Slade and Meriwether at a small table beyond ours. It only seemed neighborly to speak. If I'd been hosting our party, I'd have invited them to join us. However, Walker gave Slade a curt nod and sat next to me, with his back to him.

Slade didn't seem especially anxious to talk to us, either. All his attention was on Meriwether, who was gorgeous in black velvet. Seemed like she'd been getting even prettier recently.

Jed amiably sat between Cindy's two beautiful friends. He also steered them to seats where Meriwether could see them real well.

She wasn't looking. She was gazing at Slade like he'd personally carved the full moon outside the window and painted its reflection on the gently flowing water.

Since I was sitting where I could see both Jed and Meriwether, I watched to see if they'd start giving each other little probing looks, asking silent questions like, "Are you happy?" "Are you eating right?" Instead, they both seemed utterly content. I opened my menu and reminded myself we didn't live in Hollywood. In Hopemore, not every story has a romantic ending.

After we'd ordered, Slade called to our waiter and asked for more dressing for his salad. Apparently the waiter brought the wrong kind, because as he scurried off to replace it, Slade told

Meriwether, "Half the people in the world are below average, sweetheart, and most of them are waiters." He hadn't spoken loudly, but our tables were so close that Walker and I heard him.

Walker's head jerked up and his eyes got wide. He leaned over and murmured, "Mama, can you see that man's left hand?"

"No, why?"

Walker's nostrils flared and his face flushed. I wondered when he'd had his blood pressure checked. "I'd like to know if part of his pinkie is missing."

"I can tell you that much. It is. He caught it in a car door when he was little. Why?"

Walker pounded the table beside him lightly. "I know who he is! And why I don't like him!" He picked a roll from the basket and started picking it to bits like he used to pick the stuffing from my cushions.

"Care to share the knowledge?"

He gave me a lopsided grin. "Sure, but it's silly. Remember that trip my class took to Washington in fifth grade, when I worked my tail off earning half the money and you and Daddy put up the other half?"

"Yes."

"And remember how we had one too many people going, so I volunteered to room and buddy with somebody from another school, because I thought it would be cool to get to know somebody who wasn't from Hopemore?"

"Yes." Surely this couldn't be heading where I thought it was. I took a roll, too, and spread it with a lot of butter. I crave cholesterol when I'm nervous.

"And remember how I came home and told you I had a terrible time, because my roommate and buddy turned out to be a bully from Columbus, two years older than everybody else, who was so awful nobody from his own school would room with him?" Walker lathered the remaining roll with a lot more butter than his arteries needed, and took a savage bite.

"Slade's not from Georgia," I reminded him. "Maybe he just looks like that boy."

"No, it's him. He used to say that very same thing about anybody and everybody. 'Half the world's below average.' He embarrassed me to death everywhere we went."

He'd done a lot more than that. Walker came home complaining that they'd had to stay with their buddy the whole trip, and his would never stop to look at anything he wanted to see. He wouldn't even go to the bathroom when Walker needed to. I'd been real upset back then that the teachers hadn't assigned Walker another buddy, or added the two of them to another pair. Now he added something he hadn't told us then. "He flat out refused to sleep in a double bed with another boy. He'd have made me sleep on the *floor* if the other two boys in our room hadn't told him I had paid for my bed, and he could jolly well sleep on the floor himself. He did, but said

271

he'd break my arm if I ever fussed to the teachers about him. He could have, too. He was big, Mama. Lots bigger than I was back then." He chewed with the contentment of a man who has finally grown as big as the bullies.

I must have sat for a full minute trying to absorb all that. I found I was still furious with that child who had ruined Walker's trip. "You're sure?" I finally asked weakly.

"Danged sure. He hasn't even changed much, now that I know who he is. Except he had real long hair then. He still struts like the king of the universe and is charming with folks he wants to impress, but treats little people like dirt. Back then he sucked up to all the teachers." He gave a low chuckle. "As one of his best advertisers, I hope he finds out one day I'm that little kid he bullied all over Washington."

He hadn't spoken loudly, either, but he's got a carrying voice, and the last part of his sentence filled one of those silences that happen at meals. Slade slid back instantly and came toward us with a big grin on his face. He laid one hand on Walker's shoulder. "Are you my old roomie from the fifth-grade Washington trip? I thought you looked familiar."

I suspected he'd been waiting for the right minute to trot out that line, because I knew the very minute he'd found out who Walker was. It was the Sunday on Meriwether's porch, when Gusta said something about Walker *Crane* Yarbrough. That's why he dropped his paper in

Alice's lap, causing her to kick over my tea. Back when Walker was ten, he experimented for a few months with being called by his middle name. He'd gone on the Washington trip as Crane.

To me, Slade no longer looked like a charming newcomer who might be the answer to our prayers for Meriwether. He looked like the louse who spoiled my son's class trip.

When Slade stuck out his hand, I braced myself. I'd done my best with Walker's manners, even paid good money to send him to what Joe Riddley insisted on calling "a gentlemen's finishing school" instead of to the University of Georgia. But Walker wasn't always predictable, and anybody with any sense could read in his eyes that the memory of that trip wasn't all sweetness and light.

Slade wasn't dumb. He dropped his hand to Walker's shoulder. "I owe you an apology, buddy. I was a real brat as a kid. Forgive me?"

Walker made his mother proud. He stuck out his own hand. "Hey, it was a long time ago. No hard feelings." Both men laughed like men do when they are saying nice things and not meaning a word of it. Slade went back to Meriwether and bent near her — probably to explain. She looked our way, but not at Jed.

I don't know what Walker saw on my face, but he leaned over and said softly, "Smile, if it kills you. But there's still something in me that wishes I could knock him down just once. It would feel so good."

I gave him a big smile and murmured, "I'd like to knock him down for you." My heart twisted to remember what Walker wrote in that year's Christmas letter: *I worked very hard to earn my money, but the trip was pretty awful. I would not encourage anyone else to do this.*

I called Sheriff Gibbons when I got home and suggested he run a complete check on Slade Rutherford's background. He sure hadn't mentioned Columbus, Georgia, in any of the stories he'd told around town.

# 23

Two mornings later I left Joe Riddley at physical therapy long enough to run a van full of potted plants over to the new town center auditorium where we hold large meetings, wedding receptions, and business seminars. That day, the Junior League was having its annual fund-raising luncheon and fashion show, and I'd offered to donate ten plants for them to auction off.

As I pulled into the lot, Meriwether stood by her silver Mercedes looking uncertainly at a silver BMW and a green Saturn already parked in the lot. "Looks like we'll have some muscles to help with these plants," I called cheerfully, ignoring the way she was glaring at the BMW.

We each carried in a plant and found Jed and Maynard setting up mikes and a podium at the front. The room was set up for a luncheon much smaller than the Junior League's, and there was no stage for the fashion show.

Meriwether put down her plant with a thump. "What are you all doing?"

Maynard spoke over a mike he was carrying. "Getting ready for Rotary."

Ignoring us, Jed called from the far end of the

room, "You want three mikes up front?"

"I think two will be enough," Maynard called back.

"The Junior League has this room today," Meriwether said in an icy voice. "We've had it reserved six months."

Maynard shook his head. "Daddy's president of Rotary, and he reserved it last year."

Meriwether whipped out her cell phone, but we could tell at once that the news was not good. "We can't both meet here. You'll need to help Maynard find another place."

Meriwether held out the phone, but Maynard hadn't spent ten years in New York for nothing. "Sorry, but we're staying. Maybe you all could meet up at the motel by I-20."

"Their meeting room wouldn't hold us all. Besides, it smells of cigars. Why don't you all move up there?"

"It wouldn't hold us, either. And we've got guests coming from all over the state. This is a real important meeting." He adjusted a chair to stake his claim on the room.

Hopemore isn't like Atlanta. We don't have meeting rooms all over the place. This could get real serious. Meriwether looked mad enough to spit — except she'd never spit in public. "It's our fall fashion show, and we've sold two hundred tickets." They were getting nowhere fast.

"Is that poor woman still holding on the other end?" I asked.

Meriwether gave a snort of impatience and

said into the phone, "We'll get back to you."

Jed called, "Hey, we're gentlemen. Let me use your phone, Meri, and I'll see if the Country Club is available for you ladies. I'm sure your grandmother still belongs."

Meriwether clutched her phone to her chest like it would get cooties if he touched it. "Never mind." When she put her chin in the air like that, she was the spitting image of Gusta. "I'll call them myself." She went out in the hall, but all of us could hear her wail, "Can't you re-arrange things to accommodate us?"

"Could we meet in the church fellowship hall?" Jed asked Maynard softly.

I contributed my two cents' worth. "The women's sewing circle has it today."

"Uh-oh." Jed shook his head in defeat. "Nobody would ever get it, then."

Meriwether overheard him as she came back. "Get what?"

Jed shrugged, to show her it was a dead idea. "Nothing. I suggested you might use the church fellowship hall, but the women's sewing circle has it. There's no chance they'd move."

Her eyes flashed. "They'd move for me." She punched in another number.

It took her three calls, but she got the sewing circle to agree to meet the next day instead. "My hat is off to her," I muttered to Jed, who was standing near me. "Nothing is harder to shift than a group of church women who have staked a claim."

"She's got what it takes," he said sourly. "The hardest head in Georgia. The hardest heart, too," he added, after she called the church to tell them the *Rotary* would meet in the fellowship hall that noon.

To my surprise, Meriwether dropped by the office that afternoon. I was balancing our personal checkbook, but gladly pushed the right button to finish reconciling the account and stuffed the checks back in their envelope and into a pigeonhole. She sank into the chair by the window like she was tired to death. She had small crow's-feet around her eyes, and her hair wasn't as fluffy and soft as usual. "Good meeting?" I greeted her.

"We made a lot of money, but it was an enormous amount of work. Why, Mac, do people have to be bribed by a fashion show, a banquet, or an auction to be generous?" She rested her head against the high back of the chair and asked, "And why is it that every time I pass Pooh's house, Jed's car is there? He must be worrying her to death."

"He's worried about her. And Otis said it does her a lot of good to have company."

"Yeah, but Jed?" You'd have thought the man tracked in foot-and-mouth disease.

I leaned forward. "Have you all gone out at all since he got back? For old times' sake?"

Her laugh was as short and sharp as a stake through his heart. "For old times' sake I ought to shoot him. I don't know why he keeps

278

hanging around, embarrassing me to death. I'm trying to start a business. I don't have time to be worrying about him."

"How's that business coming?"

"We're going to send out our first catalogue in April, if I live that long. I have to run up to the Merchandise Mart to see what's available besides what I bought in China."

"You aren't going around the world in eighty days, looking for exciting things?"

She shook her head with regret. "The consultant said it's too much trouble to deal with individual suppliers in various countries. I can see that just by the trouble I'm having getting one shipment out of China. I don't know the laws for all the countries, either, and some of them expect bribes. It's a lot more sensible to buy from the Mart where I know I can get what I order, but I'll run the risk of everything looking like every other catalogue."

"Will you take the pictures yourself?" Meriwether was the photographer of choice for a lot of Hopemore organizations. She owned the best camera in town.

She laughed like I was making a joke, and some of her old sparkle returned. "You wouldn't believe what goes into taking those pictures. They create whole fake rooms to display a couple of pots. It takes days, even weeks, to shoot a catalogue. I found a photographer in Atlanta. He said he'd like to come down and shoot some of the pictures at Nana's, and I might want to use some of your rooms, too — and your barn, for the country look. What do you think?"

First, I thought it was interesting that both the Merchandise Mart and the photographer were in Atlanta, where Jed lived. Second, I thought she'd better think again if she thought Gusta would permit her home to appear in a catalogue. What I said, truthfully, was that I would be delighted to be in her catalogue. "But we aren't so much country as comfortable," I added.

"That's exactly what I want to show. My pots make people's lives more comfortable."

"What about the warehouse? I hear you've got men working on it." Even a town as small as Hopemore has a few abandoned buildings. Our biggest ones were lined up down by the railroad track, where trains no longer ran. Several, built of weather-beaten boards, were rotting and falling where they stood. One, of corrugated steel — the one Hiram begged the town council to magnetize — was slowly rusting away and watched constantly by Chief Muggins so drug dealers didn't claim it. But down at the end of the row, next to her granddaddy's old cotton gin, securely padlocked and still in pretty good shape, was a brick warehouse he'd built in 1920 to store local cotton until it was ready to ship to their mills.

Meriwether's green eyes danced with excitement. "It's going to be perfect. You can't imagine how much space there is inside —"

"I've been in that building many times with my daddy, delivering cotton. The warehouse always seemed mysterious — no windows, and that great big door where they could back a whole wagon inside to unload the bales. If I stop and think about it, I can still feel that cold concrete floor under my bare feet and the smell of cotton tickling my nose."

She laughed. "I used to love to go down there when I was little, too — for the very same reasons. And it's perfect for what I need, with the addition of heat, air conditioning, shelves for inventory, and a few lockable storage rooms for valuable merchandise."

"You sound like your daddy's daughter. Practical, wise, brave, and a little crazy. That's what Joe Riddley says a person has to be to run a business. I think you're going to make it."

For a minute she looked very young and vulnerable. "I hope so. I've never done anything as big as this." She closed her eyes and rested a minute. Then she asked without opening them, "Has Jed taken up permanent residence at Miss Hubbard's? They've had the funeral. Why doesn't he go back to Atlanta where he belongs? Looks like he'd get fired."

"He said he's got a lot of accrued vacation. I think he's waiting for the sheriff to find out who killed Hiram."

"They may never find that out. Will he stick around forever?"

"Oh, I think he'll go back eventually."

For a girl who was falling in love with Slade, she sure talked a lot about Jed.

# 24

## NOVEMBER

November blustered in with gray cloudy skies and rain. I got soaking wet putting Joe Riddley and his walker in and out of the car. Darren kept telling him he could walk without the walker, but he refused to try.

One day, driving through a neighborhood built back around 1950, I saw a "For Sale" sign in front of a one-story brick house. I slowed enough to notice a shallow step to the front door and an attached garage, and backed up for another look. No eaves to paint, no big halls to heat or cool, a dry walk to the house from the car, and a tidy little yard with two big trees. Ridd could rake or mow it in half an hour. Heck, Walker's nine-year-old, Tad, could rake and mow it. I found myself thinking about that house off and on for the rest of the day.

Sheriff Gibbons dropped by that afternoon, still convinced Darren committed the murder. "We'll get him eventually. Meanwhile, about our new editor. He's not got a criminal record, but he's told a lot of whoppers. He was born in South, not North, Carolina, in Orangeburg. His daddy was a Ford mechanic. Daddy drank and Mama called the police when he got violent. When Slade was nine, she got a divorce and moved to Columbus. Slade went to West Georgia College and worked for the LaGrange paper until he was hired by the one in Asheville." A smile flitted across his blood-hound face. "With all the lies he's told, he'd be a real good suspect, except he was in his office with three other people from seven that morning until he came to the party."

Slade being cleared as a suspect didn't make him a good marriage prospect, and Meriwether seemed headed that way. Wherever they went it was "honey" this and "sweetheart" that until it nearly made me sick. It didn't matter to me that Slade was the son of an auto mechanic, but I'll be darned if I wanted the granddaughter of my oldest friend to marry a liar.

But how could I tell Meriwether without admitting I'd asked Buster to check up on him?

Between worrying about Darren, worrying about Meriwether, worrying about Pooh, and worrying about Maynard and Selena — who might be in wheelchairs themselves before they got married — I didn't have as much time to worry about whether Joe Riddley would ever get better. Ridd didn't need to worry about me doing any detecting, either. When would I have found the time? And then, as if everything else wasn't enough . . .

Ridd dropped by one Sunday afternoon to

bring me some collard greens. He joined me for a glass of tea, and asked, "Are you taking care of the pool?" The swimming pool was in a high fenced enclosure behind our house. We didn't swim between October and May, but it still needed looking after.

I clapped both hands to my cheeks. "Oh, lordy, I haven't treated that pool since your daddy's party. I padlocked the gate the day before the party, to keep small children from drowning, and then after Hiram got shot, I plumb forgot about it."

We went to look. The blasted thing was a regular black lagoon, with a big turtle swimming around happy as a lark. I rested my head against the fence and bawled.

Ridd took my hand and led me inside. "Mama, you have got to hire more help. You need somebody to take care of the pool, to help Daddy bathe and dress, and to drive him back and forth to all these therapies. Walker and I are doing the best we can to help you keep the business going, but we can't help out here as much as we'd like to. We've got jobs."

"And families." I pulled a tissue from my pocket to blow my nose. "I know, honey. You all have been so sweet. I know you can't do more than you're doing."

"But you're not Superwoman, Mama. You've got to admit it. You can't do it all."

"Where would I find somebody who could help Joe Riddley and take care of a pool? Hired help doesn't grow on trees these days, you know."

The next morning, I got an answer to a prayer I hadn't even prayed. When we went to physical therapy, Darren wasn't there. "He's no longer with us," is all they would say. The new therapist was a jolly woman who got Joe Riddley's back up in one second by saying, "That bird will have to wait outside."

" 'Take care of Joe' is in my log," he said, agitated. "I can't do that if he's not here."

We were heading nowhere fast. "We'll come back tomorrow without the bird," I told her.

On our way home, Joe Riddley said, "I want Darren. I want Darren!"

"He's not working there anymore, honey."

"Where is he working? Take me there. Right now, Little Bit. You hear me?"

He was getting so upset, I went around the block and headed out to the apartments where Darren lived. It wasn't hard to identify his unit. The little yellow bug was parked in front.

Darren came to the door in black jeans and T-shirt. He tried to grin, but his voice cracked with anxiety. "They say people don't feel comfortable having me work with patients until this investigation is over. They didn't fire me, just gave me a leave of absence."

"How are you going to pay your bills?"

"I thought I'd ask the sheriff when my rent comes due."

I spoke on impulse. "I don't suppose you

286

know anything about pools, do you?"

"Sure. I grew up in Miami. We had a pool all my life. What do you want to know?"

"Whether you'll let me hire you. Ridd told me last night I need somebody to help with Joe Riddley — not with therapy, but driving him around, helping him bathe and dress. And I forgot to put chemicals in the pool for nearly a month, so it's full of algae and a big old turtle."

"That's bad, but not impossible to fix." He rubbed one hand across his hair. The blue had faded to gray, and the roots were half an inch long. "You sure you want somebody working for you who might have killed somebody?"

"You didn't kill anybody. When can you come?"

He shrugged; his grin looked almost normal. "Oh, I might fit you in next year."

"Want to start right now?"

"I'll get my keys."

Clarinda never had trouble stretching a meal for one more. Over dinner we agreed that Darren would pick Joe Riddley up after physical therapy each morning, bring him home, and help him exercise. I'd come home for dinner, but would get to put in a full morning's work again. While Joe Riddley napped, Darren would work on the pool and do other jobs around the house. Then he'd drive Joe Riddley to occupational therapy, bring him home, and stay long enough after supper to help Joe Riddley to bed.

"I can't remember another present that felt this good," I told him as I left for work.

At supper that night, he and Joe Riddley chatted about baseball like two old cronies. When Joe Riddley talked about a pass instead of a throw, and a touchdown instead of a home run, Darren took it in stride. When it was bedtime, he got Joe Riddley to bed without a single grumble while I sat in the study recliner with my feet up, reading a novel. I hadn't read a book in so long I felt like a parched woman taking a long, cool drink.

Darren tiptoed in and whispered, "I'm off now to see Alice."

"Looks like you two would be tired of each other by now."

He came in and perched on the edge of the love seat. "I couldn't have made it through this without her. When I get down, she reminds me they can't have a speck of evidence against me. She knows what it's like to suffer, too. Do you know her story? She's had a really sad life."

That's probably what made her so attractive to him.

I punished myself for that thought by saying, "Tell me about it. All I know is that her sister drowned before she came to work for Gusta."

"That's just the last part. First her mom and dad got married and had two kids, a brother and Alice."

"I thought it was a sister," I objected.

He held up one hand. "Wait. They had a boy and a girl, and Alice was the younger. When she was not quite one, her daddy and her brother were both killed in an automobile accident. A year later her mother married her stepfather and they had her sister. She and Terri were about three years apart. Her stepfather treated them both alike, and she adored him. He was in the Air Force and they lived all over the world. But when she was ten — no, thirteen, I think, somewhere around there — he was killed in a freak military accident. A lot of people said her mother ought to sue the Air Force, but she wouldn't. She worked at Kmart the whole time they were in junior high and senior high, and Alice had to take care of herself and her sister all that time. From what she says, her sister panicked easily and was scared of a lot of things."

"That's how she died, wasn't it?"

"Yeah. They were scuba diving, and she caught her foot and panicked. Alice says they could have gotten her out if she'd left on her respirator or breathed with a buddy, but she was too scared. Before anybody could stop her, she'd ripped off her mask and taken in too much water. Alice said watching her sister die without being able to help her was the hardest thing she ever went through. Their mom died a couple of years ago — a bad heart, I think. Now she's really alone, except for that aunt in Jacksonville. Have you ever heard a sadder story?"

"Not many," I admitted. I could imagine one, though: a young man convicted of a murder he didn't commit.

Alice didn't look sad, though, when I saw her

on my way home from the beauty parlor Saturday. She and Darren were running, and both wore wide smiles. His hair gleamed freshly blue in the sunlight, and hers was blowing alive and free around her face. That was the first time I'd seen her hair down since her first day in town. She sure was prettier that way. I wished she could loosen up a little overall.

Sunday night around nine, Ridd and Martha surprised me with a visit. "Bethany's home with Cricket," Martha told me, "and my hunk here brought his tape from this afternoon's golf match. He'll watch it and listen out for Pop if I can persuade you to go out for pie."

Were two children ever more thoughtful? I grabbed my pocketbook. "I can always be persuaded to go for pie."

Going in to Myrtle's, we ran in to Maynard and Selena coming out. "We ate all the chocolate pie," she teased me. "You'll have to settle for coconut."

"Myrtle generally keeps a piece in the back with my name on it," I informed her.

As we settled ourselves at a table, Martha sighed. "I wish those two would go on and get married. If ever two people belonged together . . ." She broke off and her eyes widened. "Don't look," she said softly, "but Jed's in the back booth with Gusta's lady-in-waiting."

I did look, of course. Alice sat in the last booth by the window, facing the door. Her hair was down, electric around her face. She wore a bright red sweater that actually fit, and when she lifted her head, I saw she was wearing mascara, blusher, and lipstick.

Jed looked spiffy, too, in a navy blazer, khaki slacks, and a white shirt open at the neck. They were eating pie with ice cream, and Jed was leaning across the table and waving his spoon around. He must have been cutting up, because she threw her head back and laughed.

"He brings out the best in her," Martha said in satisfaction.

"Poor Darren," I murmured.

"Yeah, but if Meriwether doesn't want Jed, and Darren killed Hiram . . ."

Fortunately Myrtle slapped down large wedges of chocolate pie before us right then, or I might have spoken sharply to Martha for once in my life. We each took a bite and exchanged the conspiratorial smiles of women who aren't counting calories right then.

As Myrtle poured each of us a cup of coffee, she glanced toward her door. "Uh-oh," she grunted. "Now we've got trouble."

If you grew up in the South, those words always spark an instant of fear that somebody is about to do something stupid related to race. But this time it was Meriwether, coming in with Slade. He looked like a model in white jeans and a yellow cotton sweater, and while I don't generally like a man in gold chains, his looked real good. Meriwether didn't look so bad herself, in a green corduroy pantsuit that probably cost twice as much as my Sunday best. She'd pulled her hair back at her neck with a green-and-gold silk scarf, and even had on green high heels. I do like to see a woman's shoes match her dress.

She didn't notice Jed and Alice, because she came straight across the restaurant to greet us. Slade took the booth next to Jed's and ordered two pieces of cake. Over her shoulder, Meriwether called, "I want pecan pie with ice cream. Nobody makes pecan pie like Myrtle."

"Hi, Meriwether!" Alice called from their booth, raising her spoon. "That's what we're having, too."

Meriwether turned with a smile, but when she saw Jed, her expression would have frozen a polar bear. "You know, honey," she called to Slade, "I'm not real hungry after all. Why don't we go back to my place?"

Slade hesitated, then slid from the booth. "Sure, sweetie. Anything you say."

"Anything you say, sweetie," Jed mimicked. "Or anything your grandmother says, or your daddy says. . . ." He shook his head and heaved a big sigh.

Meriwether stomped over to the booth and glared down at him. "My father is dead, you scum. I'll ask you not to mock him."

"Oh." He exhaled like she'd punched him. "When? I didn't know —"

Martha and I exchanged stricken looks. I hadn't taken the time to write Jed that Garlon died. Apparently nobody else had, either.

Meriwether obviously didn't believe him. She turned to Alice with a pitying smile. "How you can go out with this unfeeling, childish oaf is more than I can understand." She would have swept out, but as she turned, she caught her skinny heel in one of the many holes in Myrtle's linoleum. Instead of making a grand exit, she wrenched off her heel and pitched to the floor with a yelp of pain.

Martha, being a nurse, rushed right over, followed by Myrtle — avoiding my eye. Jed was already on his knees beside Meriwether. By that time on a Sunday, Myrtle's floor wasn't going to do his pants any good, but he didn't seem to care. "How bad are you hurt? Do you want me to call a doctor? Poor honey! Where does it hurt?"

"I twisted my knee." I couldn't tell if Meriwether's tears were from pain or anger. Probably a little of both. "I don't think I can get up." He bent his head and she put one arm around his neck like it was the most natural thing in the world.

Before he could help her up, though, Slade — who was hovering like he didn't know what to do — tapped Jed on the shoulder. "Pardon me, buddy, but this is my date." I noticed he squatted so his white jeans didn't touch the floor.

Meriwether took her arm off Jed and Jed backed away. But though he spoke to Slade, his eyes were still glued to hers. "Then you take real good care of her. You hear me?"

Meriwether's lips trembled, and I was afraid she was going to cry. Instead, before anybody knew she was going to do it, she'd scooped up a blob of lettuce just dripping with salad dressing that somebody had dropped on the floor. She hurled it at Jed and hit him smack in the middle of the throat where his collar lay open. "This is all your fault," she told him, her eyes glistening with tears.

I fully expected him to yell at her. Who could have blamed him if he had? Even the pain she was in didn't excuse those manners. But Jed sat down hard in his booth, dug the disgusting blob from his throat, and wiped it on his saucer. Then he picked up a piece of pie crust off his plate and threw it at her, hitting her on the shoulder. "Maybe it's all your fault."

"Stop it, you two!" Myrtle's knees popped as she bent to pick the pie crust off the floor. "I don't allow food fights in here. You oughta know that."

Martha gently probed Meriwether's knee. "Does that hurt?"

Meriwether gasped. She pressed one hand over her mouth and spoke around it. "Yeah."

"You probably tore something. You need to go straight to the emergency room to get it checked." Martha held out her hand for Myrtle to help her up.

Simultaneously, Slade asked, "You think it's that bad?" and Jed said, "Do we need an ambulance?"

Slade glared at him, then looked up at Martha. "Do we need an ambulance?"

"What do you think?" Martha bent to ask Meriwether.

Small beads of sweat were forming on her upper lip, and her eyes looked like she was in a lot of pain. Slade bent nearer. "We can get there faster if you can hop to the car."

She pressed her lips tight together, but nodded.

I saw Jed pick up his fork and jab it several times into his pie, but he didn't say a word.

Myrtle hurried to the kitchen. "I'll call to tell them you're coming."

Slade awkwardly helped Meriwether to her feet.

"Carry her!" Jed urged before he could help it.

Slade swept him a scathing glance. Meriwether bit her lip. "I think I can walk if you'll help me. It's just a little sprain." She put one arm around his neck and he held one hand at her waist. She hopped toward his sleek green Lexus in the parking lot, wincing with every hop.

"Turkey," Jed muttered, watching them drive away. "He should have carried her. Or at least brought the car to the door." Finally, he remembered Alice. "Now, where were we?"

Alice gathered up her purse. "I think I need to get back. Mrs. Wainwright would kill me if she heard about Meriwether from anybody else. But you stay and finish your pie. I'll walk — it's not far." All the light was gone from her face, and her eyes were stormy. I saw she had pulled back her hair again, too, and secured it with a brown scrunchy.

"Want to join us?" I called to Jed when the door closed behind her.

He gathered up his pie and coffee. "Might as well. All the other beautiful women in the place have deserted me."

"Looked to me like you were losing the salad wars, too," I told him, signaling Myrtle to heat up my coffee.

Jed grinned and brushed his throat. "Yeah." He puckered his forehead. His eyes strayed to the door. "You think Alice was upset because I tried to help Meriwether?"

Martha and I didn't say a word.

He sat tapping his fingers on the table, a habit he'd always had when he was little. For a while he'd worked it out by drumming in the school band, but it looked like he had a lot of pent-up drumming to get out of his system that night.

"You finding out any more about Hiram?" I asked, to make conversation. I was pretty sure Buster Gibbons would have told me anything he'd told Jed.

Jed shook his head, and his lips twisted in a rueful smile. "Poor old Hiram. I wish he'd stayed in Atlanta. He was doing real well. Working regular, too, doing yard work and a little maintenance for a small apartment complex. He had a room on a bus line, and I could keep an eye on him. We'd have dinner from time to time, so I could make sure he was all right."

Martha forked up the last of her pie crust. "Then why'd he come back?"

"Same old thing. He thought aliens were operating in those apartments. He found a stray pup wandering around and started feeding it, but one day the pup disappeared. Probably just moved on. But Hiram went all over the area looking for it. Even had me print signs to put on telephone poles. When he couldn't find it, he swore aliens had taken it."

His drumming was driving me crazy, so I put my hand over his. "Sorry," he apologized, wrapping his hands around his cup.

"You mean Hiram came home because he lost a dog?" Martha asked.

Jed's blue eyes gleamed with mischief. "Oh, that wasn't all. If it had just been the dog, I don't think he'd have given up his job. He really liked the work, felt important. The tenants counted on him to keep things running, and it was like he had finally found his niche. But a few weeks after the dog disappeared, one of the tenants died, and the family came to get the stuff at night after Hiram went home. When the furniture rental company arrived the next day, Hiram was sure the tenant had been beamed up to a spaceship. He explained to me that aliens put humans in big zoos on Venus. The last straw was when a car got stolen from the parking lot in the middle of the day, in the twenty minutes it took Hiram to walk down to the Seven-Eleven for some lunch. He passed it going out and it wasn't there when he came back. At first he thought the guy who owned it had gone out for something — he worked nights. But in a little while the guy came out to get in the car, and they realized it had been taken. The police didn't find it, either — which isn't surprising. It had probably been chopped for parts before the police started looking. But Hiram was sure aliens had stolen it. He said they had a dog, a woman, and a car, so all they needed was a man to complete the exhibit. He was terrified he'd be next. In fact, he wanted me to come back home, too. Said aliens were less likely to invade a little place like Hopemore."

"And then they did." I didn't know if I felt like laughing or crying. Poor Hiram, was there anything any of us could have done to make him feel safer on God's green earth?

"So he said." I saw in Jed's eyes some of what I was feeling. "He was convinced that night when he called me that at least one alien was walking around the streets of Hopemore wearing somebody else's skin. What they did with the skinless person, he wasn't real clear on."

"Stop it," I told him, reaching for my pocketbook. "If I start picturing skinless humans wandering around the ether in a spaceship, I'm gonna wind up as crazy as Hiram."

Jed got suddenly solemn. "I just hope nobody winds up that dead."

# 25

Tuesday I went over to the bank for change. As I came out the door, Gusta's black Cadillac pulled into the handicapped zone. Otis drove. Gusta rode beside him, and Meriwether sat sideways in the back. "Where's Alice?" I asked as Otis hurried to open the door, leaving the keys in the car.

Gusta climbed out with a puff of disgust. "That aunt in Jacksonville is poorly again. She left early and won't be back until late." You'd have thought Alice had gone to Syria for a month.

"She does deserve a little time off," I reminded my old friend and foe.

"She worked pretty hard yesterday," she admitted, patting her purse. "She's typed all my tenants' names into the computer so we can enter their checks tomorrow. But she gallivanted all over town last weekend. Out with that therapist with the odd hair Saturday until all hours, then out with a girlfriend Sunday night."

Meriwether's eyes met mine. Her mouth twitched and I had to look away not to grin. Alice was pretty savvy if she'd already learned not to mention Jed Blaine to Gusta.

Meriwether looked especially pretty that morning, but I didn't mention it. It might be pain that made her eyes bright and her cheeks pink.

Gusta was still ranting. ". . . don't know what I pay her for. Back when Granddaddy was governor —"

"Forty hours a week," I said.

That turned off her water. "What?"

"You pay her for forty hours a week. Any more and she deserves overtime."

"Nonsense. She gets room and board, and the work is practically nonexistent. But I can't stand here talking, I need to make this deposit and get Meriwether to the doctor. Claims she's torn muscles in her leg."

As Gusta stomped into the bank, I bent down to see how Meriwether was doing. She had her injured leg up on the seat. "It's hurting a lot," she admitted. "They immobilized it Sunday night and said to wait for the swelling to go down. Now I've got to see an orthopedist. Heaven knows what he'll do to it. I called Otis to see if he could drive me, and found he was already scheduled to bring Nana to the bank. She insists on coming with me."

"It's her place to do that," Otis reminded her.

"I can see why Gusta thought it was a bad time for Alice to go away, though," I said.

"Don't let Nana's grumbling fool you. She brags all the time about Alice to me."

"Letting you know you can be replaced."

"Absolutely." Meriwether's eyes twinkled. "And Alice has done marvelous things. She's persuaded Nana to put all her databases onto the computer. That's practically every organization in town, you know. And they started inputting her financial accounts yesterday. Alice even convinced Nana she ought to put me on her bank account, so I can sign checks in case anything happens to her. Daddy and I tried for years to get her to have him on the accounts, but Nana always hemmed and hawed and accused us of expecting her to get mentally incompetent."

"How did Alice convince her, then?"

"She told her Bitsy broke her hand once, and if her son hadn't been on the account, she wouldn't have had a way to sign checks. Nana's arthritis is already so bad she can scarcely hold a pen, so she finally saw the sense of it. She's getting a signature card for me this morning."

"Very wise." As I stood up to head back to the office, Otis spoke from the front seat.

"I wish Miss Winifred would put you on her account, too. It plumb worries us, Judge. We never know from one day to the next whether she's gonna be thinking clearly enough to sign her name." Appalled, I remembered I'd promised to call Pooh's lawyer, but it kept slipping my mind. But Otis and Lottie would be up a creek without a paddle if Pooh couldn't sign checks. They couldn't buy groceries or get their own paychecks, and Pooh's fears that her lights and water could be cut off might come true. He asked anxiously, "Could you talk to her about that?"

"I'll call her lawyer this morning," I promised. "Joe Riddley and I ought to put one of our boys on our account, too. He's not always reliable right now, and I could break a hand as easily as Gusta. Listen, Meriwether, do you need anything? Meals brought in, or somebody to stay with you at night? I'm sure Ridd's Bethany would be glad to move in with you for a few days."

"I'm fine, but thanks."

Seeing Gusta heading out the bank door, I said loud enough for her to hear me, "Still, that child does deserve some time off. Gusta can't expect her to work twenty-four hours a day seven days a week."

Gusta, making tracks for her car pretty fast for a woman on a cane, ignored me.

Vern, irate, hobbled three steps behind. He must have missed her arrival and was making up for lost time. As Gusta lowered herself into her seat, he bent down with a very red face and shook a finger at her. "I'm gonna have the judge here put you in jail for a hundred years."

She slammed the door and spoke through her lowered window. "I can't talk to you now. We're late for the doctor."

"You get him to give you a handicapped sticker."

"Age is its own handicap," she called as they rolled away.

★ ★ ★

Gusta wasn't the only person disgruntled with Alice. I got home after work that evening to find Darren helping Joe Riddley down the driveway on the walker. They were halfway to the road when I got there, and Darren looked as blue as his hair.

"Who ate your brownie?" I greeted him. "You were smiling big enough on Saturday, racing Miss Alice around the courthouse. You'd even gotten her to let down her hair."

"That was before that lawyer cut me out. I can't compete with BMW convertibles."

"I doubt you'll have to. Jed's old girlfriend fell right next to their table at Myrtle's, and he was on his knees helping her in a flash. Miss Alice was *not* impressed. Walked home, in fact."

That, finally, got a grin. "Great! I'll give her a call. And do you think I could have a few days off around Thanksgiving to go home? I want to ask Alice to come, too. She likes Florida."

"You can have time off as far as I'm concerned, but you'll have to wait until tomorrow to ask Alice. She's down in Jacksonville visiting her aunt again today."

"I hope she's okay. She seems to be pretty sickly."

"Since she's Alice's only relative, I expect Alice worries more than she would if she had a slew of aunts and cousins."

"You all planning on talking all day?" Joe Riddley demanded loudly. "I need to get down to the field to check Ridd's corn."

"Sic 'em!" Joe urged from the top of his cap.

"The corn is finished," I informed him. "It's November. Why don't you and Darren head back up the drive and I'll fix us some hot chocolate?" The breeze was brisk.

"Why don't you try a few steps without the walker?" Darren added. "Let Mac bring it, and I'll walk right beside you to spot you. You aren't going to fall."

"I fall easier than you know. Fell down the steps at church Sunday and it took four men to get me up."

As I shook my head to tell Darren that was another of Joe Riddley's tall tales, he told a taller one. "And last week I was helping Ridd pitch hay from our barn loft, and I fell all the way from the barn. Good thing I landed on the hay, or I coulda got hurt bad."

"And next week we're going to the Empire State Building and you can fall off there," I told him. "Let me take the walker, hon. Try taking a few steps without it."

"I can't walk." He clutched the walker defiantly. "Anybody can see I can't walk. My legs got hurt."

"Your legs are fine," Darren reminded him. "It was your head that got hurt."

"My head doesn't hurt a bit." Joe Riddley knocked on the side of it to show us how solid it was. Startled, Joe spread his wings and flew to the lowest branch of Joe Riddley's little birthday oak. He perched there swaying on the frail branches.

"Come here, bird." Joe Riddley held out his arm.

Joe didn't budge.

"Come here, I said," Joe Riddley demanded. Joe didn't budge.

"I'm coming after you," Joe Riddley warned. Still Joe didn't budge.

Joe Riddley pivoted away from his walker and walked five normal steps to the tree. "Get on that arm," he ordered, holding it out.

Joe hopped the short distance to his arm. "Good boy. Good boy," he squawked.

Darren and I hugged in pure joy.

Joe Riddley looked around and saw us. "Boy, let go of my wife. Little Bit, bring me my walker. Why'd you take it way over there? You know I can't walk a step without it."

# 26

Clarinda had baked a big chocolate cake, so that evening while Darren was settling Joe Riddley for the night, I decided to run part of it over to Meriwether with a package of stew and some of Ridd's garden vegetables from my freezer.

Jed's car sat in the driveway. I would have driven back home and gone another time, but I might be needed to sign a warrant after one of them killed the other.

Almost as soon as I rang the bell, Jed opened the door. "Hello! Come to see the wounded? She had a fight with the doctor and lost." He padded to the living room in his sock feet, apparently making himself right at home.

Poor Meriwether lay on the couch with her leg encased in an elaborate contraption of nylon and straps that started at her ankle and disappeared up her khaki skirt. She greeted me with a sour grimace. "The doctor says I have to wear this four weeks, maybe six. And I'm not to put weight on the leg that whole time."

"I'm so sorry. Will this put a crimp in starting your business?"

"I'd already had a crimp. The workmen have

another job to finish, so they're taking a week off from my warehouse. They promise it'll be ready to receive shipments by our agreed-on date, though." She waved me to a chair. "At least I can offer you a seat."

The living room had blossomed in peach, blue, and green with touches of burgundy. A new couch and two new chairs were augmented by lamps and tables I recognized from Gusta's. Several of her paintings hung on the walls and one of her Chinese carpets softened the wooden floor.

The large blue chair had Jed's loafers beside it, so I took the smaller peach one. "It's lovely, honey. Has Gusta come to see all this?"

"She sure did, and deigned to say the place looks charming for such a little house."

"Good for Gusta. She may mellow before she gets old."

Jed leaned over from his chair and took one of Meriwether's hands. "She's not the only one doing some mellowing. Meriwether and I have declared a truce."

I looked at them and ached for what could have been. Maybe it was because Joe Riddley and I met when we were so young, but I'd always had an extra soft spot for those two. They'd met at our church preschool, when she was a curly-headed four and he a towheaded five. Her family's donations paid his full scholarship, but neither of them knew that. Through their school years they were always together. A friend from India said about her happy marriage, arranged at birth to a boy she grew up with, "You treat somebody differently when you know all your life you are going to marry him." I knew what she meant. I'd gone through it with Joe Riddley and watched it between Meriwether and Jed.

However, Meriwether had a fortune and Jed was a Blaine. Somewhere around fourth grade, that fact reared its ugly head. It wasn't poverty, and it wasn't dirt. Helena kept her child scrubbed within an inch of his life, and I made sure he wore decent clothes, passing down all Walker outgrew, and Walker was a fussy dresser. It was little things — birthday parties to which he wasn't invited, social events he didn't know had happened until they were over.

The year she was nine, he asked what she wanted for Christmas and she said, "A gold locket with your picture," with the blissful ignorance of a child who'd always gotten anything she wanted. He came into my office that afternoon asking if I had any work he could do to earn money to buy a gold locket. I knew he'd never earn enough to buy the kind of locket her family and friends would admire. Worried about that, I confided in Pooh.

As I had hoped, she found a solution. "I've got a child's locket that belonged to my little sister. Let me see if Lottie can find it." We agreed Jed would rake her leaves for two weeks to earn it, and he was glad to do it. Meriwether loved the locket, wore it everywhere. But Pooh and I knew we couldn't always rescue him.

Through high school, though, Meriwether continued to have a mind of her own. She defied both Gusta and Garlon to go with Jed to every dance, every football game, and every party. She was perfectly happy sipping milkshakes with him at Hardee's while her friends danced at the country club. Jed was her escort when she was homecoming queen, and she went to Georgia Wesleyan because he was at Mercer.

During their college years, even Joe Riddley started to worry about how Jed could support Meriwether in the style she was used to, but at spring break of her junior year they came by the store, glowing. "Jed's been accepted to Mercer Law School next fall," she told us proudly.

"And we're getting married the next summer," he added. "We'll be poor at first, but one day I can give her anything." At that point all he could give her was a diamond so tiny it looked like the head of a pin.

"I don't want anything except him," she assured us.

They planned an August wedding. Then, right before her graduation, we heard the wedding was off. Meriwether came home and turned to Georgia granite if anyone so much as mentioned his name. The closest she'd come to saying what happened was once when she told me, "You're lucky all your family likes each other."

That all ran through my head in far less time than it takes to tell it, while they sat and smiled at one another. Finally he asked her a silent question and she nodded with a smile. "We're getting married the week before Christmas," he informed me. "You're the first to know."

I held on to the arms of my chair in case it started levitating. "What happened?"

Meriwether looked like she used to, not merely charming but radiant. "He stayed under my skin all these years, I guess. And Sunday night when I fell and he came to help me, looking so worried, I knew his feelings hadn't changed, either."

"You threw salad at him," I reminded her.

Jed guffawed. "She was saying she loved me. We used to have food fights all the time, starting in junior high. Just little ones — we never disrupted the cafeteria. But throwing a small piece of food and saying 'it's all your fault' was our secret code. As soon as she lobbed me with that lettuce, I knew things were going to be all right. That's why I threw the pie crust back." Their expressions would have made me sick if I weren't a sentimental old softie.

"I figured I'd better let the editor take her to the hospital, though," Jed added. "I didn't want to make a scene. So I came over after she got home, and we got things straight between us."

"Have you told Gusta?"

"Not yet," Meriwether began.

"But we're working up our courage." He

rubbed one cheek with his palm. "I wish I could find out who my daddy was before we tell her. Do you know anything — anything at all, Mac?"

"I always figured Helena found you under a bush."

"Or floating down the river in a basket. But if she didn't?"

I shook my head doubtfully. "I don't know. We all assumed he was in the Air Force, or another civilian at Warner Robbins, but she never said. His name isn't on your birth certificate?"

He leaned forward and clasped his hands between his knees. "No, but Hiram kept hinting at something for the past several months. The first time was when I took him up to see my offices." Seeing my startled look, he laughed. "Oh, I took him after work. I wouldn't expose the firm's partners or clients to Hiram. But anyway, he looked around and nodded like a wise old owl, and he said, 'Boy, you done got where you was born to be.' I thought at the time he meant I'd gotten what I went to law school for, but every time we met after that he'd say things like, 'Your daddy and mama would be real proud of you' or 'If Miss High and Mighty knew what I know, she'd climb off her high horse and beg you to marry her granddaughter.' "

Jed rumpled Meriwether's hair and she swatted him playfully. "Not unless your daddy was a president she voted for."

"Hey, I aim that high." He leaned over and kissed her.

"Hiram never told you anything else?" I asked, to remind them I was there.

He went back to his chair. "Nothing I could understand. Several times I said, 'Hiram, tell me what you know.' But he'd screw up his mouth and promise, 'I'll tell you sometime.' He never said what he was waiting for. Probably for Martians to land."

"Probably," I agreed. "And he might have been making it up."

"Maybe. But he told me all sorts of things I didn't know before. Like, he said Hector threw a fit when Mama brought home another mouth to feed, and wanted her to take me back where I belonged."

"As if Hector ever did a lick of work to feed you," I said sourly.

"You got that right. But Hiram said they fought about it a lot at first, until Hector had to go do some time — his first stint in jail, I think."

"Yeah, that was about the time Helena came to work for us. You were around a year old, not walking yet, and Hiram volunteered to look after you."

"Oh, no!" Meriwether exclaimed.

I chuckled. "That's what Helena and I said, too. We scurried around pretty smart finding somebody else to keep Jed, then we told Hiram that Helena got free child care with her job." She did, too, until he entered preschool, but I didn't bother to tell them that. I just added,

"Hiram was real put out with us for not leaving you with him."

Jed chuckled. "He told me he never minded having a little bugger around the house, and was always glad Mama got to keep me."

"The fact that he said Helena 'got to keep' you" — Meriwether took her hand from Jed's long enough to sketch quotation marks — "makes me wonder if she was even your mother."

"Have you asked Hector about this since you got back?" I asked.

"Yeah, but he said, 'Helena never told me a *thang,*' which is true. He and Mama never got along, and she never spoke to him unless she had to."

"Which brings us back to the bush," I joked.

"I hope it was a bush with decent family roots. You don't think anybody would have killed Hiram to keep him from telling me who I am, do you?"

"That's pretty far-fetched. We don't run to missing royalty in Hopemore. Now if it had been *Hiram* claiming to be their relative, I can see the point in somebody's getting him out of the way. But you clean up real good. Any family would be proud to own you."

"Except one," he said ruefully.

Meriwether leaned over and punched him. "Don't be mean. I told you I'll marry you this time, Nana or no Nana."

My opportunity had come. I could be the first in Hope County to know. "Was Gusta the reason you didn't get married before?"

Meriwether nodded, and Jed shook his head, "You can't both be right," I informed them.

"Nana was objecting, and I begged Jed to wait until she came around."

"But she doesn't get to take all the blame." Jed squeezed her hand. "I told Meriwether Miss Gusta would never agree to her marrying me, and we'd have to do it in spite of her whenever we did it. She begged me to wait one more year, and I got on my own high horse and said if she wouldn't marry me when we planned to do it, it was off." He groaned. "We were such fools. How could I have been so dumb?"

"Hardheaded," I told him. "Your daddy must be southern, at least. Southern men have heads harder than the granite beneath our soil."

For several minutes we sat in silence. They held hands and looked at each other like they couldn't get enough of it. Jed was so happy his freckles glowed. I don't know what they were thinking but I was thinking about twelve wasted years. Their children could be up in school by now. I was so busy picturing little girls with Meriwether's green eyes and curls and little boys with Jed's freckles — except the boys would probably get the curls and the girls the freckles — that I was startled when Jed heaved a big sigh and said softly, "I think Mama really was my mother. At least my birth certificate tells us that."

"You're lucky to have a birth certificate at all," I informed him. "Helena lost your first one, and had to get a new one when you started school. A friend of hers in the courthouse helped, I remember, and they had trouble locating the original. Finally Helena had to swear an affidavit, and —"

"You're leaking!" Meriwether exclaimed, pointing at me.

"Oh, laws a mercy." I held up my dripping plastic bag. "I brought you some stew and frozen vegetables. Now you'll need to cook them tomorrow."

Jed grabbed the food and took it to the kitchen. I looked ruefully at my lap. "I need to go, so I can get out of this sopping skirt." But before I got up, the doorbell rang.

Meriwether peered through the lace sheers at her window. "It's Nana and Slade. Don't leave us, Mac. We need moral support."

"I can't answer the door like this."

"Jed?" she called. "Can you get that?"

As he ushered them in, it was obvious that I was the only person in the room universally welcome. Jed and Slade carried in chairs from the dining room and each took his seat like he was prepared to wait the other out. Gusta opened battle as soon as she set a basket covered with a red napkin on the floor and settled her gray skirts to her satisfaction in the blue chair. "What is he doing here?" Only good breeding kept her from pointing at Jed.

"He brought me supper," Meriwether replied cooly.

"I've brought you supper. Florine had meat loaf and I've brought you some."

Slade rose to his feet. "Let me take that to the refrigerator, Augusta."

Point to Slade. Jed would never be able to call Gusta by her given name if he lived to be a hundred. And, as I have said, nobody but Slade called her Augusta.

She gave him her wintry smile. "You are so *kind,* Slade."

He sauntered into the kitchen like it was his house. "Do you need a glass of tea or anything while I'm here, honey?" he called.

Meriwether didn't reply.

Gusta leaned from the wing chair and said softly, "I hope you aren't encouraging *him,* dear." She gave a slight sideways nod toward Jed, as if he couldn't hear every word.

Jed stretched out on his chair and spread out his blue sock feet. "Oh, she's been pretty encouraging, Miss Gusta. Pretty encouraging." He clasped his hands behind his head and grinned.

Meriwether started to frown at him, then changed her mind and lifted her chin. "Jed and I are getting married the week before Christmas." Oh, I was proud of her!

Slade, coming back from the kitchen, made a short strangled sound. Gusta sat like she'd turned to stone. Then she turned to me and asked, "How is dear Joe Riddley?"

"Dear Joe Riddley actually took five steps on

316

his own this afternoon. But I don't think that's what Meriwether wants to talk about."

"Meriwether is ill."

Slade went to the couch and knelt beside her. He spoke so softly I had to strain my ears to hear. "You don't have to marry him. I was going to ask you at Thanksgiving, but I'll do it right here in front of everybody if that's what you want."

Meriwether shook her head and said, equally softly, "I'm sorry, Slade. But I'm going to marry Jed."

"You can't throw yourself away on him. I offer you my heart and my good name."

I figured an interruption might be in order. "The Rutherfords from South Carolina?"

"North Carolina." Gusta's tone implied that I may be southern, but my family wasn't exactly quality. Her gnarled hands clutched the arms of the chair so tightly that her veins stood out like wisteria.

Any family who survived the mosquitoes, malaria, heat, humidity, gnats, and boll weevils of early Georgia, as mine did, counts as quality, so I ignored her. "I believe Mr. Rutherford was raised in Orangeburg. Isn't that right, Slade?"

Slade slid out from that like butter between hot pancakes. He stood and gave me a friendly nod. "That's partly right. Daddy worked in Orangeburg for a while, and I was born down there."

Jed waved Slade back to his seat. "Even if you

were born in Buckingham Palace, Meriwether is going to marry me. And Miss Gusta knows everything there is to know about my lack of pedigree." An impish grin creased his freckled face. Jed wasn't anywhere near as handsome as Slade, but anybody would have to admit he was cute — with one notable exception.

The exception gave him a chilling stare. "I think you ought to be going."

Jed leaned forward like he was about to tell Gusta a secret. "You'd better be nice to me, Miss Gusta. I'm fixing to endow your granddaughter with my good name, the purity of my heart, and all my worldly goods."

"A parrot?" Her voice would have frozen poor Joe in two seconds flat.

"Oh, he's got more than that." I gave a grand wave. "He's also got some books at my place that belonged to his grandmother."

Jed's blue eyes widened in surprise. "Virgil?" He sounded like he'd found an old friend.

"I think so. There's also a book of poetry, a Latin grammar, and a couple of others. Your mother left them with us for you."

"Then let's go get them! Honey," he said deliberately, leaning over Meriwether and giving her a conspiratorial smile, "this room is a bit full. I'll go with Mac now and come back tomorrow. But hold fast to your courage, you hear me?"

She reached up and stroked his cheek. "It's screwed to the mast."

Jed squeezed her hand, then slipped on his loafers. "Ready, Mac?"

I said my good-byes and trotted after him down the walk. "I don't know what your hurry is," I grumbled. "Those books have been there fifteen years."

"I wanted out of there. Besides, they are mine, right? And they were Mama's?"

"They were your grandmother's. Helena left them with us for you." He was going to be disappointed when he saw what a pitiful legacy it was, but I was touched that he was that sentimental about his mother. "Follow me home, and don't tailgate," I commanded. "I can't speed. I'm a judge."

Darren was in our living room watching television. "J.R.'s fast asleep and Joe's in the barn." As he let himself out the back, the dogs didn't even bark.

"Where are the books?" Jed looked around the kitchen like I kept them with the cookbooks.

"They're in the study, and you'll have to reach them. I certainly can't."

I pointed to the five books on the top shelf. "That red one, the two short ones in the middle, the big green one, and the poetry book at the end."

He glanced at all the others, then held the Virgil like it was made of gold. "If you're thinking that book is valuable," I warned, "it's not. None of them are that old."

"I know, but Granny, Mama, and I all loved

Virgil. Granny used to read him to me at bed-time. In Latin, before I was six." His lips twisted in a sad smile. "Mama said Granny was a Latin teacher who fell for a man who looked like Paris of Troy but had no more brains than the horse. When did she give them to you?"

I touched the four books on the desk gently. "When she first found out she was dying. She brought them to the store and asked us to give them to you for your twenty-first birthday. Then you didn't come home after that birthday, and we plumb forgot. I am so sorry."

"Hey, it's all right." He stroked that old green book. "When Mama was dying, that very last morning, she was talking about this book. 'Virgil,' she'd say, turning her head back and forth on the pillow. 'Mama's Virgil.' I went home at noon and turned the house upside down looking for it, but the only books I found besides my own were Hector's girlie maga-zines." Unconsciously he echoed his mother. "I figured Hector had used it to light fires. Then they called to say she was going, so I rushed back. I hadn't thought about old Virgil for years." He gave me a crooked, sad smile. "Like you and Gusta said, I don't have much to offer Meriwether. But believe me, I'll give her the moon if I can."

"Just give her yourself, hon. That's all she's ever wanted. Back when I was in college I had a car accident, and that night Joe Riddley drove three hours and sweet-talked the nurses into letting him come in after hours. He bent over my bed and whispered, 'Don't scare me like that, Little Bit. You're the only thing in the world I want.' That was one of the sweetest things he ever said." If I wasn't careful, I was going to get maudlin.

Jed settled that with a grin. "Well, if I gave Meriwether the moon, Miss Gusta would just put me on it and send it back into orbit." He hefted his books. "I'll see you later. Sleep well."

I went up to bed thinking that some things, at least, turn out better than we expect.

Others, of course, do not.

# 27

Meriwether called early the next morning. "Good morning, Mac. I need a favor."

"Sure, what is it?"

"Could you go by Nana's? She's so upset she's going to make herself sick."

"I'll go by after I take Joe Riddley to therapy. Is the wedding still on?"

For a girl with a bum leg, she was downright cheerful. "Of course!"

As I hung up, Joe Riddley reached for the log near his plate and laboriously read the page. "Says here 'Go to therapy.' Doesn't say 'go by' or 'have wedding.'"

"That's your log, honey. If I kept a log, I'd need a book per day."

He gave me a long look, then his face crinkled into his old Joe Riddley grin. "Don't you be getting married, Little Bit. You're already married." He held out his arms, and I slid onto his lap for the first really good hug we'd had in ages. He rubbed his cheek on the top of my head like he used to. "I love you, Little Bit."

"I love you, too, Joe Riddley."

I got to Gusta's to find Darren's yellow Volkswagen backed up the drive, but I didn't see him as Florine showed me to the sun porch, which was fitted with windows for winter. Gusta sat amid the floral cushions like a yard ornament in gray corduroy. Pooh sat in her wheelchair beside her. The day was cool, but the porch pleasant, warmed by the sun.

"That maple is particularly lovely this year," I greeted them, gesturing to the view.

Pooh opened her blue eyes wide and beamed. "I was just saying the very same thing!"

Gusta smoothed her skirt. "Yes, some things in life are reliable." She touched her hair, as if to reassure herself that every lacquered curl was in place. Whatever Gusta's hairdresser did, her hairdos always lasted longer than anybody else's.

"Meriwether asked me to come," I told her. "She's worried about you."

Her old gray eyes were not angry, but bleak. "I cannot understand how she can throw herself away on Jed. It's nothing more than a childhood infatuation. That's all it ever was."

I looked questioningly at Pooh.

"I've told her all about it. After all, Pooh is my oldest friend."

Pooh pooched out her lips like she was thinking. "I don't think you are right to call it an infatuation, dear. They've had a long time to think it over, and Jed has become a fine young man. If they still want one another —"

I jumped in to second that motion. "If Jed was

a stranger who'd moved to town and showed up at church, you'd have been mighty proud for Meriwether to be seen with him."

"I cannot forget he is a Blaine." Seeing me make a sharp impatient move, Gusta held up one hand. "I am not quite the snob you think me. I had two cousins, sisters. One married a boy from a fine family who beat her until she died much too young. The other married a boy from very modest beginnings, but he was a good husband and she has been very happy. I would not mind if Meriwether merely wanted to marry out of her class."

Pooh chortled. "You make us sound like an English country village."

"In many ways, we are. We all know there are different circles in which people move. Sometimes people rise above their beginnings — I'll grant you that."

"Slade Rutherford has apparently managed," I contributed.

Pooh leaned forward in distress. "I thought he was one of the *North Carolina Rutherfords*." I doubted if Pooh had known there were North Carolina Rutherfords until Slade came to town, and I still wasn't certain they existed except as a figment of Gusta's imagination. But clearly, debunking him would crush Pooh almost as much as telling her the Queen of England was really only Elizabeth Smith.

Gusta must have thought the same thing, because she first asked, "Do you know that for a fact?" and then, before I could answer, she'd flapped her hand. "We'll talk about that another time. You are perfectly right that if Jed Blaine had come here from another place and I had not known his family, I might have been proud for him to date Meriwether. But if I had afterward learned that his family for generations had been liars, thieves, and degenerates —"

Pooh pressed one plump hand to her chest. "Surely not degenerates, Gusta!"

Gusta pinched her lips together and drew herself up. "I have never told a soul, but my husband whipped Hector for trying to rape Helena when she was barely thirteen."

"Oh, no!" Pooh was providing all the chorus Gusta needed. I sat back and listened.

"Oh, yes. Lamar found them in the cotton gin after closing one evening. He grabbed the boy by his collar, threw him to the ground, seized a piece of rope hanging on a post, and beat the tar out of him. The poor girl was so grateful she followed Lamar home. I gave her a bath in my own tub and found her some clean clothes, but I had to send her home. She had nowhere else to go. If we'd had a shelter then like we do now —" Now I realized why Gusta had worked so hard to build a shelter for abused women and children. I wanted to kick her, though, when she added, "For all we know, Jed is the product of Helena and one of her dreadful brothers."

"No!" Finally I joined Pooh in the chorus.

"I know what I am talking about, Mac. I know

what is boiling in that boy's genes. It is deadly. I cannot bear for him to touch Meriwether." For the first time in my life, I saw Augusta Wainwright burst into tears.

What I could not bear was to see my old friend in such distress with Pooh fluttering helplessly beside her.

"Whatever is boiling in Jed's genes, as you put it, he's worked as hard as Jacob in the Bible proving that he can and will take care of Meriwether. Trust her wisdom, Gusta. You raised her. Start thinking about their wedding."

"Six weeks." Gusta flapped her hands in despair and dabbed her eyes with a white linen handkerchief. "How can she expect me to do a wedding in six weeks?"

"You can do it," Pooh said encouragingly.

Gusta sniffed and became her usual autocratic self. "As crazy as she's been lately, she may try something like going to the preacher's office on a Wednesday afternoon."

Feet clattered down the stairs and Alice's and Darren's voices mingled in the front hall. "It's time he was leaving." Gusta pulled a silver ball on a chain from her dress to consult the small clock it held. "He told me he was merely coming by to pick up something. He's been here twenty-four minutes."

"I need to go home, too." Pooh looked up at me. "If Gusta will ask Florine to call Otis to come get me, would you push me down the ramp and to the bottom of her drive? I'm always afraid the chair will fly away from him going down."

"I'll come on my walker. I need the exercise." As Gusta reached for the blue walker near her chair, I hoped Pooh's chair wouldn't fly away from me down the drive with Gusta and her walker running behind.

I pushed Pooh through the kitchen and down Lamar Wainwright's ramp to the back of the drive. In the open garage, Gusta's Cadillac and Alice's white Acura sat side by side. Darren's Volkswagen still squatted in the drive, rear end facing us, and he and Alice were loading things into the back. Gusta's drive was lined with nandina bushes and the fall berries were the same deep orange as Darren's hair today.

"Orange hair!" Gusta muttered. "I do not know what Alice sees in him."

"I understand his ancestors may have been nobles in Spain," I murmured, steering Pooh around a bump. They might have been cockroaches, too. You really can't tell about ancestors.

As we reached the Volkswagen, Darren hefted a large bag into his car. It landed with a thump. Alice — with her back to us — worried aloud, "I'm not sure I'm ready to start again."

"It's like getting back on a horse when you fall off," he urged.

"I guess so." She still didn't sound convinced.

"Is she moving out?" Pooh inquired. Alice turned, obviously startled.

"No, that's my diving stuff," Darren explained.

"I didn't know you dived — dove — whatever," I told him.

"What do you have in that bag?" Pooh asked, inquisitive as a child. "Rocks?"

He unzipped it and lifted out a mesh belt with pockets sewn along it. "Weights, to hold me down. Each pocket has a bag of buckshot. Here, Mac, feel." He handed them to me.

"Whoa!" The belt was so heavy I nearly dropped it.

"You don't notice the weight in the water." He tucked it back in his bag, pointing out the rest of what he had. "Mask, fins, a wet suit, and my vest."

It still had a price tag on it, which Pooh could read from her chair. "That is a very expensive garment!"

"It's a buoyancy control device — a BCD," Alice explained. "It controls your buoyancy underwater."

"Alice persuaded me to buy one." Darren zipped back up his bag and slammed his trunk. "We're making a lake dive Saturday with a group from Gwinnett County. That's why I came over — she was checking my BCD and I had to get her P.A.D.I. card for the dive master."

Surely that made sense to somebody in the world.

"Miss Gusta gave me the day off," Alice added with a shy quick look at her employer.

Gusta give a genteel snort. "Didn't expect

you to spend it at the bottom of a lake."

Alice responded to her voice like a dog who graduated at the head of obedience class. "I was just going back to work." She took a couple of steps, then told Darren over one shoulder, "I'll be ready Saturday morning at six." She started for the front porch steps.

As I maneuvered Pooh's chair past the car to wait for Otis down on the sidewalk, I called to Alice up on the steps, "I remember you telling me how much you looked forward to your first dive with your sister. But don't go down again until you truly feel ready."

Alice froze. I was dreadfully sorry I'd brought up her sister. Darren, short on tact, made it worse. "First dive?" he said scornfully. "She's a lot more experienced than me. It was her sister who was the novice. That's why she panicked and drowned."

Now Alice was trembling like a nervous bird dog.

Gusta got her moving, calling crossly, "You said you were going back to work. You know you have the month's rent checks to enter today."

"Yes, ma'am." Alice hurried across the porch and scurried inside.

I pushed Pooh down to the bottom of the drive and installed her on the sidewalk. She and Gusta got into a discussion about whose chrysanthemums were lasting longer, and I didn't want to get dragged in, since I sold them all. "I need to be going," I told them.

I was about to back out when Slade's green Lexus pulled in behind me. The green Lexus, blue Nissan, and little yellow Beetle filled the drive like a colorful food chain.

As he climbed out, Slade's eyes met mine in my side mirror. His were full of uncertainty. But he reached in and pulled out flowers, then strode down the drive and gave Gusta a courtly bow. "I owe you an apology, Miss Augusta, and an explanation. When you first mentioned the North Carolina Rutherfords in the bank, I was reluctant to say we are only distant relations, particularly since you obviously admired them so much. Next thing I knew, the whole town thought that's who I was. And I confess, since you are also related to those distant cousins of mine, I couldn't resist a chance to be related to you." He held out the flowers. "Forgive me?"

Pooh clapped her hands. "Very prettily said!"

I would never have fallen for a line like that, but then, I don't look in the mirror every day and see an aristocrat. Gusta lapped it up like rich cream. It had been a master stroke to point out, truthfully enough, that it was she who had spread the rumor in the first place. And if he was not going to marry Meriwether, she could afford to be gracious.

"Come in and we'll talk about it," she said brusquely, "as soon as Otis comes for Pooh."

"Let us out first," I called. "Unless Gusta wants us driving across her lawn."

Slade hurried to his car a much sprightlier

man than the one who had climbed out, but his eyes were cold as he sketched me a little salute. "At your service, Judge. I want to talk with you later." He backed down the drive so quickly he nearly ran smack into Otis, who was slowing to two miles an hour before turning into the drive.

Slade laid on the horn and shouted. "He can't hear a thing," Pooh called to him. "Otis never wears his hearing aids when he drives. He says all those blowing horns distract him."

Finally Otis backed, Slade backed, MacLaren backed, and Darren backed. Historic Oglethorpe Street, as exciting as a first-grade reader.

# 28

A dirty gray drizzle started to fall around two, with neither the comfort of a gentle patter nor the excitement of a downpour. I sat in my office staring out the window and thinking how ugly our parking lot was, how pitiful Joe Riddley was, how discontent I was. I wanted to be sailing in the Greek Islands or flying over an Alaskan glacier. Anything except paying bills in Hopemore. The phone was a welcome distraction.

"Judge Yarbrough?" Alice Fulton sounded harassed — as well she might, with Gusta's monthly checks to enter. "Meriwether asked me to call and see if you can meet her down at her warehouse at three. She says it's real important."

I'd been wanting to see that warehouse, and a rainy day is a great time to look at a big dry building. "Sure. Tell her I'll be there."

At ten minutes to three I grabbed a big green-and-white umbrella a tourist forgot in the store on his way home from the last Masters Tournament. I didn't bother with a coat because I was just going half a mile. And I didn't bother to tell anybody where I was going because we weren't busy, with the rain, and the clerks had gone to the back for a group break.

Meriwether's parking lot was still full of potholes and clumps of grass, so I parked at the curb in front near the door. The workmen, I remembered, were taking a week off to finish another job. But the door was standing open, so Jed must have already brought Meriwether.

I dashed across the sidewalk and was fully in the store before I lowered the umbrella and blinked to adjust to the dimness. "Meriwether?" The warehouse smelled both the same and different; musty memories of cotton overlaid with fresh sawdust. It was chilly, though, with the concrete floor, and except for the light from the door, the place was dark. Old Mr. Wainwright hadn't wasted money on windows. "Makes thieves' business easier," I'd heard him say more than once. Puzzled, I turned to go back out and wait in my car.

I heard a slight movement, then everything went black.

I woke with sand beneath my palms. Why was my bed full of grit? And why was I on my back? I never sleep on my back. I also had a headache that practically sang.

I opened my eyes, but couldn't see a thing. No night sky beyond the window. No bulky bedroom furniture. My eyes were open and I could not see. That was one of the most terrifying moments of my life. I thought I had gone totally blind. I had no idea where I was, or what dangers might surround me. But I was cold.

I reached up to adjust my pillow, and found none. That, finally, woke me up. I wasn't in bed. I was lying on a hard concrete floor in a room that smelled like sawdust. My head ached fit to burst. I rolled over and climbed to my hands and knees. Nothing felt broken. Had I fallen? I carefully pulled myself to a kneeling position. The world became a carnival teacup ride, spinning around and around. I sat back on my calves, ignoring my complaining muscles, and held my head in both hands until things spun slower and I remembered where I'd been: Meriwether's warehouse. I had gone there to meet her.

Holding on to a sawhorse I tried to haul myself to my feet, but a wave of nausea drove me back to my knees. It seemed like a good position for a prayer, but "Help!" was all I could muster. I rested my head against the sawhorse while truth floated toward me on a great gray cloud of pain. Somebody persuaded Alice to call and say Meriwether wanted to meet me, so they could hit me. But who? And why?

Alice was most likely, of course, but what motive could she have? And she was busy with Gusta's checks. I didn't think for a second that Meriwether had any reason to get me out of the way, but her two suitors — I didn't really know what Jed had been doing in Atlanta all these years, and a freckled friendly face was no guarantee of honesty. And Slade had been distinctly chilly that morning when he said he'd see me later. Was this what he had in mind? Did he ask Alice to call, telling her the message was from Meriwether? She'd have believed him, if Gusta hadn't told her about Meriwether and Jed. Knowing Gusta, she wouldn't tell anybody but Pooh until the announcement was in the paper. She'd be hoping the wedding wouldn't happen.

One thing was obvious. Nobody was going to come rescue me. Not for a long time, anyway. The folks in my office wouldn't bother me all afternoon, thinking I was working on the books. Walker would come and presume I'd gone on errands. Ridd would come by like he did every day after school and he'd lock up, shaking his head that his mama was getting so forgetful she didn't let people know where she was going. Darren and Joe Riddley wouldn't worry until seven, at least. They would eventually call Ridd, and when he'd checked all the places I might have stopped off and gotten too busy talking to get on home, he'd finally call Sheriff Gibbons.

Because I was a judge and a good friend, Buster would know I hadn't abandoned my family, so he'd get a search under way immediately. But unless he questioned Alice, who would ever think to look at Meriwether's warehouse?

I had no doubt that a person smart enough to get me there would be smart enough to take my keys and move my car where it wouldn't be found. Our county was full of convenient cattle ponds and old logging roads.

I couldn't remember how long a person could live without food and water, but wished I hadn't turned down Clarinda's second biscuit and had thought to bring my coat. My jersey knit pantsuit wasn't enough. And how long had I been there? I fumbled to find the button on my watch to illuminate the dial, hoping I wasn't resetting the time by pushing the wrong button. Four-thirty, the same afternoon. I welcomed that glow of green light like a friend. But it made the edges of darkness just that much blacker.

I had no intention of sitting there waiting for somebody to miss me, initiate a search, and eventually try Meriwether's warehouse. I wanted out, and I wanted out *now*. Shivering, I slowly forced myself to stand, fighting nausea and dizziness. I could find a door if I felt around all the walls. Granted the warehouse was a big place, but I had time to explore. I shored up my spirits by making a bet with myself: I could find an outside door before anybody found me.

So long as whoever it was wasn't somewhere inside, too, waiting for me to wake up.

My heart sank when I finally found the door. It wasn't an outside door, but a metal inside door, and it was locked. I must be in one of Meriwether's new secure storerooms.

Using my dim watch light, I felt my way around the room, stumbling over blocks of wood and, once, a hammer. The space was about twelve by fifteen, and had that one solid door. I felt no light switches at all. Trapped, I slid to the floor with my back against the door and had a pity party for one. How could I have been that dumb? If I'm reading a book and a heroine climbs a dark tower alone at midnight, I get furious with the author. If she goes to an isolated spot far from town to meet somebody in a shady glade, I lose all respect for her intelligence. So how did I get myself in this fix? Because Meriwether's warehouse was half a mile from my office, smack in the middle of town. Because I presumed Meriwether was inside and didn't verify that. Because — finally I had to face it — because I'd been proud that Meriwether called me with her problem instead of Gusta. Pride not only goeth before a fall. Sometimes it goeth before a heck of a mess.

Mama used to say there's no use crying over spilt milk, but go ahead if it makes you feel better. Shaking with cold, I sniffled like a brokenhearted three-year-old. I cried because I'd been dumb enough to come to that deserted warehouse by myself. I cried because I realized somebody could be coming back any minute to finish me off. And I cried because my head hurt so bad, if I didn't get an aspirin pretty soon I was going to scream and nobody would hear.

I massaged the back of my neck and tried to figure out why anybody had lured me to the warehouse in the first place. Did somebody think I knew something I didn't? What? Or did somebody need time to do some dastardly deed — snatch Meriwether and ride off to marry her, rob my house, even commit another murder?

I had a lot of time to answer those questions. Alternating between sitting against the wall and walking when my bottom got numb, I thought about everything that had been happening in Hopemore that fall. I began to get an idea that was so outrageous, it almost had to be true.

When I got that far, I realized I had to go to the bathroom so bad I was about to pop. "I am fixing to get out of this warehouse or die in the attempt," I said aloud to God. "It's just you and me, and I need some help here."

To my dying day, I'll believe that remembering the hammer was an answer to prayer. If I could only find it, in the darkness, a hammer and new walls were a winning combination. I groped around until my hands finally touched it, and held it claw out. I'd gladly buy Meriwether a new wall. I just hoped I didn't hit a power wire and electrocute myself.

I felt my way to the door, then moved over three feet and attacked the wall. Again and again I savaged it with the hammer claw. Bits of Sheetrock hit my face and lodged in my hair. Sometimes my headache was so bad I had to stop and breathe deeply to keep from throwing up. That was one mess I would rather not leave on Meriwether's floor.

Eventually I hacked and pulled open a hole with my bare hands. The studs were so close it was a tight fit, but I wriggled through, ignoring ripping sounds in my jersey shirt and pants. I slowly climbed to my feet and hoped I was in the warehouse, not in another locked room. I wasn't sure how many walls my strength was equal to.

Trying to be silent, I felt my way along the wall to a corner and, to my relief, felt a brick outer wall. I inched along the bricks to a door already fitted with fire bars. Thank God for safety codes.

One minute I was in darkness, the next I stumbled into the prettiest rainwashed sunset I ever saw. I knew exactly how Lazarus felt coming out of the tomb. Oh, the world was beautiful!

I squinted against the light. My forest-green pantsuit was covered with sawdust and white Sheetrock dust, a big blister was rising at the base of my right thumb, and my head still swam. As I had expected, my car was gone, and I didn't have my pocketbook with my keys, anyway. But in the light of the open door, I saw a fire alarm box on the inside wall of the warehouse.

I had always wanted to pull one of those little levers.

It helps to have lived in a small town all your life and handed out suckers over the counter to every child in town. When the fire truck came screaming down the street and screeched to a stop by the warehouse door, I limped from where I'd been propping up the wall and re-membered the driver as a girl who liked grape suckers. "It's not a fire, it's an emergency. I got kidnapped, and I need to get to Sheriff Gib-bons's office on the double."

"Yes, ma'am, Judge." She turned on her siren as her partner pulled me up to the high front seat. We were moving before I got settled good.

"Want a comb?" the partner asked, offering one from his pocket.

"Thanks." Not that a comb could do much to restore my former glory.

When we arrived at the station, I staggered into the ladies' room with what dignity I could muster and tried to wash some of the filth off my face and hands. Then I collapsed into Sheriff Gibbons's visitor's chair and told him everything that had happened to me, what I had figured out, and a couple of things we might try to prove it. "You'd better hurry, though," I warned him. "The perpetrator has a two-hour head start, and we don't have a clue in which di-rection."

At last I got to take something for my head-ache, drink a Sprite for my nausea, and sit back in that uncomfortable vinyl chair with closed eyes. He got on the phone and alerted south-eastern law officers who to look for and why.

When he finished, I held up my bare arm. "I wish we could go see if my pocketbook is still in the warehouse. I feel naked without it."

I don't know what Sheriff Gibbons told

Meriwether, but she let him borrow her keys. He told me to wait in his car while he went inside. He came back with not only my pocketbook, but also a plastic grocery bag.

"You sure you came through that little bitty hole?" he greeted me.

I shuddered. "I'm not going back through to prove it."

"Well, you weren't meant to suffer." He held up the grocery bag. "This was under the light switch. It's got a couple of apples, three cartons of yogurt, two chocolate bars, a six-pack of water, even a spoon and a few napkins."

I was more interested in what he'd said before. "What light switch? I didn't find one."

"They are set low, to comply with the disabilities act. Old dogs have to learn new tricks, Judge. But you wouldn't have starved."

"If you are suggesting I need to feel grateful, let me tell you something. I have never known such terror in my life as when I woke in this dark place. Any compassion I might have been born with has plumb dried up."

"It'll come back. The person doesn't live you can't feel sorry for."

I rubbed the back of my head, where a large lump was forming. "Try me tomorrow. Right now I'm fresh out of sympathy."

He handed me the pocketbook. A typed note was just inside: "I am very sorry."

I was furious to feel tears of sympathy stin my eyes. "Oh, this is such a mess!"

Sheriff Gibbons offered to take me home, but as we passed Yarbrough's, I saw my Nissan sitting in its usual place, smug as you please. "I've got extra keys in my bottom desk drawer. If you'll go in and get them, so I don't have to see anybody, I'll drive myself home," I told him. "I feel fine." We both knew that was a lie, but he let it pass.

I arrived home to find Darren's yellow Beetle and Alice's white Acura beside Joe Riddley's silver Towncar. Inside, the three of them sat at our kitchen table finishing peanut butter sandwiches, applesauce, and yogurt.

Alice's eyes widened.

"What happened to you?" Darren demanded.

Joe Riddley gave me a judicious appraisal. "You look awful."

"I got stuck in a tight place," I told them grimly. "I badly need a bath."

I needed to make some calls, too, and preferred to use my bedside phone.

When I came back, clean and with most of the debris brushed from my hair, Joe Riddley said, "Sit down. Shall I get you some tea?"

It was the first thing he had offered to do for anybody else since he got shot. "That would be great," I told him, taking a seat like a queen and reaching for the bread and peanut butter.

He rubbed his knuckles in my hair as he passed. "You got powder in your hair."

"I'll call Phyllis tomorrow and see if she can

work me in." I made my sandwich and started to stretch, then put my arms down. I was very sore. I must have been dragged.

"Sic 'em," Joe advised from high on the curtain rod. Lulu whined at my feet.

Joe Riddley filled my glass with ice, then tried to remember what came next. "Tea," I reminded him gently. "Pour in some tea."

"Oh, yeah." It took a little more coaching for him to put lemon in the glass and set it before me, but he did it. I gave him a grateful kiss on the cheek.

"Since you're home, could we go to an early movie?" Darren asked.

Alice hadn't said a word.

"Could you help Joe Riddley to bed, first?" That took almost as much energy as putting a child to bed, and I didn't think I could do it.

"Sure. You ready, J.R.?" The two of them went happily toward the back of the house. I realized after they were gone that Joe Riddley had not been pushing his walker, he had been carrying it in front of him.

Finally I took a deep breath and turned to the woman beside me. "We've got some talking to do, Terri."

# 29

She swallowed hard and glanced desperately around, but she'd seen me lock the back door and pocket the key as I came in.

I made my voice calm and reasonable. "I should have guessed before. When I first saw you, you seemed spunkier than you sounded on the phone, but I figured you'd been upset about your boss's death the day I called. You could have told Gusta the truth. She'd probably have hired you anyway."

She nodded, her voice little more than a whisper. "I know that now, but I was afraid she wouldn't, and I needed a job. I knew I could do it better than Alice could, anyway. Alice —" She swallowed hard. "Alice was a little slow. Miss Bitsy mostly had her answer the phone, stock shelves, and dust. She wouldn't have been able to do everything I've done here."

"How did you get away with burying her as you, though? Looks like *somebody* would have found out."

"They worked on her so long, I had a lot of time to think it out. We'd just gotten to Clearwater the night before, so nobody knew us apart. We look — looked a lot alike." She pulled her wallet from the purse by her chair and handed me a photograph. Alice was stockier, plainer, and had a slightly vacant look in her eyes, but they had the same dark eyes and hair.

She went on, as she put back the picture, "When they asked who she was, I said she was Terri. I filled out all the forms, and because I was her sister, they never questioned it. I had her cremated and buried down there, so nobody who knew us could come, then I sent a notice to the Atlanta paper."

"But when you closed down the apartments, didn't you have to see the landlords?"

"I typed a letter to Alice's landlord, saying I had found a new job where I lived in the house, so would he please give my stuff away. That's the kind of thing Alice would have done. She was very generous." Her voice wobbled. I had no doubt that Terri had been very fond of her sister. "Before he got the letter, I went for her clothes. She didn't have much else."

It was a sad, empty epitaph for a young woman's life.

"What about your own apartment?"

"I called the furniture rental place and arranged for them to pick it up, then I went that night to get my stuff. The next day I called the landlord as Alice and told them Terri was dead and that somebody would pick up the furniture."

Her room at Gusta's, I recalled, had a mahogany bed with matching chest and dresser, a small escritoire, and a little chair. Graceful rose valances hung above lace sheers, a soft blue and rose rug covered the floor, lovely landscapes in gilt frames decorated the rose-papered walls. What a haven it must have seemed after rented furniture.

Terri's glance flicked toward me, then away, but she didn't bother to stare at the ground like she had when impersonating Alice. Instead she sat tensely on her chair and watched me warily. In a fluffy white top and dark skirt, she looked frail in the soft glow of the Tiffany light over our table. Her eyes were large disks of chocolate, her hair a living cloud around her face. Anybody who didn't know better would think she'd never committed any crime worse than taking her sister's identity.

We heard a car approach and turn into our gravel drive. "That will be Gusta," I said. She flinched. I stood to answer the door. In passing her, I gave her open purse a swift kick. It turned over, and among the things that tumbled out was a rubber stamp. Terri grabbed for it, but I kicked it out of her reach and got it first. When I pressed it hard on my white countertop, red words sprang to life: *Pay to the account of Augusta Wainwright*. The account number's last three digits were the same as my phone number.

She jumped from her chair and ran through the house. I heard the front door slam behind her as Gusta tapped on the back door glass. Otis

346

was with her, pushing Meriwether in Pooh's wheelchair.

"What's going on?" Gusta came in shedding a gray all-weather coat and a gray silk scarf misted with rain. "It's raining again, and Meriwether showed up with Otis a few minutes ago and said you wanted us down here for something. Is that Alice's car outside?"

Hearing a motor start, I said, "It was. She just left."

"That girl has been jumpy all day. Worried about that dive, I think. She was jittery as a Mexican jumping bean while she was entering my checks in the computer, then she asked if she could go for a drive. I haven't seen her since."

"Let's go in the living room." I took the wheelchair from Otis and pushed Meriwether ahead of her grandmother. I turned on enough lamps to make it pleasant without being bright. Otis waited in the kitchen.

"Can I get you some tea?" I asked the women.

They didn't want tea, they wanted ice water, but that took as long as I had hoped it would. I was just picking up the tray to carry it in when I heard more tires on gravel. Quickly I printed a piece of paper from my telephone pad with Gusta's stamp, pocketed the paper, and opened the back door.

Jed's BMW pulled in under our light. He climbed out, opened the passenger door, and grasped Terri by one wrist. Maynard climbed out and grabbed the other. "We got her, per instructions," he called. The woman wriggled like an eel, but together the two men persuaded her up the walk and into the kitchen.

"We're in the living room," I told them. "Otis, you come, too." I slid both heavy pocket doors closed so Joe Riddley couldn't hear. Otis took a seat in the dimmest corner. When we were all seated, Terri on the couch between the two men, I turned to Gusta. "I want to talk to you about Teresa Civilis."

"Who's that?" Gusta snapped.

"This is Teresa Civilis. She's Alice Fulton's younger sister, and she's been working for you. This afternoon she lured me to Meriwether's warehouse, hit me with a blunt instrument — probably diving weights — and left me there." I turned and pointed. "See the bump?"

"That's awful," Meriwether exclaimed. "Did you really hit her, Alice?" Her dark brows drew together, puzzled. "And how did you get in my warehouse?"

"She's Terri," I reminded her. "I suspect you sent her over there on an errand sometime, and she got keys made."

"I sent her to open up one day when I had a meeting," Meriwether admitted faintly.

"She *looks* like *Alice*." Gusta peered at the girl on the couch. "What's happened to Alice?"

"Alice drowned," I told her bluntly. "Before you ever saw her. Teresa, her sister, took her identification and buried Alice as herself. They looked a bit alike."

Gusta glowered from Terri to me. "What makes you think she isn't Alice?"

"For one thing, Alice was looking forward to her first dive. This woman spoke knowledgeably about diving equipment this morning and has some kind of diving card. She knows how to use computers and business procedures, which she learned when she got a business degree. Alice never finished her first year of community college. She likes to party when she gets out of town. Oh, there were a lot of clues, if we'd been looking for them."

"Alice wasn't murdered, was she?" Gusta drew slightly away from Terri.

"No!" Terri's one breathed word was a cry of pain. Maynard put a quick hand of sympathy over hers, but she snatched hers away.

"Alice's death wasn't intentional," I granted. "But what followed was. She intentionally came here as Alice Fulton to work for you."

Terri's breaths were short and shallow. One finger twirled a piece of hair.

"You can't take somebody else's identify for long. *Somebody* was sure to recognize her." Meriwether always had a fine brain. "Besides, what difference does it make who she really is by now, when Nana so obviously adores her? Yes, you do," she said, answering the quick jerk of Gusta's head. "She does an enormous amount of work for you, and does it well. She's put all your addresses into the computer, and all your properties, so you don't have to keep that tedious ledger every month —"

I touched her. "That tedious ledger is one reason we are here. Gusta, do you have your checkbook with you? Would you get it out?"

Gusta grudgingly allowed that she did, and pulled it from her pocketbook.

"Is this your account number?" I handed her the stamped paper from my pocket.

As Gusta compared the two, Terri held her breath. Gusta gave a perplexed grunt. "No. No, it's not. And I don't have but one bank account, so why does this stamp say, 'Deposit to the account of Augusta Wainwright'?"

"Did you get her purse?" I asked. Maynard held it out. Terri made a grab for it, but he pulled it away. "Look inside," I instructed, "and see if there's a checkbook. Then compare these two numbers." I handed him the stamped paper.

"They're the same," he announced. When Terri looked at me, it was a good thing looks weren't fire. I would be charcoal.

"I never agreed to open an account with her," Gusta objected.

"You didn't have to," I told her. "All Terri had to do was get a signature card from her own bank, sign your name on it, and take it back. That gave you permission to write checks and deposit funds to her account."

"I don't have checks to her account." Gusta still didn't understand.

"Of course not. But once your name was on the account, nobody would be surprised when you deposited money into it. All she had to do was make a second deposit stamp with your name and her account number on it. I suspect we'll find she's already deposited a number of your checks."

Gusta's eyes bored into me like gray drill bits. "You said that rubber stamp was a good idea."

"It was. It saved you endorsing all those checks. But we didn't either one expect Terri to have two stamps made."

"I told you I didn't want a stranger handling my money," Gusta snapped at Meriwether.

In his corner, Otis raised a hand in protest. "You got no cause to fuss at the judge and Meriwether 'cause you didn't take care of your own business."

Gusta whirled toward him, madder than a rattler in a bucket, but she wasn't the only one in that room who was mad. Before she could speak, Terri lashed out, eyes blazing. "With all the money you've got, you'd never have missed it. I wasn't going to bleed you dry." She looked around the room in amazement. "Do you know how much rent she collects every single month? Nearly sixty-five thousand dollars! Would she miss a few thousand a month?"

"It wasn't your money." Otis spoke again from his corner, in a gentle tone of reason.

Terri poured her rage over him. "You ought to understand, if anybody does. What have you ever had? What have I ever had? Daddy died in a crazy accident. Mama could have sued and lived comfortable, but she wouldn't. Instead, she worked herself to death and we had *nothing*. How much work did she" — she pointed to Gusta — "ever do for all that money? Tell me that!"

"Now, now," Otis remonstrated, patting the air with his thin old hands.

She gave him a furious look. "Somebody owes me!"

Otis spoke again, real soft. "You ain't mad at Miss Gusta, child, you're mad at God. You think God oughta arranged your life a mite fairer. Now I ain't sayin' you haven't had a hard row to hoe. You have. But we each got our own row, and if you don't like yours, tell the Boss. Don't take it out on Miss Gusta, here. I ain't sayin' she's perfect. She ain't." Gusta gasped, but Otis went placidly on, "But she never did you a speck of harm. It ain't right for you to take your mad out on her. That's one of the devil's favorite little games. He loves it when we pick and tear at one another. Doesn't make *us* feel any better — in fact, we usually feel a whole lot worse. But we sure feel justified." He rubbed his old gray head like he was getting all that wisdom out of a genie's lamp. "And when we feel justified hurting somebody else? Umm-umm. We're dancing with the devil, for sure." He gave his head one more rub, then let his hand stroke the back of his neck and drop to his lap. "Who you're really mad at is God, so go ahead and tell Him. God can take it. God can even make hard things bearable." He bent his head and his lips moved silently.

As Terri looked at the floor, she looked a lot more like the Alice I used to know and like.

Jed cleared his throat. "Thank you, Otis. Now let's —"

Gusta stood and glared at Terri. "I hope they put you underneath the jail. Come, Meriwether." She stomped toward the door on her cane. I will always find that hard to forgive. The child could have done with a little charity. But I understood, too. Gusta had let herself get fond of a criminal. It was not just Terri whom Gusta would not forgive. It was also herself.

Jed called her back. "Miss Gusta? We're not quite finished. Would you come back for just a minute, please?"

Her tall old frame wavered. Gusta wasn't accustomed to changing her mind. At last she gave a curt nod. "Might as well, since we're here." She stomped back to her seat.

Jed looked around the room and finished with his eyes on Terri. "Mac called me this evening and asked me three questions. First, she asked where my uncle Hiram worked in Atlanta." Terri grew very still. "I could answer that. He did maintenance for an apartment complex. She asked if Teresa Civilis lived in that complex, and if she knew Hiram. I verified tonight, by a call to the manager, that Teresa Civilis did live there until her death, and that Hiram fixed her sink and spoke with her often. Apparently there are several people who can testify he knew her and she knew him — at least to speak to. When he found her apartment empty one morning, he was told she had died and her family had come for her things. But Hiram didn't believe it. He called me and told me aliens had taken her away."

Meriwether's voice was soft and sad. "Poor Hiram and his aliens."

Jed nodded. "Hiram was so worried about aliens in Atlanta that he came home to Hopemore, where he thought he'd be safer."

I picked up the story. "But one of the first people he saw, the Friday after he got back, was Teresa Civilis, at the wheel of Gusta's car. I was with him at the time and heard him exclaim, 'Ms. Civilis!' " Terri shifted uneasily in her chair. "I didn't know what he meant, at the time, so I ignored him." I didn't see any point in telling them what I thought he'd said.

Gusta leaned forward on her cane and contributed her bit. "He came by one Friday night while we were eating and insisted that Florine call Alice — Terri, whoever she is — from the table." I wasn't surprised she remembered. For Gusta, leaving the table during a meal ranks on her Poor Taste list right up there with wearing white shoes after Labor Day. "You came back and said he had you mixed up with somebody else. Florine said she gave him a glass of water afterwards, and he was talking wild about people from Mars."

Jed nodded. "He called me that same evening and said an alien was walking around Hopemore in somebody else's skin. He said as a lawyer, I could get the proof we'd need." Jed apparently remembered then that he *was* a lawyer, not supposed to commit himself to anything, because he added, "He was not, however, more specific than that."

I picked up the story tentatively. "You already had a gun you'd found on Gusta's closet shelf —" This was the part where we were waltzing on roller skates and anything could happen.

Gusta huffed, appalled. "Are you saying Alice used my gun to shoot Hiram?"

Darren slid open one door in time to hear. "You're crazy, *vieja!* Alice hasn't shot anybody." I didn't know Spanish, but the word was pepper on his tongue.

Terri's scorn was so thick she could have poured it on pancakes. "They don't have a shred of evidence. Just because I knew that filthy old man doesn't prove I killed him."

She was absolutely right, of course. Nevertheless, I plunged on, hoping — what? That she would confess? "We have the gun. I found it in Joe Riddley's boot and gave it to the sheriff. And your prints are on my closet door."

Darren's eyes blazed, and blistering words poured over me like lava. "Half the county left *huellas* on that door! Why should Alice kill that old man? That's ridiculous!" He waved both hands in the air and spun from one of us to the other, blasting each with his fury.

Jed reached one arm across Alice to restrain him, and Darren whirled toward him. "Don't you touch her! It's a frame-up, that's what it is. Because we are outsiders. But we didn't do this murder! Neither of us!" He whipped back to me. "Where is your compassion? How could you think such a thing about Alice, who's had the worst life you ever imagined? How could you? *Cosmo se atreve?*" He was loud, he was incoherent, he was magnificent.

In the middle of all that commotion, before any of us could stop her, Terri sprinted through the narrow opening in the door.

Everybody except Meriwether and Darren jumped up to follow her. We wound up in a jumble at the doorway. Jed pushed the hardest and I was right on his heels. As we reached the front porch, we saw a blur of white as Terri raced across the lawn and jumped into Gusta's Cadillac. As usual, Otis had left the keys in the ignition.

She made ruts in our lawn as she turned and peeled out of the yard. Jed ran to the BMW, me close behind. He had the engine roaring before I slammed my door. "The sheriff will get her," I promised. "I told him she might try to leave my house tonight. He's got a deputy stationed at the end of the road."

Jed didn't slow a whit. He raced backward down our drive like one of the Petty boys. On the road he spun gravel as he made the turn. The misty rain was still falling.

My hands clenched into fists as we rocketed through the night. I saw Terri's own car beside the road near Hubert's, where Jed and Maynard had waylaid her. Up at the highway, I heard a siren open up. When we reached the corner, we followed the sound — turning right, away from town. "She's heading for I-20," I said unnecessarily. "Probably making for Atlanta."

Ahead of us, Buster's deputy wailed in her wake.

Our part of Georgia is along the geological fall line where the Piedmont drops to the coastal plain. Since our county hasn't felt a need for many four-lane roads, the road we were on was hilly and narrow, dropping off at the side in some places nearly thirty feet. But Jed grew up on Hope County roads. He just gunned his motor and raced after them. I found myself sneaking peeks at the speedometer and whispering, *"DearGoddearGoddearGod."* I didn't know if I was praying that we'd catch her or that we'd all be safe. Once in a while a suspicion flitted through my head that I even hoped she'd get away.

I kept sneaking peeks at Jed, too. I'd known him since he was knee-high to a gnat, but that night he was fueled with a fury I hadn't seen before. Was it for his uncle or for Meriwether's grandmother that he felt such rage? He hunched his shoulders and clutched the wheel as the speedometer climbed to heights I never hope to experience again.

Terri was a nerveless driver. I had to give her credit for that. She pushed Gusta's old Cadillac harder than anybody knew it would go. Our speedometer was hovering over one hundred when we suddenly saw her swerve from the right lane into the left. A slow car was dead ahead. At the top of the next hill, we could see another approaching.

I still live those three seconds in my nightmares. The deputy and Jed slammed on brakes, fought to keep their cars on the slick road. Terri sped up and jerked her wheel to the right.

She overcompensated, fishtailed all over that wet road, and then, in a heart-stopping second, plunged into an abyss of kudzu.

# 30

It took a lifetime for the deputy and Jed to both stop, turn, and get back to where Terri went over. The other two cars had stopped as well.

As soon as Jed stopped, I jumped out my side and peered over into one of those places where Georgia soil is still following Sherman to the sea. In summer the deep, eroded gash of earth would be filled with kudzu, that pernicious vine somebody brought from China to prevent erosion. It now overruns the South, thick green leaves that climb our pines and snake down our hillsides. By late autumn, kudzu was nothing but thick ropy vines, but they had broken Terri's fall.

In the dimness, the Cadillac lay on its back, tires still spinning, looking like Lulu hoping to get her belly scratched. Terri, little more than a glimmer of white top and white face, lay on her back in kudzu vines, flung a good twenty feet from the car. She hadn't bothered with a seatbelt.

The drivers of the other two cars, one elderly farmer and an excited teen, were making sharp little grunts of dismay. "She's gotta be twenty feet down there, and there's no good way to get to her." Without a word, the deputy dashed back to his cruiser and grabbed the phone.

I stood on the side of the road shaking like a kudzu leaf in the wind, except the kudzu had lost its leaves and there was no wind. Jed peered all along the bank, hoping for a miraculous staircase — or at least an easy way down.

I got the miracle, but it wasn't stairs. I was peering through the dimness at Terri when suddenly I saw a flash of white. "She flung out her arm! She's alive!" I yelled to the deputy in the car. "My God, she's alive!" I bent over the gully and shouted down, whether she could hear or not, "Help's coming, honey. Hang on! Help's coming."

But there was no way down. No way down at all. The red clay banks were crumbly and pitted where rivulets of rain had washed them out.

A second cruiser slid to a stop behind ours and a red-faced beefy deputy jumped out. He hurried toward me, took one look down, and sucked in a long whistle. "Boy! We had a gully like that on our place, growing up. Try and climb down there, and you'd plunge under the kudzu and never be seen again." He didn't seem to expect me to answer, because he turned at once and went to talk to the first deputy.

They and the other men were still by the cruiser scratching their heads when Sheriff Gibbons pulled up. I stayed where I could see Terri.

Like I said, Buster is a marvelous officer of

the law. In less than a minute he'd gotten on his radio requesting a helicopter rescue. I remembered how he had fought for three counties to go together and buy a helicopter for this very sort of thing a year back, and how much opposition he'd had before they bought it. As I stood on the gully bank praying for Terri, I sent up a word of thanks for Buster.

A sizable crowd gathered before the helicopter arrived. Folks are real friendly about stopping for wrecks around where we live — and real curious. Buster had to send the deputies out to light flares to protect rescue workers and flag traffic on its way. Everybody's face looked tense and worried in the flashing lights. I saw Darren's yellow Beetle pass several times, but they wouldn't let him stop. If I hadn't been a judge, they'd have tried to send me home — but they wouldn't have succeeded. I was also a mother, and as long as Terri lay like a rag doll below us, I planned to stay. I kept my eyes on the sky and my ears tuned for the first thunk-thunk-thunk in the sky.

Watching that rescue was like watching a miracle. I couldn't believe it when the technicians swung down from the belly of the 'copter and actually managed to lift Terri inside. They flew off into the night sky like a giant mosquito rising from the swamps.

Seeing the sheriff nearby, I said, "Your deputy deserves a commendation for good driving. He didn't drive her off the road. She swerved to avoid another car and overcompensated."

He took off his hat and ran his hand over his hair, then put the hat back on. "You deserve a paddling for being here. Do you know what Joe Riddley would do to me if anything happened to you?"

"I didn't exactly think," I admitted.

"I hope you think up a better story than that before you meet up with Walker and Ridd." He gave me another look and shook his head. "This is a historic moment. You went off without your pocketbook."

I called Ridd and asked him to send Bethany down to sleep at our house. "I may have to be out late, and I don't want Joe Riddley waking up with nobody there." Bethany had done that before and not minded. By way of explanation, I said that Miss Gusta's assistant had been in a bad wreck and I needed to check on her in the hospital. "Martha's working tonight," he told me.

If anybody could get Terri in and out of an emergency room in record time, Martha could. But her brown eyes were worried when I got there, and she shook her head when she saw me. "She's not good, Mac. Not good at all."

"Can I see her?"

"The sheriff's got a deputy at the curtain, but we can ask him."

He stepped aside to let me in. "Sheriff said you'd probably be here. Her boyfriend's in there already."

I found Darren in a chair holding one of Terri's hands. Her head was bandaged, her face white beneath it. An IV went in one arm and a monitor overhead graphed her heartbeat. It was, I saw, erratic and fast. Her head was restless on her pillow.

Darren turned, his eyes enormous and accusing. "What happened?"

I breathed a prayer for wisdom before I answered. "She was trying to outrun a deputy, and had to swerve to miss a slow car in her lane. She lost control and wound up in a gully."

"She didn't kill anybody," he insisted. "I know she wouldn't." His orange hair blazed like a torch in the room. "Alice wouldn't!"

"She isn't Alice, Darren. She's Terri, Alice's sister. It was Alice who drowned."

"No way!" He breathed the words like an angry dragon.

"Yes, way," I said automatically, echoing little Cricket's favorite response.

"Darren?" The word was little more than a breath on the wind. We both bent to the bed. Terri's eyes flickered open. "Don't hate me," she whispered. "I had to kill him. I had to. He —"

"Don't talk," Darren urged. "Rest. You can talk later."

She shook her head. "No. Now." She closed her eyes and seemed to gather strength, but tears squeezed between her closed lashes. "I thought he'd ruin everything." A sob tore itself from her throat. She took a couple of deep breaths. Behind me, I felt the deputy come into the room.

"Why did you choose my house?" I simply had to know.

"I didn't know. I meant to take him . . . deserted road. Say we were going to my spaceship. I went to Bi-Lo for plastic gloves." She stopped and spoke in short raspy phrases. "I saw him . . . walk down a road. . . . I followed . . . picked him up . . . told him . . . show him my spaceship." She paused again to catch her breath.

"That's weird," Darren muttered. "This whole thing is weird."

Terri opened her eyes and gave him a special smile. "You're not weird. Just me." She rested so long I thought she was finished, but she was just gathering strength again.

She looked pleadingly at me. "He said . . . not your name . . ." Again she stopped.

" 'Mizzoner'? Is that what he said?"

"Yeah. Mizzoner . . . said he promised to mow. Made me stop at a house. I saw your name . . . on mailbox. He said he had to go in to say he'd be back . . . gone a long time . . . I went in, too, and . . . dining room screen . . ."

Again her head tossed on the pillow. Martha came in to put something in the IV. "She's tiring. You all need to go."

"Wait!" Terri raised one arm and winced with pain. Her chest heaved with the effort to breathe. ". . . told him. . . . lie on mail . . . close his eyes . . . I'd beam him up. He never knew a thing."

She sighed again, and her head flopped to one side. Martha hurried to take her pulse. "Out!" she said. "All of you. She must rest."

Terri's eyes fluttered open once more. "Darren's good. So very good. . . ." The last word was no more than a sigh.

We had turned to leave when we heard her give a sharp little cry. "Mama!"

Teresa Civilis was gone.

# 31

## DECEMBER

The first Sunday in December, Gusta called to say she was coming to see me. She surprised me by arriving in a taxi. "I've decided not to buy another car," she said, unbuttoning her coat. "I don't know a thing about buying cars, and who would drive it? Otis's license has been pulled, and he refuses to drive again anyway — he's certain that everything that happened was his fault for leaving the keys in the car. Pooh and I have decided we'll take taxis from now on."

That day was unusually warm, so I suggested we sit on the side porch, out of the wind but in the sunshine. We each chose a rocker, and I handed her a mug of coffee.

"I still can't believe that girl was taking my money." Her gnarled hands shook at her own incompetence. "Do you know that she had deposited all of that month's rent checks into her own account that afternoon? Over in Sandersville. Meriwether says she was planning to leave in a day or two, close her account, and vanish."

"You'll get the money back," I reminded her. "And you've still got her computer with your ledger entered into it. Once you learn to use the program, you can enter checks yourself. You can stamp them, and you can deposit them. You won't need an Alice or even Meriwether."

"She didn't even have an aunt in Jacksonville."

"She must have gone out of town to deposit checks in different towns."

"And have a holiday at my expense."

Something in her tone made me ask, "You miss her, don't you?"

She sipped her tea, then confessed. "I do. I'd gotten used to having her around."

"You paid for her funeral, too, didn't you?"

Her gray eyes slewed my way. "How'd you know that?"

"I know you."

"Somebody had to. They buried her in Macon, beside her mother and sister."

I looked down the drive, where Joe Riddley and Darren were coming back from a slow walk to Hubert's pond. "I don't know how long it will be before Darren recovers. He wanders around here like a shadow of his old self."

"But Joe Riddley's getting stronger every day, isn't he?"

"Yes. Once he gave his brain permission to let him walk, he started getting stronger at once. He even thinks more clearly."

"But he looks old. We're all getting old."

I started to remind her that I was sixteen years younger than she, but I didn't. I couldn't remember the last time Gusta came to my house and acted so human.

"Have you heard what Pooh's doing now?" She didn't wait for me to answer. "She's taking in boarders. Hubert's moving in with her, and she's using his first year's rent to put in an elevator. Makes her whole upstairs accessible."

"I deserve a little credit for that," I boasted. "Martha and I worked on him some, getting him to admit his big house was expensive to keep up when he wasn't using half of it." I didn't tell Gusta, but I also told Hubert that Joe Riddley and I might be buying a smaller house in town. I hadn't made up my mind to do it, but I'd told him I was considering it.

"Why did you suggest he move in with Pooh?" Gusta demanded.

I laughed. "We didn't. Martha suggested he let Maynard fix him up a place in Maynard's new house in town, so Maynard and Selena could get married. Hubert said he'd move to town, but he wasn't living with lovebirds. Then one day he went to fix Pooh's television. They got to talking about rattling around in big houses, and the next thing we knew, they had it all fixed up between them. He plans to move right after Christmas, and brags he can see the roof of his store from his new window."

Gusta gave what started out as a disdainful huff and wound up a sad little sigh. "Now that Otis doesn't drive, Pooh doesn't come to see me much anymore."

"Why don't you move in with Pooh, too?" I spoke without thinking, but once I said it, it made a lot of sense. "She's got lots of room. And Martha says that if Pooh had five people in her house, together they could hire a full-time nurse, housekeeper, and a cook cheaper than they could eventually all go into assisted living facilities."

"Life isn't only about money, MacLaren," Gusta told me severely. "What on earth would I do with my own house? And Florine —" Did I detect a wistfulness behind the protest?

"Florine could help Lottie. And Maynard is drooling to turn your house into a first-rate antique shop. You could stipulate that he call it Wainwright House."

She gave an impatient huff, but she had a thoughtful look in her eye.

Meriwether and Jed got married a week before Christmas, as soon as she could walk again. She was a radiant bride. I didn't see any crow's-feet. Jed was a happy groom, too, and when the minister said, "You may kiss the bride," he did it rather thoroughly.

Darren agreed to go, although he was still fragile. I expected him to sit with us, but just as we got to the church, Kelly Keane joined him. "Will you sit with me? I don't know many people."

Maynard and Selena sat in front of us, and I don't think they even knew who was getting married. Selena had a gorgeous diamond on her finger, and the way they kept looking at each other, I think they viewed the whole process as a rehearsal for their own wedding in January.

Joe Riddley walked into the church without a walker, and held my hand during the whole ceremony. When the preacher asked, "Will you take this woman to be your lawfully wedded wife?" he leaned over, kissed my temple, and whispered, "I sure do."

Everybody seemed to have a good time at the reception except Gusta, who was heard to remark acidly that once a girl decided to throw herself away, there wasn't a thing anybody could do about it.

After the reception, Jed and Meriwether went to change into their going-away clothes. They sent an usher to ask if I would join them in the church parlor in ten minutes.

They looked splendid together, she in dusty rose wool and he in gray, but so nervous that I joked, "It's already legal. I don't have to marry you again." They smiled, but they were still jumpy as kittens chasing butterflies.

Jed reached into his pocket and brought out an old envelope. "We have a big favor to ask. I'm going to give you something, and after we're gone, I want you to show it to Miss Gusta. But only after we're gone. Do you understand?"

"Not yet, but I'm working on it."

"Remember the Virgil you gave me last month? This was in it." He took two yellowing sheets from the envelope and handed me one. It was a birth certificate for Jedediah Lafayette

DuBose, born to Mary Helen Whitsett and Zachary Lafayette DuBose.

My eyes widened. "What —" He interrupted by handing me the second paper. Now, his eyes were brimming with tears.

*Dear Jed,* Helena wrote in her large, sloppy scrawl,

*I ought to of told you sooner, but I couldn't bring myself to do it. Please forgive me. I know I'm selfish, but I think of you as mine and want to die with you at my side. The fact is, honey, you are not my child. Your daddy was Zach DuBose, son of Mr. Lafette and Miss Pooh. Your mother was the only nice boss I ever had before Miss Mac. She and Zach loved each other a lot, but he didn't think his daddy would take to her. She was not only a Yankee, but kin to General Sherman. When Zach got killed in Nam, Mary was so upset, you came early. She got so sick the Army hospital kept her, so she asked me to take you to her house and look after you until she got there. But she died.*

*She had told me she was an orfan, and I didn't know what to do with you, so I took you back to Hopemore. I tried to give you to Zach's folks, but Mister Lafette ordered me off the porch before I could tell him about Mary. I got so mad I took you home with me and did a terrible thing. I kept you. I have tried hard to keep you clean and nice, but I'm sorry you didn't have all you could have. I did love you. Please forgive me.*

371

At the end she had written *Mama,* then scratched it out and put *Helena Blaine.*

I stared at him through a haze of my own tears. Poor Helena. But how could we have missed that line of Zach's jaw, the clear blue of Pooh's own eyes? Once you knew, the signs were there. We'd just none of us ever looked at a Blaine that way. "Helena tried to tell us near the end. It wasn't 'sack' she was trying to say, it was 'Zach.' Oh, honey!" I held out my arms to hug him.

He held me with one arm and Meriwether with the other. "Don't cry, Mac. Do you realize what this means? I get to take care of Pooh!"

But then I got so upset I had to back into a convenient chair. "You should have known years ago. If we hadn't forgotten the books — but it never occurred to us she might have put anything in them. I am so sorry. How can I ever make it up to you?"

He grinned. "You are about to. You are to wait until we get out of here, then you are to sit Miss Gusta down and tell her."

"You don't want to tell her yourself, right now?"

He shook his head and grinned. "Nope."

"What —" I had to clear my throat to get my voice working again. "What about Pooh?"

"We'll tell Pooh when we get back from the honeymoon."

Meriwether touched his arm, and he nodded. "I didn't forget." He pulled a second envelope out of his pocket. "Give Miss Gusta these. They are copies. Don't you dare let her touch the originals."

"And you're sure you don't want to tell her now?"

He and Meriwether shook their heads simultaneously. Then he threw back his head and laughed. "I found these the night you gave me the books, and I knew Hiram was right. Miss High and Mighty would come crawling, begging me to marry Meriwether, if she knew I was Pooh's grandson. But I won't have her fawning all over me on my wedding day."

They departed in a shower of rice.

I decided to take Joe Riddley home and be with him a little while before I went back to tell Gusta. She'd need a nap after the wedding. Besides, she looked so sour, watching them go, I decided she'd enjoy a little more misery.

After we got home, Joe Riddley and I sat for a while on our porch, Joe on his shoulder and Lulu at my feet. The doctor had ordered Hubert to walk every evening, so he moseyed down to our place and sat a spell, too. He told us he often went over to Pooh's for lunch now, and she joined him on his walk in her motorized chair. "We went as far as the square not long ago," he bragged, getting himself together to head back home. "I figure by spring we'll be able to walk as far as your new house."

"Not to worry. Not to worry," Joe advised, preening his left wing.

"We don't have a new house," Joe Riddley objected. But after Hubert left, he caught my hand with a thoughtful expression. "You know what, Little Bit? When we get old — real old, like Pooh and Hubert there — I think we ought to get us a littler place. Let Ridd and Martha have this big house, and get a little place, just for us."

"We'll do that," I promised, squeezing his hand, "when we get as old as Hubert."

The employees of Thorndike Press hope you have enjoyed this Large Print book. All our Thorndike and Wheeler Large Print titles are designed for easy reading, and all our books are made to last. Other Thorndike Press Large Print books are available at your library, through selected bookstores, or directly from us.

For information about titles, please call:

(800) 223-1244

or visit our Web site at:

www.gale.com/thorndike
www.gale.com/wheeler

To share your comments, please write:

Publisher
Thorndike Press
295 Kennedy Memorial Drive
Waterville, ME   04901

X